come back

Lacey Furr

To my Rooby Tuesday, my favorite person, I love you

come back

Come Back
She knew when she closed her eyes
She would feel him there
His touch burned her flesh
Hot tears erupted from her eyes
He suckled her neck and let his hands fall
She knew when she opened her eyes he would be gone
Come back Come back Come back
She screamed

Chapter 1

2016

Gwen felt the panic rise within her. She tried to focus her thoughts on anything she could in an effort to calm herself. But the panic took up its regular place in her chest. She labored for breath and a cool sweat coated her chest. Gwen knew what happened if she didn't find a task to focus her mind on and soon. She looked around her apartment to find something to distract her, rushed over to her desk and shuffled the papers around. She reached for a pen and pad of paper.

"A to-do list! Yes, I need to make a to-do list." She said it out loud hoping the sound would steady her hands. Ignoring the crack in her voice and the tears stinging the back of her eyes, she began making her to-do list in shaky script. The moving van would arrive the following afternoon and there was much to accomplish. She promised her landlord she would leave the place clean since he already had it leased to a visiting college professor. Instead of providing order and direction, the menial tasks trickling out onto the page were soon forgotten.

A face took shape in her mind, clouding her vision. He was beautiful. Smiling and laughing as if he were there with her. Gwen saw his lips move and could imagine the warmth of his voice as the words fell from his mouth. Her hand lifted; the fingertips gently brushed his cheek. She knew the words he was speaking. She knew the tone and sound of his voice and exactly how she felt the first time he spoke them. Standing beside her desk with paper and pen in hand she felt the same rush of love she felt for him that day— remembered exactly what it felt like to be that girl. The memory took over, pushing aside all her practiced control.

The memories she had spent the past few years trying to forget took their rightful place in her mind and in her heart, invading the present.

Gwen threw the pen and paper across the room and with a frustrated scream dropped to the floor. She drew her knees into her chest, wrapped around them and fastened her fingers. As the tears spilled from her eyes, Gwen felt the anger rise up inside her chest. She had known this move was going to be hard, that leaving the place he knew would be upsetting. It was a final goodbye but she was ready for goodbye. She had spent the last several years focused on strengthening herself so she would be ready enough to conquer her anxiety. She was prepared. She was strong enough. Yet she found herself curled on the floor and that motivated her to take back control.

Focusing on her breath, she felt the tension ebb away. Slowly, she looked around the room, gathered her emotions as if they were a bunch of touch-me-nots ready to explode. She placed a firm grip on the desk beside her and pulled herself up to sit in the desk chair relieved the panic attack was held at bay.

This is it, she thought. Her last night in these rooms had come at last. She would never sleep here again, or eat here, or study here. She would never have to tap the bathroom faucet twice to get the water to stop dripping. She wouldn't need a sound machine to drown out the neighbor's loud music and voices as they partied several nights a week. She was losing this constant reminder of a time when her life should have headed in a different direction.

She remembered so many nights hidden in the comfort of these rooms with nothing but her memories to keep her from being lonely. This was her refuge. Here in these rooms she could pretend to participate in life when mostly she was hiding out. She came to college with expectations of adventure, of love, and dreams to conquer. She planned to go out and talk about politics and laugh at stupid jokes. She imagined herself as an activist fighting against some social injustice, forcing change. These were the years she should have fallen in love for the first time, met her life-long best friends, traveled, made big life-altering decisions and survived her mistakes. These were the years she would start living her life. She would become the person she always dreamed of being. Some of those things happened, but most did not.

She fell in love. She experienced the fluttering of her heart, the racing of her pulse. She knew what it felt like to see her future in someone else's eyes. She wanted all that for herself. But she learned she couldn't have everything she wanted. She made big decisions which led to the one mistake that would define her life. She knew what loss felt like. She knew it would eat you from the inside out if you didn't pay careful attention. She knew that loss could kill you although you were still breathing and walking and talking and living.

She also knew that no matter how much you wanted something you would never know what you were getting until you had it and lost it. Gwen understood how a person could smile and laugh and live while feeling absolutely nothing. She knew that she could live through the panic attacks and the fear that bordered on phobia every time she left the confines of her apartment. She knew because that was her life. The combination of that knowledge defined the person she had become: a survivor.

As these thoughts swelled around her, growing bigger and more dramatic, Gwen couldn't stand being in the room a minute longer. She grabbed her sweater and ran from the tiny apartment.

Walking briskly, she set out toward the river. Although the urge to run was strong, she kept a steady pace. She wanted to be in control of herself. Controlling her urges, especially when her anxiety was high, made her feel powerful. The cool spring air slightly tickled her nostrils as she walked. She started counting in English to one hundred. A habit she had developed to clear her mind. She had read about it in a meditation book. She started in English, then Spanish and then French. She stopped counting when she felt her mind and body relax. The technique worked well for her. In the beginning she went through all three languages, but recently she would relax into the rhythm at some point in the first hundred.

As her anxiety subsided, Gwen noticed the other people on the street. A woman walking toward her pushed a stroller. The child inside screamed, obviously unhappy with his current situation. Twice he tossed his cup onto the sidewalk, while his mother stopped to hand it back to him. Gwen hid a smile as she imagined a child with her eyes throwing the same fit. The woman looked at Gwen with tired eyes and smiled. "Terrible twos," she said. A simple explanation of an age-old dilemma parents everywhere encounter. Gwen returned her smile without speaking. The urge to count returned.

She approached the pier, assessed the groups of people, then headed toward the stone stairs to the left. She didn't want to be in earshot of any of the groups. She needed to sit and watch the river ripple without the rumble of voices interrupting her. Water comforted her.

When she was little girl her dad would take her fishing with him every Saturday morning before most of the city had risen from sleep. She liked to sit quietly and watch the water and listen for the fish. She loved how close she felt to her dad as they sat in silence and waited. She had never thought it strange that he rarely talked to her. She was simply thankful he allowed her to share the time with him. And she found the time peaceful and empowering. Her dad teased her that since she was a Pisces she was basically a fish. He used to whisper to her, so the mermaids in the water could not hear, that if she wasn't careful, one day she may turn into a mermaid, too. She loved her dad and loved the silly things he would tell her.

After he died, she was angry with her mom for not burying his body in the river. The memory made her smile. She had been nine and had not understood how her mom could be so thoughtless. She knew her dad would want to be with the fishes. And although she did not speak it aloud, she was certain that if her father was in the river she would turn into a mermaid and get to be with him again. Her mom had been horrified at her daughter and devastated by the loss of her husband. Gwen had apologized years later for her constant nagging and fit-throwing throughout their first year without him. The mercy her mom showed her the year her dad died taught Gwen how to be empathetic and the importance forgiveness plays in relationships.

She felt relief in the fact that there wasn't too much of a crowd today. It wasn't often that she could come down here in the spring and not see crowds of people playing on the green lawns, hanging out on the pier, passing by in their boats. This spot on the river was why she loved Chattanooga so much. Gwen breathed in deeply, freshness and energy swelling within her. The air filled her lungs with oxygen then swooshed out of her mouth. Relief replaced anxiety. She tilted her face up and let the sun heal her.

Gwen's dad first brought her to visit the city when she was seven. It was about a three-hour drive from Berry, Alabama, where they lived. Her dad entered a biannual fishing tournament and agreed to let her go with him as a reward for getting all A's on her report card. Her mom didn't understand why she loved fishing with her dad so much but it made her smile when he took Gwen with him. Every time they went fishing for a day they came home to their favorite meal: steak, salad, green beans, and mashed potatoes. Sometimes Gwen thought dinner was her favorite part of the fishing trips because they all sat together sharing stories from the day.

That first visit to Chattanooga stole her imagination. It was a sleepy city hugged by mountains with a river splitting its heart right down the middle. It was a quiet place that echoed with the energy of Cherokee Indians who once roamed the countryside. The fishermen filled her head with stories about how dirty it once had been; manufacturers polluted the air and the water. They told her how several families came together and demanded change. The community rallied behind them and the city quickly noticed change and development. She daydreamed about princes and princesses who lived on Lookout Mountain rescuing the city from evil dragons with the help of river mermaids.

She remembered clearly her dad's Bass boat racing down the river at top speed. She was nestled into the seat in the rear of the boat. She had to stretch her spine and neck like a crane to see the landscape flashing by them. When she saw the large triangle-topped building come into view she stretched as tall as she could make her body rise and pointed at it. There were blue lights twinkling down the roofline lighting the sky. Her dad did not see her pointing. The boat hit a wave, knocking her back into her seat. She didn't get to see the building up close that visit but the image of it played a role in the stories she made up while sitting quietly fishing with her dad.

A face crept into her mind. She tried to stop herself from remembering the night they sat together dreaming about the beach houses they would buy. They couldn't decide which ocean so they laughingly conceded that a house on each coast was the way to go. He knew how much she loved the water. But he didn't want to live in a small town in Alabama or a small city in Tennessee. He wanted to live in big cities and travel the world. Gwen rested her head in his lap as they talked about all the places they would go. Shaking her head, she released the memory and focused on maintaining control. She began to think about her own plans for the future as she watched the ripples push each other toward the river bank. Now was the time for her to move forward away from the past.

Gwen had completed her Master's and was preparing to sit for her CPA exam. She was excited about her new job; it was a great opportunity. She was starting her career working as an assistant in one of the largest global accounting firms in America. If all went well, she would have the opportunity to travel to Europe and work for their international trade division. She knew it wouldn't be easy there was a lot to learn and her mentor would be hard on her. She had already heard the rumors about how tough her mentor was on mentees in the human resource office while she finished her paperwork. They warned her not to expect to have a life outside the office. She knew his last mentee had quit and gone to work in a bank. Yet she was confident she'd be able to handle it. The long hours would help to fill her days. She was stubborn, so she knew the more pressure he put on her the more determined she'd be to succeed.

A cool breeze pulled her back to the present. She pulled her sweater tightly around her shivering shoulders and wondered what time it was. Without warning her breath caught in her throat. Her heart began to race and tears erupted from her eyes. Her body broke out in a cold sweat. She wrapped her arms tightly across her chest, resting her hands on the back of her neck as if holding herself together. She rocked her body forward and backward while she fought for control. No matter how hard she tried to fill her lungs with air she could not get enough. Advice from her therapist rolled through her mind: There are times when you have to go with the flow. No one has all the answers and no one can be in control at all times. The best you can do is to know when to fight for control and when to find strength in letting go. With those words comforting her she submitted to the panic attack and let the tears fall.

The attack overcame her and left her quickly. The air began to flow easily through her lungs. She felt the tension leave her back. She wiped the tears off her face and she shook her head from side to side to free herself of the last remnants of tension.

Gwen had started shaking her head to clear it when she was in kindergarten. The first time was when she was trying to recite the alphabet. She kept mixing up the L, M, N, O, P with the X, Y, Z. One day she shook her head from side to side in frustration. When she started again, she got it right. The habit remained a constant from then on. Whenever she needed to start over, clear her head, or refresh her mind, she shook her head from side to side.

A memory of her mom telling her she looked like a wet puppy trying to get water out of her ears made her smile. Whenever her mom witnessed the movement she would reach behind her ears and use her nails to tickle her. Her mom also told her that if she pretended to be happy long and hard enough one day she would wake up and truly be happy. She tried it every day, even while thinking the idea was crazy and would never work.

Just then a bluebird landed a few feet from her and snatched a worm from the ground. Gwen watched as the bird flew high into the trees. It landed in a nest, sharing the juicy worm with several chirping babies. Watching the mamma bird feeding her babies made

Gwen smile. The smile stretched her check muscles. She felt her laugh lines dip into her face and her cheeks swelled under her eyes. It felt amazing. She imagined it was similar to standing for the first time, engaging muscles in your body you did not know were there. Standing was the first step in personal freedom, smiling was her first step in being happy.

"I can't let what happened keep me from moving on." Gwen stood and headed back to her apartment feeling completely confident and smiling.

When she returned to her apartment she changed into her favorite sweats and put on a kettle of water. She had already packed most of her kitchen items, so she had to rummage through a couple of boxes to find a mug to put her tea in. The smell of the tea bag steeping helped calm her nerves even more. When she started to feel steady again an idea came to her. She took her tea and went to her desk. She found her pad sat and wrote him a final letter.

When she reread it, she knew it didn't say enough of what she wanted to communicate. She wished she could yell at him. Accuse him of being a coward. She thought about telling him where she was moving. But she didn't want to wonder if he would show up. Besides, if he wanted to find her it would be easy enough.

Hurriedly she addressed an envelope and stuffed the letter in. She went straight to the mail drop and released it into the black hole before she could change her mind. This was goodbye to her past.

With that gesture she felt like an adult full-grown. No turning back, no second guessing herself.

She squared her shoulders, expanded her chest with oxygen, and went back to her apartment. Her heart felt heavy and hollow at the same time. She turned the lights off and climbed into bed, hoping for a peaceful night's sleep. As she lay staring at the shadows on the wall she wondered if first loves were meant to be so painful. Was the lesson they taught you to learn to live with pain and loss? Were they meant to teach you about mercy, forgiveness, kindness? Those questions swirled through her mind as she drifted off to sleep.

Chapter 2

2016

The next month left Gwen exhausted at the end of each day. She woke at five in the morning and ran a mile to the yoga studio. She would take an hour-long hot yoga class and then spend fifteen minutes meditating before running back to her condo to get ready for work. Sometimes she would stop at the Happy Monkey and grab a coffee and pastry and walk back, forsaking her two-mile run for the day. She usually arrived at her office before nine and would work well into the evening. A peacefulness began to live inside her, providing her the confidence to open herself up to new experiences.

The accounting firm she worked for was located five blocks from her condo so she often walked to work. Her mentor was tough but fair. She learned quickly she had to pay attention to the tiny details. He set up little tests for her without her knowledge. If she found the missing file or noticed a number that didn't fit with the rest of the data, he would be quick to reward and complement. The couple of times she failed his tests she learned his favorite motivator was public embarrassment. Gwen spent a lot of time each day looking for his hidden tests. The office was diverse. There were a group of women who had formed a knitted-together family unit. They supported each other emotionally and hung out together. Gwen's first week they invited her to join them for drinks. She only hesitated a few seconds before accepting. They folded her into their group with several lunches and after-work drinks a week.

Carol was in her late fifties and had two sons; she constantly told stories of their crazy adventures. She tried to talk Gwen into going on a date with her oldest son. But Gwen politely explained she didn't date. Jenny was in her late twenties and was the fun one. She always had something amusing to say about everything and was the life of the party—even if the party was a none thirty staff meeting. She was also single, but rarely without a date. Sarah was in her thirties and was married with three children. Her husband, an artist, stayed at home with the kids. Becky was Gwen's favorite. Becky was a year older than Gwen. She was quiet but when she did speak, she was always kind and interesting. Gwen found that she could talk to Becky about lots of topics. They often sat together at lunch in the park across from the office. They talked about work, career goals, decorating, books, and traveling. Recently they started to share more intimate details with each other but Gwen wasn't ready to open up completely about her past.

The tedious work often left Gwen deliriously tired, but she enjoyed it. She was always immersed in numbers. She impressed her mentor with her ability to quickly pick out discrepancies. She'd helped find an error on a large account and made the company thousands in revenue. She proudly called her mother and James right away to tell them how she had picked the error out before she even really analyzed the numbers. Gwen could hear the joy in her mother's voice as she congratulated her and she knew the joy was because of more than just the success at work. Gwen felt herself hugged in nostalgia as they chatted like they had before her accident. The words of an invite rolled off her tongue before she realized the thought had formed in her mind. And of course, her mother didn't allow even a moment to pass between the invite and the acceptance. There was no way out.

Gwen had been in her new condo for two months and hadn't finished unpacking. Living out of boxes and on take-out were new to her, but she enjoyed the peace of her evenings reading and exercising. However, now that her mother and James, her stepdad, were coming for a visit, she needed to make the condo presentable. She wanted to show them she was okay. Even better than okay, she managed her anxiety and had a life. Even if she didn't keep a full social calendar her life fit her just fine. She didn't want her life overrun with people and events. She was happier standing on the sidelines watching the game of life at a safe distance. But she did reserve the right to call a play or two every so often.

***

Gwen stood in the kitchen looking from one empty cabinet to the next trying to decide which would be better for her glasses and which she should use for her plates when she noticed she was humming. She paused and smiled. When she was in high school, she was an avid music fan. She loved all types and constantly had music playing. Her mother never understood how she studied with her iPod earphones stuffed in her ears. But since her accident she'd gotten used to silence. It had been so long since she had listened to music. It usually brought back memories she didn't want to have. She'd also learned to use silence to manage her anxiety. Yet she stood in her kitchen humming as she worked through such menial decisions as where to put her glasses verses her plates and bowls. She wasn't even sure what the song was in her head. She had learned how to not hear music in restaurants, in stores, when passing street musicians. She learned to find solace in quiet moments. Later, after the panic attacks were well on their way to controlling her, she became a fan of art museums. The art was spectacular. She enjoyed standing in front of pieces and imagining what the artist was feeling while they painted. If it was a portrait, she'd study their faces and try to understand their stories. She would imagine their whole life in her mind. She thought her own hidden truth contributed to her ability to see what was hidden behind the smiles. While she became a huge fan of abstracts and photography as art, she mostly loved how quiet and peaceful the museums were. Patrons generally knew to ponder the art in silence. There was never an awkward moment when someone shared an unexpected greeting and she wasn't sure how much of a response was truly expected of her. In museums most patrons nodded as they moved from one piece of work to the next.

Sometimes the rare amateur would indulge in a casual comment about a piece but mostly everyone understood the rules of solitude and private enjoyment of the artist's work.

"I am happy." She said the words aloud, trying out how they sounded. She smiled and knew exactly what she wanted to do. She ran into the living room and hurriedly unpacked her stereo.

After an hour of trying to figure out which cords went to what connection she finally sat back and decided the music could wait. Gwen was frustrated with herself for turning down James' offer to help her move. As she sat there wondering who could help her with the mess of wires so she would have her television and stereo hooked up she heard a knock.

Thinking it must be a delivery man of some sort knocking at the wrong door she thought about ignoring it. But as the knocking persisted, she stood and went to the door.

"Who's there?"

"Hi, I'm Jason, your neighbor in 3A," a pleasant voice answered.

Slowly, Gwen opened the door, surprised to see a tall handsome man standing before her. He had a red oven mitt on his right hand balancing a glass casserole. His other hand was holding a small pitcher of tea.

"Hi. Let me help you." She took the pitcher from him and stepped back giving him space to pass. "Come in."

"My mother taught me that if I wanted good relationships with my neighbors, I should feed them." He spoke as he followed her to the kitchen. He set the casserole dish on the counter and looked around the condo.

Gwen felt a wave of embarrassment roll over her as her eyes took in the scene he was looking at; open boxes full of contents, open cabinet doors revealing bare shelves, plain walls, vases sitting empty on the counter. In the adjoining living area pictures rested against walls where she was thinking about hanging them, a bundle of tangled wires in a heap on the floor. His eyes circled back and met hers. His eyes were a deep blue green; she could get lost swimming in them.

"Apparently, unpacking isn't my strength." She laughed. "I'm Gwen, by the way." She held out her hand to shake his.

"It's great to meet you. I thought it would be nice of me to give you a little time to get settled before I came over..." his smile dazzled her.

"Yeah." She glanced around again. "Jason, how are you with at hooking up electronics?"

"Pretty good. Want me to help with these?" He pointed at the wire pile in her living room.

"That would be amazing—if you have time."

He glanced at her with eyes that reminded her of the ocean. "I have time." He grinned. "Where do you want to set up the TV and stereo?" He walked toward the mess of wires and started the untangling process.

"I was thinking here." Gwen stood in front of the small wall that separated the kitchen and living area. "Or do you think over here?" she went to the far side of the room near the fireplace. The room was a large, open space. The outside wall was all floor to ceiling windows.

"My layout is similar except I have a wall separating the dining area and living room." He looked around her space. "And that's where I put my TV."

Gwen watched him as he sorted out her dilemma.

"I think over the fireplace. Then you could position the couch to face it." He walked over to the space.

"I like that idea. The chairs can face the windows." She stood there a minute. "I have a bench seat in my bedroom; I could put it here and complete the sitting area." She was getting excited.

"I like it. Let's get started." Jason handed her one untangled cord. "What about the pictures?"

"Did my mom send you?" she laughed.

He laughed along with her. They spent the next hour rearranging the furniture and hanging the TV. Jason went back to his condo twice for the right tools. Gwen knew he was saving her big-time. But more than that she was enjoying spending time with him. They chatted easily about the city, their jobs, and general conversation.

"I moved here with my company to work on a large acquisition deal." He told her.

"What company?"

"Hebrelen Corp."

"Are you working on the Southside Project?"

"Yes. If I land this deal, I'll probably make partner. Then I'll move back to Atlanta." She couldn't read the look he gave her.

"I'm working on some reports for that project."

"Really? My livelihood is in your hands?"

She laughed, "Not exactly. I still work under a mentor. I do the work he gets the credit kind of thing. But it's a great opportunity for me."

"What type of opportunities are you looking for?"

"I would love to travel. Our firm has an international division headquartered in Ireland. I'd love the opportunity to work in that office."

"That's great. Maybe when I make partner, I can extend our business there and we can work on a real project together without your mentor."

Gwen wondered if he was flirting with her. She took in his profile. He had a strong jaw line. He had a small amount of stubble on his face. When the light danced off him it looked like golden specks, like a gold powder, was brushed along his jaw line. She smiled and stood. She pretended to dust off invisible dirt from her pants. "Are you hungry? I have a great smelling casserole in the kitchen. I can heat us up some." She flashed him what she hoped was a dazzling smile.

"I am famished. I almost have this hooked up. Want me to put some music on?"

"Yes, that would be great."

"What do you want to hear?" he asked her.

Gwen paused, trying to remember what her favorite songs were. "I like lots of different music. Maybe try the Hits station."

She went to the kitchen and made them plates. A few minutes later music filled the condo. She stood in the kitchen letting the sound become familiar. The song seemed familiar from playing in the background at store and restaurants. She picked up the plates and headed back into the living room. Jason was feeling around on the wall for a stud to hang a picture for her.

"I don't know if this is going to work here. It won't be centered."

The DJ announced another band, the music changed.

Gwen stopped in her tracks. The plates in her hands began to shake. His voice filled the condo with the most beautiful song. Memories of him singing to her, strumming his guitar for her, overloaded her mind. She stood motionless, listening, and remembering.

Jason turned toward her asking something else about the picture.

"Gwen, what is it? Are you okay?" he took several steps to her, he took the plates from her trembling hands and sat them on a nearby box.

Tears ran down her face. She tried to pull herself together but this was not a panic attack, this felt like her heart breaking all over again. She looked at Jason trying to think of what to say. Her breathing became shallow. Jason went to her, pulled her body into his chest, and wrapped his arms around her. She heard him making shush noises like you would to an upset child. She focused on his sounds; she matched her breathing to the noise he made. His hand rubbed up and down her back. Slowly, the pressure of the pent-up sobs loosened in her chest. She relaxed, letting the weight of her body rest into him. Jason tightened his hold her on her. Gwen let herself be comforted in his arms.

After a few minutes she pulled back from him slightly. She looked up and met his gaze. She felt all her pain and hurt shine out of her eyes. He seemed to absorb the depths of her pain, drinking it in as if he could carry it for her. She felt the tears start to roll down her face again. "I can't breathe." She pulled away from him, wrapped her arms around herself, and sat down on the couch.

"I'll get you some water." Jason watched her for a few seconds before he strode into the kitchen.

Gwen gazed at the stereo listening to his voice. "It can't be. It can't be him. I would have known. Someone would have told me. How could I have not known?" she spoke to herself.

> *I know I will leave you but forgive my selfish heart*
> *I must take all you got*

Gwen knew his voice, she recognized it as the voice in her dreams. It was the voice she prayed to forget. She didn't want to listen but she couldn't turn it off. The song washed over and through her. She closed her eyes and felt his words, felt the message in them. He did have a selfish heart. He left her alone when she needed him most. He never even told her goodbye. He just left. Memories flooded her mind. They flowed in and out: days lounging at the park, flying her kite, fishing at the river, picnics, him singing and writing while she read. The memories came and went too quick for her grab onto any of them. They played like a movie on fast forward through her mind. Hearing his voice for the first time in years both exhilarated and hurt her. She found she no longer wanted to ignore the past or wash out the memories. She wanted to memorize his song. She listened as if the last years hadn't happened.

As the song ended, she opened her eyes. She looked around the room and let reality come in. She was not the girl who loved Soary anymore. She was the woman who would finally let him go. This moment felt like the beginning of the end of her healing process.

The song reminded her of their time together. Their time together was full of love and laughter. Until he left, they were happy. They never got around to having their first fight.

"Here you go." Jason handed her a glass of water and Tylenol. She wasn't sure where he found them but she was glad to take them.

"Thank you." She smiled at him. He walked over to the radio and flipped the off switch then went to the picture he was working on before. Gwen followed him with her eyes, grateful he was here with her.

He held the picture up. "What do you think? Here?" He looked over his shoulder waiting for her response.

"I think that looks good." She got the hammer for him. "Should I mark the spot?"

"Yep." He winked at her making her blush.

They stood back and admired the picture he had hung. "Thank you, it looks good."

"You're welcome."

Gwen still felt unsettled. "Jason, do you want to go for a walk?" She tried to keep her voice steady. She knew tears were threatening again.

She had been doing so well the past few months and she wasn't going to let her progress halt by breaking down because she heard his voice on the radio. She knew Soary dreamed of being a musician and if she was honest with herself, she knew a part of the reason he left her was to chase that dream. There was never a doubt he was talented and he was going to be a star. Isn't that why she avoided listening to music? Isn't her past with him the reason music was a trigger for her panic attacks? She could lie to others and she could even pretend to herself for a time but when confronted with reality she needed to make a choice, own up to the truth and heal herself or live a lie waiting for something she couldn't define. Soary was meant to be a musician and musicians were on the radio. That's why she had avoided turning one on for so long. And today was the beginning of accepting that truth and turning toward her future.

"Yes, I would like that." He looked relieved.

***

Their condo building was nestled in a corner of the Art District. It was only a couple of blocks from the University but felt secluded from the hustle and bustle. A developer had remodeled an old stone mansion into condos. The backside of the property over looked the river, the west side overlooked the art museum and had a smaller view of the river and the sculpture garden, the front condos had a glorious view of the city and the triangular roof of the aquarium, and the east side looked out over the large flower garden surrounded by magnolia trees and a minimum view of the river where the trees opened up to a short path to the Riverwalk. It was a peaceful area. The city had invested millions into beautifying the riverfront. Part of the project was to build river walk pathways across the city leading people to the river. On a nice evening you could find various people and groups gathering or passing along the river front. In the water fishermen were waiting for their big catch.

Jason and Gwen passed through the trees and came out on the Riverwalk across from a small fishing pier. When they reached the pier, Jason broke the silence, "Do you want sit here a while and see what they catch?" he waved his hand in the direction of the boats.

"Yes." They settled onto a bench near the end of the pier that was still warm from the sun. "I'm sorry. You come by to make your mother proud and you get yourself caught up with a weird person who cries over a silly song on the radio." Jason noticed the effort she made to make her voice sound light-hearted. "Thank you," she whispered.

"This is one thing I really love about this city. You can be by the water in no time. It's so peaceful and quiet, not like being in a city at all. I fell in love with the river the first week I was here. I don't know if I will ever be happy going back to the high-rises of Atlanta. Even though that's home and I'll have to eventually." He gazed at the water while he spoke. He felt Gwen watching him. He sensed she needed to be distracted; he was willing to oblige.

"We lived most of the year in a penthouse in the city. My dad was an executive in a production company. He worked about fifteen hours a day at the office and even more when he was home. My mom liked to spend time with him even if their alone time was very limited. She loved the parties too. There were always dinners and parties entertaining new directors, celebrating a shows success, recruiting the next big star."

"That sounds fun and exhausting." Gwen told him.

"Yeah, it was. We had a farm also, in Dallas, Georgia. We would go there a few times a year. It was more like a resort where my parents entertained their most important guests. I loved it there. We still entertained but it was more relaxing." He paused remembering different moments. "We had horses and there was a pond I could fish in. It was nice. I love my parents.

They taught me a lot about business, success, loyalty, and love. They loved each other very much and supported each other." He rattled on giving her time to find her balance. He didn't know why he talked of his parents. They were usually the last people he wanted to talk about. He wanted to share with her more than the superficial.

"My father was work-a-holic and my mother was a socialite. My mom made me feel like she just barely tolerated me unless she was showing me off. And my dad was only proud of me because my accomplishments gave him something to brag about among his peers." He paused.

"They are great people overall. They just live in a sphere where love is only big enough for the two of them." He wondered how cynical that sounded to her.

He looked over at her and saw she was staring at him. She smiled but it fell short of her eyes. "I fished in the pond at the farm but it always felt kind of like a carnival. My dad hired someone to fill it up with fish several times a season. It was rare someone tossed a line and didn't catch a fish. You know that carnival duck game where everyone is a winner? It reminded me of that. I preferred spending time with the horses. I loved going on long rides. That's how I found my peace of mind. Maybe one day I could take you there, you could fish in the pond and we could go horseback riding." He realized he may have jumped too far ahead with the invite and suddenly went silent.

"That actually sounds great." Her voice was full of sadness but it was steady. Jason kept his eyes on the fisherman. He watched as he struggled with his fishing line; his catch had gotten away and his line was tangled. Gwen's body was tense beside him. He could feel that she was preparing to say more.

"It has been a long time since I have heard his voice."

He heard her voice crack slightly. She coughed to cover it up. Jason knew he needed to wait for her to find the words she wanted to share.

He had heard the song before. He thought it was one of the saddest love songs he'd ever heard. It always made him wonder if it was written for someone. And sometimes he would think of his ex when he heard it. He knew about Soary and The Deuces, they were the hottest new group. They were all over the radio, country stations and pop stations. Jason was pretty sure they were nominated for some award but he couldn't remember which one. He couldn't help but be surprised that Gwen hadn't heard the song before. He was always on a talk show, on the cover of magazines, even if he wasn't the one promoting himself; the tabloids were enamored with him and his bandmates. But then he remembered her condo and realized she'd lived there for several weeks without having taken her radio and TV out of the boxes. Wasn't that the first thing most people unpacked? Even if she had a rare ability to live without the sounds of the TV and radio how could she walk around in the world and not hear his songs in stores or restaurants?

"Yeah, he's really popular right now. I think he's nominated for some music awards. Maybe the new artist of the year one." As he spoke, he was lost in his own thoughts, thinking he sounded lame; he didn't notice her wince at his words.

"We were friends once. We met in my hometown the summer after my freshman year of college." She reached over and patted his hand. As she went to move her hand away, he intertwined his fingers in hers and rested their hands on the bench between them. She looked up at him and this time he met her gaze with his own.

She smiled before looking away toward the water. They sat like that, fingers interlocked, watching the fishermen in silence.

***

"I should take you back and feed you since you were so nice to cook for me."

"Yeah, I am hungry." Jason suddenly remembered his secret.

"So," he started slowly, "I think it is time I came clean." He turned to her with a serious look. Gwen looked nervously at him.

"Okay." She nodded for him to continue.

"I didn't really cook the casserole. I bought it at one of those we prepare it and you cook it dinner places." He gave her a sheepish smile and laid his free hand on his heart. "If you forgive me, I promise never to mislead you again."

Gwen looked into his eyes for a full minute. Then she let a smile escape and leaned her head back and laughed. "What a scoundrel. What would your mother say?"

Laughing too, he said, "Who do you think I learned it from?"

Jason held her hand on the walk back to the condo. They walked companionably with few words being exchanged. He felt Gwen relax beside him. He thought they might actually start to enjoy the night again.

Radio Interview: FM 103.3
New York May 20, 2016

DJ JoanieS: Good evening people! We are here tonight with two members of the hottest band The Deuces! They are here to debut a new single off their upcoming third album, *Not Lost*. Soary, Jeff, welcome!

Soary: Thank you.

Jeff: Thanks.

DJ JoanieS: You all just stopped touring, what, like a month ago?

Laughing

Soary: No, we wish. We have a few more stops on the tour before we get to rest.

Jeff: Yeah, the tour will never end. It's been non-stop. But we love it so it's good.

DJ JoanieS: Your second album received a lot of attention, single of the year, album of the year, best new artist. How has that influenced your upcoming album?

Soary: Yes, but we lost most of those awards, remember?

DJ JoanieS: But being nominated was great, right?

Jeff: Yeah, of course. It was an honor. We were very pleased. I don't think about those things when we're working though.

Soary: I don't think the nominations influence our music really. We write what we feel and we just hope the fans love it.

DJ JoanieS:　How did you all have time to record while constantly touring and performing?

Jeff:　Well, we tour on the same bus. Soary and I both write lyrics and then we use the guitar to find melodies. We wrote most of the songs for the second album on the road and then we perfected them in the studio afterwards.

DJ JoanieS:　Soary, there's been much speculation over the years about who you write your songs about. There is such a sadness and loss to them. Is there a particular person you write for?

Soary:　Hmmm, no. *Pause.* Sad and lost? No, I am a pretty laid-back person, I think. I'm not lost or sad.

Jeff:　Yeah, we aren't sad.

DJ JoanieS:　So, there isn't someone who is at the root of your lyrics?

Soary:　Of course, there's always a someone. We write from experience, but not always our own experiences. We're good.

Pause

DJ JoanieS:　Okay, after the break we will hear a song from their upcoming album. Stay tuned.

After the break DJ JoanieS plays a song from their newest album, Not Lost, *called "Waiting."*

DJ JoanieS:　That was fantastic! I loved it. Did you write this one together?

Jeff:　Soary wrote this one, we worked the arrangement out together, though.

DJ JoanieS: Soary, you know what I'm going to ask.

Soary: Pass.

Laughs

DJ JoanieS: Which one of you are single?

Jeff: We're both single.

DJ JoanieS: Well, ladies, what are you waiting on?

Laughs

DJ JoanieS: When does the new album release?

Jeff: We don't have an official date yet. A lot of the songs are still being recorded. A few are being reworked with our producer, too.

DJ JoanieS: Guys, thank you for coming out tonight. It was great. For those of you lucky enough to have scored tickets to our after-party you're in store for a treat because we've talked these two into an encore acoustic performance.

Chapter 3

2016

<handwritten>We find out
Mentor's name</handwritten>

The following week Gwen spent most of her time at work. Her mentor, Roger, was working with a manufacturing company that was losing money in one of its divisions. They were thinking about selling it since they had an offer from a competitor to purchase it. Gwen was responsible for separating the financials to show the impact to the company if they sold it. She needed her work to clearly show how much the profit or loss would be if they kept the division and made minor improvements verses their profit or loss if they sold it and reallocated their resources to the three remaining divisions. Wednesday evening, she accepted Jenny's invite to go to dinner with the girls. Gwen was so absorbed in her work she skipped lunch. It wasn't until her mind kept filling up with

<handwritten>Who?
Coworke
Single
ma om</handwritten>

thoughts of Jason that she realized she was starving. She could never focus when she was hungry. She had spent the last hour on the same form because she was daydreaming ways to run into Jason on the elevator, in the hallway, in the nearby coffee shop.

When Jenny told her it was time to pack it up Gwen didn't hesitate. It was six o'clock and the earliest she had left the office all week.

Jenny and Gwen walked to a new restaurant on the west side of town called Duke's. It was a tapas bar. The atmosphere was casual with dark wood paneling and accents. Candles were lit on all the tables and string lights hung low on the heated patios. The tables were low and the seats were couches and benches with a few chairs scattered around. The setting was inviting and encouraged guests to linger. Gwen really liked it and felt the stress from the week start to slip away as she settled in with her glass of wine.

"You will never believe how much in back taxes my client owes." Jenny went into a long gripe session about her client and how they never do what she advises.

"Well, I think you should raise their fee. That might make them think about going to another firm and then you won't have to deal with them anymore." Carol told her half kiddingly.

"Well that's a thought."

"Gwen, how is your work going?" Sarah leaned over the table and took a piece of the pork that was brought out to them. "Oh, this is amazing!"

"It is going well. I am just logging a lot of hours right now." Gwen followed Sarah's lead and took a bite of the pork as well. "Oh, my goodness, this is amazing."

"Well, I for one want to know when you are going to go out on the town with me and let loose."

"Leave her alone, Jenny. She is not into your scene." Becky told her.

"Woah. What's wrong with my scene?"

"Nothing really. Just Gwen isn't into bar hopping and going home with random men she doesn't know." *except when they show up w/ chocolate*

Tossing a wadded-up cocktail napkin at Becky, Jenny snapped, "Me either! That is not a nice way to describe my nights out." Smiling she turned to Gwen, "I always know the men. At least I know their full name before I let them take me home." She finished laughing.

Gwen loved how they bantered, teased, laughed, and were serious. It was a random mash up of women but the friendship they were creating was important and strong. *weird that women = friendship, Roger = career*

Sipping her third glass of wine Gwen felt a nostalgia overcome her. She was having a great time and the memories of similar times with her high school friends tickled the back of her mind. "So, I actually have met someone I am interested in." She surprised the group and herself with her outburst. Carol and Becky were in a debate about who the best actor was but stopped mid-conversation and stared at her.

"Why the heck has it taken you so long to tell us?" Jenny whined as she reached for her martini. *have we confirmed?*

"He lives in my condo building. He actually lives right down the hall from me." Gwen felt shy now that an image of Jason was in her head. She blushed and sipped her wine. *She owns a condo.*

"Tell us all about him." Sarah demanded.

"Well, his name is Jason. He works in business acquisitions for Hebrelen Inc. He brought me dinner this past last week as a welcome gift."

"He sounds like a nice man. I haven't heard of men doing that before." Carol sounded skeptical.

"Is he gay?" Jenny asked.

"No!" Gwen wished she had not mentioned anything about Jason.

"Stop teasing her. I want to hear more about him. What does he look like, what did you all talk about?"

Gwen hesitated but she knew she had to give them more. "He is tall with blonde hair. His eyes are greenish with grey. They are gorgeous, actually. But it's more the way he looked at me than his actual eyes that was so..." She couldn't think of the words to describe the way he looked at her. She had started to convince herself she had imagined it.

"Wow. You are already crushing on him." Jenny signaled for the waiter to bring another round. "We have something to celebrate."

"No, I can't have another. Two is my limit and I'm already on three."

"Tell us more about Jason." Carol leaned forward to hear better over the growing crowd.

"He helped me hang my TV and hook up the stereo. We rearranged some of my living room furniture and hang a few pictures. We went for a walk and ate the pasta he brought over. We had a good time. I had a good time. But I have not seen him or heard from him since." She realized their advice would be skewed since she didn't tell them about her panic attack. But they didn't know about her anxiety, it just wasn't something you led with when talking to new friends.

"He lives next door?" Carol questioned "It's simple, take him a meal back as a thank you for helping you."

"No!" Jenny wailed. "Just go knock on his door and ask if he has eaten or if wants to grab a drink. Tell him you hate to drink alone but you could use a glass of wine. I promise there isn't a man who can say no to that."

"I actually agree with Jenny on this one." Becky looked at Carol apologetically. "If she takes him dinner as a thank you it could become this weird dinner exchange. But being direct and asking him to have a drink with her and disguising it with she doesn't want to drink alone gives them a chance to see if they are attracted to each other."

Sarah looked thoughtful and added, "I just think you should go down and knock on his door and say hi. Ask him over, ask him for a drink, whatever. If you like him the important thing is you make an effort." She shrugged. "Ladies, it is time for me to call it a night. Gwen, we will give you three days. Monday you need to update us on how it went when you went and knocked on his door." She hugged each of them before heading to the door.

"Yes! I'll put thirty dollars down it goes great. Look at you, you're gorgeous, smart, and nice. There isn't a man alive who could resist you at his door." Jenny stated.

Liked friendly advice exchange

***

Thur

The next evening when Gwen got home from work, she stood at her door staring down the hall toward his condo. She wanted to go knock. She was hungry; maybe she could ask him to dinner. Or maybe Jenny was right just asking him for a drink was the best choice. As she stood there, she knew she didn't have the nerve to go knock on his door. Eventually they would run into each other she reasoned. She turned the key in her door. "Such a coward." *She said to herself*

She immediately heard laughter behind her and froze her hand on her doorknob. She recognized his laugh; butterflies danced in her stomach. A thought flashed through her mind; she could turn the knob and disappear inside her condo as if she had not heard him. As the seconds ticked by, she knew she had to stay and face him.

"Not a very nice thing to say, Gwen." His voice made the hair prickle down her spine.

"Hi. I was actually just thinking about you." She spoke the words as she turned to face Jason knowing her face was flushed and her smile was a bit too big.

"Ah, so I'm the coward?" he teased.

"No. No. I, uh, was actually thinking of..." She couldn't think quick enough to make anything sound believable so she just smiled at him and shrugged her shoulders.

"Well, I think I will let you buy me a beer for calling me a coward. Do you have plans tonight?" He smiled at her, enjoying her discomfort.

"No, actually I don't."

"Perfect. Want to meet me right here in ten minutes? We can go down to the Boat House. Have you eaten there? It's great."

He was already heading to his door before she had a chance to answer. "I'll let you buy the first beer but I am buying dinner. We are celebrating. I closed the Southside Project deal today." And with that he disappeared into his condo.

Hurrying inside Gwen felt nervous energy growing in her. She was excited to run into Jason and even more excited that he wanted to spend time with her. Trying to focus, she headed into her bedroom closet to change her clothes. As she surveyed her options she began to wonder if it was a date or just two neighbors hanging out because they didn't have other plans. It occurred to her that she hadn't been asked out on a date since returning to college her junior year. She had taken an internship the summer before at a small finance firm in South Georgia near Savannah. It was located about thirty minutes from a secluded beach with public access off the highway.

Every evening and weekend when the weather was nice, she would drive to the beach. She used that time to work on her mental health. She practiced yoga and breathing techniques. She started running. She swam a lot. When she returned to Chattanooga, she was lean and tan and happier than she had been in a long while. She found herself engaging with other people a little bit more.

One day after a class a guy she knew was talking to her on the way out of the building about their latest assignment. When he suddenly asked her to go out that weekend, she was surprised. She hesitated an unbearable amount of time. The guy broke the silence by telling her never mind and quickly walked away. Gwen felt horrible for how awful her response had been and wanted to apologize to him. She tried to approach him a couple of times but both times he saw her coming he headed in a different direction. He even started sitting on the other side of the lecture hall. The thought occurred to her that she responded to Jason differently than other men. Jason made her nervous but not anxious.

She pulled on a pair of jeans with a hole in one knee. They hugged her body but weren't too tight. She paired them with a black linen tie-front tank top and tan wedge sandals. Hurrying to the bathroom, she freed her hair from the loose bun, letting it cascade onto her shoulders. She applied some lip gloss, glanced at her reflection in the mirror and headed back to the hall to meet Jason.

"Ready?" Jason reached for her hand as she closed the door behind her. "Do you mind walking?" He tried not to stare at her but he found it hard. She was so stunning. She had let her hair down and it fell in soft curls on her shoulders. Her skin was translucent against her black top. He liked that she had put on jeans. She was possibly the most attractive woman he had ever met but she didn't seem to be aware of how beautiful she was. Her beauty was effortless and startling because it was more than physical. There was a surrealness about her.

"I don't mind. The exercise will be good. I sit so much at work it feels good to stretch my legs and walk. So, tell me about the project." She was trying not to notice how nice it felt for him to hold her hand. He had a strong but soft grip.

***

holding hands = date

"And that's what we're celebrating." He grinned at her. Jason was amused at her expression. She had listened intently to every word. He was certain she could have repeated it back to him almost verbatim. She asked questions at the appropriate times and was interested in the more complex parts of his deal. He was intrigued by her intelligence. Their first day together had been light-hearted until the incident, which is how he had started to think of it, so he hadn't realized how smart she was. He knew she worked for an international accounting firm but didn't have a clue what she did. He realized he hadn't given any thought to her career. But he had thought of her. He was so relieved to finally run into her in the hall because it saved him from having to knock on her door. He was glad they could be casual instead of formal. He wanted to spend time with her but wasn't sure if he wanted to ask her out. He was certain he'd thought about her more than he had any of the other women he'd dated. He remembered how her eyes disappeared when she laughed and how her lips quivered when she cried. But what he kept thinking about most was how he felt when he saw her cry. He had an overwhelming need to make everything all right for her. He wanted to sweep her up, take her in his arms and make the pain disappear.

hm

The intensity of the desire he felt for her unbalanced him. He began to second guess himself. *to what?*

As the days went by his desire to see her grew. He regretted that he didn't go by the day after meeting her to say hi. He kept thinking it would be awkward just to knock on her door to say hi. Every time he didn't pass her in the hall or at the mailboxes or the lobby he felt disappointment. As he left for work that Thursday morning, he decided he would go by her condo and ask her out to dinner. So, when she was at her door he jumped at the opportunity. What was better was that she didn't seem to notice how over-zealous he was to spend time with her.

Throughout the meal, Gwen continued to ask him questions about his company and his plans. He found she was easy to talk to. She understood the complex set-up of his firm and understood why building this territory was crucial to his moving up with the company. After dinner Jason realized that again they had talked about him all evening and he didn't know any more about her than when he met her in the hall.

"Share a piece of chocolate cake with me and tell me about your work." Jason ordered the cake and leaned over the table to give his full attention to Gwen. He wanted to show her the same intense interest she had shown him.

"My job isn't nearly as interesting as mergers and acquisitions. Most people find accounting boring. And really it isn't that interesting at all, but I like it. It keeps me busy. Numbers are easy. They are unemotional and they leave no room for interpretation." She paused. Jason noticed her take in how close they were. Her chest expanded as she took a deep breath then she leaned back creating space between them and continued.

"Basically, I spend half of my days studying. I read up on the all the new tax laws as well as the best reporting and tracking methods in the mornings. Then after lunch I do a lot of client research and put together portfolios for my mentor. In the afternoons I sit in meetings both internal and external. My favorite part is the clients though. I love the way you can help them turn their whole life around by finding errors in their reporting. The down-side is I usually find errors that aren't in their favor and have to tell them they have less than they thought. But I have to work under a mentor for a year, then I can decide if I want to go international or stay domestic. My heart is set on international though. I'm interested in learning about different cultures and how businesses prosper differently based on cultural differences. We have an office in Belfast.

Ireland would be my first choice. I studied Irish history in college and would love to live there for a year or two. The city is recovering nicely from the years of the troubles. The people seem to have a spirit of determined hope that is pushing them toward success. I would love to experience it firsthand."

Jason watched her expressions change as she talked. The smile, the frown, the glistening in her eyes, each one made him want to know more about her. Without thinking about what he was doing, he reached over and wiped some chocolate from the corner of her mouth with his fingertip. Gwen jumped back in her chair. He saw fear flash in her eyes.

reaction to touch Jason

She recovered quickly and mumbled, "I have always been a messy eater. Thank you." She used her napkin to wipe her lips.

"I am sorry. I didn't mean to..." He wasn't sure what else to say or how to appropriately apologize for it.

"Jason, I uh, I am not used to being touched. Honestly, you have touched me more than anyone other than my parents in a really long time." She looked up at him. She managed a big smile and took another bite of cake. She didn't want to explain why she hadn't been close to anyone. She didn't feel comfortable with being intimate.

Jason noticed the change in the atmosphere. He watched as Gwen's chest rose and fell more rapidly. She was chewing her cake, fiddling with her napkin, doing her best to act like nothing had changed. His touch killed the mood. In an effort to salvage the night he said, "Let's get out of here." He stood up from the table. "Want to walk along the pier before we head back?" He pulled her chair out for her and wondered whether he should hold her hand. He decided it wasn't the best idea so he motioned to her to lead the way. As he followed her from the restaurant, he vowed to himself that he would remember to go slow with her. She had a history he knew almost nothing about. He wanted to ask her one hundred questions and get it all out so they could move through it. The thought of them moving forward in a relationship made him pause his thoughts. Where was forward, he wondered. He'd only known her a week. He needed to get control of his feelings so his actions would be appropriate towards her.

They walked along the pier looking at various boats. After a few minutes they were deep in a guessing game of who owned which vessel. Naturally, Jason grabbed her hand to cross the street, he was relieved that she didn't pull away. Instead she smiled and squeezed his hand gently.

Jason felt his heart race when she squeezed his hand. The small gesture on her part encouraged him. The need to protect her was so natural he barely noticed his reaction to grab her hand until he felt her fingers interlocked with his.

"Come in with me. I will make us some tea and we can sit on the deck and watch the stars come out." She invited.

"That sounds nice, Gwen. But I have some work to finish up so I better go home. Thanks for the beer." He smiled and turned toward his own door.

"Thanks for dinner." She said as he turned back to her. She had not released his hand. He looked down at their clasped fingers and back to her eyes.

"Good night." Jason wasn't sure what he was doing when he leaned in and kissed her cheek.

She didn't flinch away. She closed her eyes and leaned her cheek to him. He released her hand and straightened up. He watched as she brought her hand to touch where his lips had warmed her cheek. She smiled at him and whispered "goodnight" then she disappeared in her condo.

That night Gwen couldn't sleep. She replayed the kiss over and over in her mind. Her emotions felt all jumbled up. She had no idea what she felt. When Jason's lips touched brushed against her skin, she felt a slow burn spread through her body followed by guilt. She refused to give the guilt any of her energy. She had no reason to feel guilt. She gently rubbed her cheek where the burn from his lips was still present. Soary's face kept pushing against the outside of her thoughts trying to break through the happiness she was feeling. But Gwen didn't want to let him in. She didn't want him to be a part of this memory with Jason.

Lying in bed she felt at a loss, restless. She was tired but her body felt tense; she couldn't be still. The energy inside her was rustling around causing her to toss and turn.

She tossed over on her side and sighed. She pictured Jason's face. She was attracted to him. His face was handsome. He had a strong jaw line and wide eyes. His eyes were kind and his laugh was brassy and friendly. She liked the way he had looked in his suit this afternoon. But she thought he had looked even better in the khakis and t-shirt he had worn to dinner. He was strong and kind. He had the manners of a gentleman. He opened doors for her, guided her in front of him when they were walking, he stayed on the outside of the sidewalk. He was protective, she felt safe with him.

Surprise joined her restlessness when Gwen recognized the feelings rolling around inside of her. She couldn't stand lying there any longer. Tossing back the cover she got up from the bed and went to the kitchen. She fixed a cup of chamomile hoping it would dull her energy. She went out on her deck and curled onto her futon. Staring up at the stars, she tried to re-focus her thoughts on the weekend ahead.

She was looking forward to spending time with her mom and James. When her mom had messaged to confirm their visit, Gwen fought off her normal annoyance at her mom for pushing her too hard. After making the plans though she found she was excited. Her attitude and annoyance were more a habit formed to protect herself than how she truly felt.

With each star she counted she attached a to-do item for tomorrow to prepare for their visit. After she ran out of things to do, she started attaching comments her mother was likely to make that would upset Gwen. She wanted to be prepared.

She was exhausted in the morning when she woke and was thankful she had decided to take the day off. She had a lot to do so she forced herself to get up. It was important to her for her mom and James to be comfortable. Gwen's mom worried about her living alone in another city. She was concerned Gwen would have a panic attack and not be able to find out her way out of it. Gwen tried to assure her she was fine but because she hated talking about herself, she knew she wasn't convincing. Gwen wanted her parents to see she was getting her life back together. She wanted them to visit without her anxiety being the center of their time together. Before she left the condo, she put her list to paper so she wouldn't forget anything then headed out to get her shopping done. As she stepped into the hall, she couldn't help but steal a quick glance at Jason's door. She felt shy and excited. Smiling she slowly turned and headed out.

When she got back, she was surprised to see a note on her door. She dropped several of her bags on the floor so she could open the note. Her heart fluttered as she reached for it. It was a man's writing. She tried to control her breathing as she studied the handwriting. It couldn't be, she thought as reached for the note. Steadying her hand, she opened the note and looked at the words written for her.   *um, what?*

Gwen, come next door. Your mom's here. - Jason

Her breathing returned to normal before her raced again. Her mom was early and Jason was having to entertain her. "Oh, my goodness." Picking up her bags she hurried in her condo. "So much for making the place look nice." She mumbled. She debated setting the flowers and candles out before going to Jason's. She was still trying to steady her nerves after the rush of butterflies from seeing the note. Where had the hope come from, she wondered. And would she ever get past wanting to see him again? She decided to take sometime to calm her nervous stomach so she found a vase and put the flowers in some water. She carried it and the candles to the guest room. She was sure her mom would love the blue walls and white furniture. She also thought the black and white comforter looked nice. She would have to ask her mom to go shopping with her for pictures to put on the walls. She was hoping to find some nice black and white boating pictures. After she situated the candles, she decided to change her clothes before heading to Jason's. She pulled on a paisley patterned maxi dress and a light sweater.

She took the magnum bottle of beer from one of her bags. She bought it as a thank you present for Jason. She planned to give it to him after her parents visit but decided to take it with her to collect them. She could hear her mom laughing as she approached Jason's door. She became nervous as she listened. It had been a long time since she had heard her mom really laugh. Gwen felt sorry as she realized this was because she had not been fun to be around the last few years. She took a few deep breaths and made a silent promise she would do better. She would be a better daughter. And even though she made the same promise to herself before, she believed this time was different. She knocked lightly on the door, feeling timid and slightly embarrassed.

"Gwen, hey." Jason smiled at her. "I came home early today and found these two hanging out by your door." He moved out of the doorway to let Gwen in. She saw her mom perched on the arm of an oversized chair with her arm draped over James' shoulder.

"Gwen." She stood and approached slowly. It pained Gwen when she saw her mom's hesitation to hug her.

"Mom." Gwen went to her and threw her arms around her and squeezed. She ignored the tensing of her mother's body and gasp that escaped her as Gwen surprised with the embrace. She also ignored the look exchanged by her mom and James as she embraced James in the same manner.

"I'm so glad you two are here. I'm sorry I wasn't home to greet you. I thought you were going to be here around three." She looked at her watch and saw it was only one. "I was out picking up a few things." Remembering the bottle in her hand she turned back to Jason.

Extending her arm to offer him the bottle she said, "Thank you for helping me get my TV set up." She could feel her parents taking in all the details. Jason took that bottle from her and smiled as he read the label.

"You're a great listener." His smile spread. He leaned in and kissed her cheek. "Thank you."

Gwen felt all the blood rush to her head. His touch was waking up something inside of her she didn't realize she missed. As Jason walked away toward the kitchen, she turned back to her parents hoping her face wasn't shining bright red. "So, what have you two been up to?"

James broke the awkward pause.

"Your mom was up early and couldn't sit still so we decided to head up early. We should have called first. But we thought we'd surprise you. When we got here we realized how early we really were and were trying to decide where to go for a couple of hours when Jason came home and invited us over."

"He was so nice to entertain us." Her mom rested her hand on Jason's arm as they exchanged a smile. "Let's all go to lunch. You haven't eaten, have you? Jason, let us take you to lunch. Then we'll get out of your way," she added as Jason rejoined them.

"Sarah, that's nice of you to invite me but I don't want to intrude." Jason looked to Gwen for affirmation.

"Nonsense. It isn't intruding. I insist. We passed a cute little diner on the way here. What was it called, James, Maggie's? Let's go there." With that said she grabbed her purse and headed to the door. The rest had no choice but to follow. Gwen glanced at Jason and saw he was watching her. Their eyes met and her heart immediately started to hammer in her chest.

"Thank you for keeping them company." She said after James and her mother were already out of earshot.

"It's been fun. Your mom wanted to hear all about how we met. She thought it was hilarious that you had the wires all tangled. And then gave poor James a hard time. Apparently, she had wanted to help you move and he supported your decision to do it yourself." His look told her he hadn't told them all about their first meeting. She was thankful but she wondered how he knew she wouldn't want her mom to know. Her mind was racing. Of course, he would know that she didn't want her mom to know she'd lost it the day they met.

James was waiting at the lobby door. He held it open for her mother and as Gwen passed through, he wrapped his arm around her shoulder and gave her a squeeze, walking in step with her, "You look good kid. I knew this move was going to be good for you. You're practically glowing." He squeezed her and then ran up to open the car door for her mom.

***

Jason watched her. He wanted to know what had broken her. He noticed her flinch when he'd mentioned telling her parents about their initial meeting. Why was her mom so nervous about her and why were her stepdad and mom watching her closely? Jason wondered if she had enough time to heal from whatever wounded her. He knew it had something to do with Soary. But it seemed like so much more than just a break-up. Her pain and their reaction to her were deeper than that. Whatever was haunting Gwen wasn't a broken heart.

He hadn't missed the look of surprise then relief flood Sarah's face when her daughter embraced her. The look had made him feel sorry for her. Although he and his mother had their problems, she never had to fear embracing him. Without looking he reached for Gwen's hand. She didn't flinch. She simply intertwined her fingers with his. When he gave her hand a squeeze she squeezed back. But she didn't look at him either. She walked to the car and got in as he followed behind her. He held her hand until they got to the restaurant as he enjoyed the chatter between her and her family.

He picked up on the fact that James seemed to know more about Gwen's life than Sarah. It appeared to Jason he was caught in the middle of protecting them both from the pain they caused each other. It was a strange dynamic. He could tell Gwen and Sarah cared deeply for each other and wanted to make each other happy. But as James added commentary to both their dialogs Jason realized Gwen and her mother didn't know what made the other happy.

[handwritten margin note: most obscural guy ever too much]

He didn't want to release Gwen's hand but he had to as he climbed out of the car. There was something about the way he felt when he was touching her that he wanted to keep feeling. Gwen stood close to him as they were waiting for their table allowing him to inhale the smell of herand his heart fluttered.

During lunch they all became more relaxed and chatted more freely. Gwen talked about work and Sarah talked about old friends. James added commentary now and then but mostly watched. Sarah politely asked about Jason and his family. Jason found he was really enjoying himself and was thinking he would ask Gwen out on an official date—one where he could give her a proper kiss.

"Now Gwen, I think it would be a great idea if you brought Jason to visit. I think he would really enjoy our small town. I was telling him about the annual art festival. We could even take a drive down to the beach one morning." Sarah said all this as she was buttering a piece of bread.

Jason saw Gwen stiffen and watched as James surveyed her face. He wasn't sure what Sarah had said to cause the reaction. Maybe it was the invite of him visiting her home; he wasn't sure but he knew he was right about the change in her.

"Mom, I don't know when I'll make it home for a visit." Gwen mumbled as she excused herself from the table.

"I thought she seemed so much better. I didn't know the suggestion would upset her." She mumbled.

James reached over and patted Sarah's hand. "I know, I know. She is fine. Jason, I'm sorry." James looked at him with sad eyes. "Gwen hasn't been home in a while. She just has..." he trailed off not knowing what else to say.

"Well, she's not alright. It's not alright. Your child should be able to come home." Sarah snapped as she too departed the table.

James sighed and leaned back in his chair. "Jason, you haven't known Gwen long." It was a statement not a question but Jason decided to answer it any way.

"No. But I know something or someone has wounded her. She hasn't talked of it and I haven't asked." He was taking a risk in approaching the subject but was instantly glad he did.

"No, she wouldn't talk of it." James took a sip of his Bloody Mary then shrugged as if to say why not. "I try not to meddle. I actually do a pretty good job at it. But I worry about her too. It was nice to see her with you. She seemed so different, relaxed the way she used to be. Then I saw you two holding hands and I told Sarah things were different. She hasn't let us hold her in so long. And today just felt good. I know Sarah wouldn't have mentioned it if she had thought it would upset Gwen. It's just been hard not having our daughter home."

He took another sip of his drink. "She had her heart broken."

He said it as if that explained it neatly but Jason knew there was more to it so he waited. "Gwen had just turned nineteen. She was home for the summer when she met him. His mother had moved to town from Nashville They were instantly in love. It was exciting and scary to watch it happen. Gwen and Soary became one person. She had never been with anyone before him or after, I am sure." He paused and looked at Jason as if for confirmation. "She fell hard and fast. They made plans to spend the rest of their lives together. Then summer ended and she had to go back to school. And he went to Nashville to record his album. He was working on securing a record deal. He hadn't planned to be home for the summer until he met Gwen. He was just helping his mom move. Gwen was so happy. But then, well, then nothing. He never called her again. He disappeared. She wrote and called but nothing. Then she showed up at home and went to his mom's house. Judy tried to help Gwen but he is her son." He took a sip of water before continuing.

"Gwen stayed with her two nights waiting for him to call home but he didn't. One morning Judy woke up to a thank you note from her. We didn't know where she went. We stayed up worried about her for a week. Then we got the call that Gwen was in the hospital. She had been in an accident and she was hurt." His voice cracked. "She refused to come home with us or talk about what happened. She wanted to go back to school so Sarah took her back. She stayed with Gwen for a month. Gwen got into a routine and put up walls around herself. Music became a trigger that caused panic attacks so she stopped turning on the radio. And she hasn't been home since. We only know what happened to her that night because the nurses talked to us. Gwen hasn't ever talked about it.

Sarah and I have done the best we can to help her move on. But it's been hard. And then today she seemed so—fine. Happy even."

Jason didn't know what to say. He watched James as he talked and could see the love for Gwen in his eyes; he could feel his hurt bleeding out with every word. He noticed he twisted the napkin in his hands as he talked and at one point, he was surprised the man didn't cry. He wondered about the accident, he wanted to know what she went through that night. He felt the need to find her now and hold her tight. He felt protective and nervous.

"Why did he leave her?" He knew there wouldn't be an answer to that question but he couldn't help but speak it. He thought of how Gwen looked that first night when she heard the song on the radio. She went from a beautiful woman to a frightened girl. It was eerie how vulnerable she became in an instant. He recognized the signs of her holding herself together as a coping technique. She must do it to try to keep the world from taking any more from her. If that day had been the first time she had heard Soary's voice or had known he'd made his dreams come true he was amazed she pulled herself together so quickly.

No shit "I shouldn't have told you. But I see the way you look at her. And, well, I like it. I want her to be happy. I think she can be. She just has to let go. We don't know why he left. But I know he loved her too. I hear his songs on the radio, you can hear the angst and heartbreak. Sarah has kept up with him. She wants to be prepared if he gets married or has kids. But he is pretty mellow for a musician. He hasn't been linked to any women in the tabloids. I almost went to Nashville to get answers but I knew it wouldn't do any good. In the end I didn't."

Why didn't Gwen? Where's home?

Sarah and Gwen returned to the table arm in arm. James stood to greet them. The relief Jason saw on James' face told him they were okay.

"Gwen and I had a nice chat in the bathroom and we decided that my birthday would be the perfect time for Gwen to come home for a visit." She seemed pleased as she made the statement.

Gwen smiled sheepishly at Jason and reached for his hand as she settled herself back into her seat. He took it immediately and placed a gentle kiss on it. She didn't pull away. He noticed she flinched but she smiled. He wanted to be alone with her. He wanted to ask her if she was okay. He wanted to hold her until she was able to enjoy it as much as he did. He wanted to take her face in his hands and look into her eyes until he was certain her pain was dissolved. The desire that built in him shocked him so much he released her hand and looked away. In that moment he realized that he was in love with her.

The rest of the weekend went by in a blur. Gwen took James and Sarah sightseeing the next day and Jason met them at the park for a picnic by the river. They were enjoying each other.

Gwen told them all about her new friends from work and Jason told them about his family. They shared jokes and laughter. There was no tension and no more tears.

Sunday morning Jason helped James load their bags in the car. "Jason, thank you." James said it without glancing up at him. But Jason knew he was not thanking him for helping load the car. There was more meaning in his words.

"My pleasure." Jason tried to sound upbeat and relaxed. The two men finished with the bags, stopped to look at each other. Jason wasn't sure what James was thinking but suddenly the older man leaned over and leaned in for a quick hug and clap on the back. Then he moved off to join Gwen and Sarah.

"Now, Gwen, don't work too hard. I want you to make sure to spend plenty of time relaxing and playing. Jason, you make sure she doesn't lock herself in her apartment working all night every night. Our little genius needs to have fun too." Sarah was using a light-hearted tone but they all knew she was giving a warning.

Gwen embraced her. "I am fine, Mom. I promise. Better every day." Gwen whispered the words into her ear but Jason heard them and smiled.

Jason stood by Gwen as she watched her parent's car disappear into traffic. She turned to him looked up into his eyes and smiled. "You must be exhausted." She laughed.

"Why is that?" He placed his hand on the small of her back as he guided her back into the building.

"Oh, I don't know. The crazy neighbor-girl's parents' long weekend visit that you got entangled in. More drama than I am sure you wanted." She laughed again and peeked at him out the corner of her eye as they got on the elevator. *Pretty low drama*

"Yeah, I guess it was more than I expected. But I always wanted to have a crazy neighbor. Makes for more interesting conversation at parties." He looked seriously at her then laughed at her expression. "I'm kidding. Your parents were great. Fun, loving, welcoming. I felt like I've known them forever."

"Thanks." Gwen laughed. "They loved you."

They stopped at her door.

"I'm sure you're tired." Gwen shuffled her feet and wrung her hands. She looked nervous to Jason. He hid a smile as he picked up on the energy circling her.

"A little."

Jason wanted to kiss her. He wasn't sure if he should but the desire burned him from the inside out. He reached his hand up and cupped her face. He stroked her cheek with his thumb. He looked deep in her eyes; he saw a flash of fear. He wanted to kiss it away. He leaned in slowly. He kept his eyes on hers. When he was sure she wasn't going to pull away he gently placed his lips on her forehead. His heart was racing and he heard her breath catch then quicken. Without thinking he released her. "Good night, Gwen." One last look and he disappeared behind the closed door of his condo.

***

Gwen was having trouble catching her breath. She could hear her gasps as she struggled with the door. She wasn't sure exactly what she had wanted but she knew her body craved more. His hand had burned her cheek. She felt places in her come alive in a way she had forgotten was possible. She thought about knocking on his door and throwing herself in his arms. She even took a step in that direction when another face clouded her eyes. In an instant her desire was replaced with anxiety. She felt the old ache in her chest and she knew she wouldn't go to Jason. Instead she threw herself on her bed and sobbed.

Article printed in Rolling Stone Magazine: June 21, 2016
Written by: Julie Cutter

My Day with Soary

The Deuces lead singer Soary has been elusive over the span of his career. Often when he is interviewed, he gives short answers that trigger momentary satisfaction for the interviewer until they realize later, they did not garner any additional information about the man or the band. You can imagine my surprise when he granted me a 'day in the life' interview.

My editor told me to meet him outside of Feed the People, a community kitchen and shelter for homeless people. When I arrived Soary was already there with several members of the band. Noticeably missing was bassist and sometimes singer, Jeff. When I asked where he was, I received a non-committal reply about prior commitments but he would join us later. Soary wore running shoes, athletic shorts and a Cure t-shirt. Interesting shirt for a pop/country star; I made a mental note to ask about it later. After a short greeting with the director we were assigned tasks and sent off to work. I was grouped with Soary and we were sent into the warehouse to organize food that was delivered from a recent food drive. After an hour we finally took a break and I was able to get my first question in.

"Why are we here?" I was tired and hot. While I am in support of volunteering, this was not my idea of a day in the life of a musician. I felt his intense stare as he considered my question. His dark eyes bored through me, making me squirm uncomfortably.

"It's important to me to spend time supporting people and communities."

I felt chastised and embarrassed. I searched for a way to come back from my insensitive question. But after a moment he let me off the hook by chuckling.

This I could handle; I have a great sense of humor.

"Standard answer? Okay, honestly, my mom instilled in me at a young age that the bigger the blessings I am bestowed, the bigger my responsibility to give to others becomes. When I was young I used to volunteer in retirement homes, play games and sing. I wrote a few songs in nursing homes."

He gave me a mom story. One of the sexy men in show business just got sexier. I was momentarily stunned. I mean a musician who was spending his day volunteering because his mom told him to was a bit of a shock. "So, there's no publicity tied to you being here?"

"No. There is not." He sounded offended. "If you decide to mention it in your article it'll be the only way this makes it to print."

"Then why am I here?" Could I be crazy enough to hope he was a fan of my work?

"Because my manager said I was doing this 'day in the life' interview and I refused to change my plans for today to entertain you." And with that comment he went back to sorting. He was still a bit grumpy. I decided to focus on the experience.

We worked for five hours! Afterward he offered me for me to ride with him back to the hotel. Instead of going straight back he asked if I was hungry. After all that work, I was famished so we stopped off the Burger Joint. You know the one of Highway 1-11? A true old-fashioned grease pit.

"I love a good burger." He said as he took a big bite.

"Me too." I squirmed as I took a tiny bite thinking of all the extra time in the gym it would take to get rid of this meal. "You've been traveling a lot since your first album released in 2012. Where is the best burger?"

He wiped his mouth, gazed out the window as he gave my question some thought. "It would have to be in a small town in Alabama."

"I didn't know you played shows in small towns."

"My mom lives there."

"Do you and your mom go for burgers when you visit?"

"No. A girl I knew took me there."

His voice was softer, his eyes were wistful. There it is, I thought to myself, there is the heart to some of these songs. If I was careful, I just might have a story here.

"Does she take you there when go visit?"

He continued to eat his burger. I couldn't tell if he was ignoring my question or if he was contemplating his answer. The silence grew but I knew from experience the first to speak often gives something away. I needed him to give me something. So far, I had very little to print anyone would care to read.

"I don't go back often. No, we don't go for burgers anymore."

Well, I didn't gain much except for a full belly. Soary spent the rest of the meal talking sports and answering emails on his phone.

When we arrived back at the hotel we went to his suite. Jeff was there lounging on the sofa. He greeted me with a quick hello. After the introductions and pleasantries, we settled down on the veranda to chat.

"Why were you not at the community kitchen today?" Soary gay?

"I wasn't feeling well this morning. I think I'm coming down with something. So I rested up for tonight's show."

"Are you feeling better now?"

"A bit but I'll make it."

"Some of the songs on the new album have more of a dark tone to them. That's unlike the first album which was more pop/love songs. Why is that?"

Jeff looked at Soary and waited for him to answer. "Love isn't always joyful and full of light."

"Your fans seem to love the darker version. You sold over a million copies. What do you have planned next?"

"Yes, the fans are great. We will finish this tour out then take some time off to focus on the third album." Jeff answered.

"Yes, we'll be going home and taking a break." Soary added. "We've spent most of the last five years touring. The second album was written primarily on the tour bus. So, it'll be great to actually spend time in the studio."

"Do you ever get lonely? Being single on the road?"

They exchanged looks.

"We aren't single, we have each other and the rest of the band." Soary told me. GAY

Jeff tossed a napkin at him. "Speak for yourself. We are definitely not a couple." Or are you?

We all got a good laugh and they successfully avoided yet again opening up. The afternoon was turning into evening; I knew it would be time to get ready for the show soon. I was going to join them backstage for the VIP session.

"I read somewhere that you're dating someone." I said to Jeff.

"Oh, I date off and on. Sure. I do have a lady friend who is very special to me. But we aren't committed and I want her to be able to keep her privacy so I won't tell you more than that."

"What about you Soary? Are you dating? Is there someone special in your life?"

The tension was obvious. Jeff stared at his hands and Soary looked out at the city. The sun was starting to set, light was changing, filtering shadows across our quaint sitting area.

"Yes, there is someone very special to me. But I don't talk about her." And with that the interview ended.

I took my car over to the stadium and was escorted backstage to the VIP area. I watched as Jeff, Soary, and the band posed for pictures and chatted with fans. It was a sold-out show. The energy and excitement were contagious as they took the stage. The cheers were deafening. The floor shook as the sound vibrated out of each fan in the arena. The Deuces are going to be around for a long time, I thought to myself. Then I remembered that Cure t-shirt. I guess I will have to get that story next time.

Chapter 4

2016

"Come back, Come back, Come back," she screamed.

The dreams started after her parents' visit. They were different every night but the intensity was always the same. Gwen would wake in tears and always touch her chest. She had to make sure that there wasn't a hole where her heart was supposed to be. Unlike most people she didn't want to remember her dreams when she woke but some snippets would always find a way into her mind. She remembered telling him bye at the airport and she was screaming for him not to go. Sometimes she would dream of the beach and how it felt to be in his arms but always in the end she was losing him and he never looked back. There was one dream that upset her so much she barely slept for two nights following it.

[handwritten margin notes: "it was a good visit?" and "legit but doesn't fit?"]

She figured her therapist would have told her the dreams were brought on by the anxiety of her pending visit home. Although she knew it was unlikely that she would see Soary, she was still fearful of it. That's what was so strange about the pain she still felt. There was a time she wanted to see him. Casually, run into him on the street, at the bookstore, or at a concert. But now, she knew without a doubt she did not want to ever see him again. Especially now that she was living her life again. She did not want to face her past.

She only wanted to look forward. The dreams were causing memories she repressed to haunt her days.

She liked to sit in the conference room and study different companies' financials. She liked to witness the quiet mornings turn into the rush of business. Gwen had made it a habit to make herself enough of the group without being an active participant. She would also make sure to fix coffee and set out the fruit and bagels when the caterer arrived. She was always there when the morning rush began and as a result was usually included in invites from breakfast meetings to after-hour cocktails. She was careful which invites she accepted, focusing on surrounding herself with people she could learn from. She watched her superiors and she learned how to interact with clients with confidence and humility. She made notes of who was an expert at what and who trusted and leaned on whom. By the end of her second quarter she had read all the product manuals, taken all the tests, and written dozens of proposals. She knew who the top clients were and what characteristics would get her in the top spot.

After work she often met with Jason. He was helping her paint her condo. Gwen enjoyed being around Jason tremendously. She often found herself glancing at her watch in the afternoon counting down the hours till she would see him. He was constantly making her laugh and she appreciated that he never once offered to turn on the radio or TV. She knew he must wonder what was wrong with her but she just didn't trust herself to open up to him. They never seemed at a loss for things to talk about. The days flowed easily into each other; she enjoyed her routine. She was excited about her life.

but also haunted by past?

Although things were going well there were often moments of tension with Jason when she wanted him to take her in his arms and kiss her. But she was also relieved when he didn't. She was attracted to him so when his arm grazed hers while they were painting or fixing dinner or walking along the pier, she would feel her heart flutter. They often held hands; the warmth of his fingers intertwined with hers would cause a rush of excitement flow through her. At the end of their evenings he would cup her face in his hands and kiss her forehead leaving her breathless.

She was at ease with him but never at peace. There was a longing for more and a fear of more that kept her dancing on edge.

One evening as she was about to unlock her door and head in to relax for the night, she abruptly changed her mind. She headed to Jason's condo and knocked. She had a sudden overwhelming desire to touch him, to be with him. She ignored the warning in her head. She wanted him. She was tired of being scared. Over the past four months she had spent almost every day with Jason. He made her laugh and he was kind to her. She wanted him. She wanted more of him; without hesitating she knocked on his door.

"Hey." He greeted her with a warm smile.

"Let's go away this weekend."

"Go away? And what do you have in mind?" He was completely taken aback.

Gwen reached for his hand and placed it on her hip. As she stepped in closer to him, she saw his look of surprise. They were just friends. He had never made any move to indicate he wanted anything more. She watched his eyes. She was sure she saw them darken with desire as he realized what she was doing. But he didn't step into her. He waited for her to continue what she started. She was in more control of herself in that moment than she had been in years. She could see herself as if she was outside her body looking down, witnessing the scene as a passerby. She urged herself on.

Jason tightened his grip on her hip as her face looked up into his. And still he waited on her. Gwen reached up to him on the tips of her toes. She had to remind herself to breathe. Their lips were so close they could feel the moisture of each other's breath. She wanted him to kiss her. He wanted her to kiss him. But they were frozen neither moved.

"So, where do you want to go?" He asked again. His voice was barely a whisper. As his lips moved, she felt them on her own which caused a shiver to run down her spine.

Gwen felt the rush of desire engulf her body. Her body became alive and she wanted him more than she could remember wanting anything. She stood tall and pressed her lips to his. For a moment he just stood there and then he pulled her close and slowly began to kiss her. He was gentle with her as he drew her in his condo and closed the door, never moving his lips from hers. She could feel his excitement but he pulled back from her and kissed her hair, her forehead. She laid her head on his chest to regain her balance.

"I want to be with you." As she said the words she looked up into his eyes and kissed his lips softly.

She felt him grow harder against her as he pulled her body closer. He wrapped her in his arms and kissed her deeply. He pulled back but did not remove his lips from hers. He kissed her gently and watched her face. "Are you sure?" His lips never left hers. He kissed her over and over. Gently biting her lips as he did.

"Yes. Please." She wasn't sure how she was able to get the words out. They were muffled under his mouth. Dizziness made her sway as he quickly released her.

Jason took her hand and led her to his room. He turned to her and reached for her jacket.

Gwen realized she still had her purse slung over her shoulder. She smiled at him. She watched as he hung her jacket over the back of nearby chair and set her purse down.

"May I?" his voice was husky. His hands stretched out toward the buttons on her blouse.

Gwen's mouth was dry. She nodded. Jason smiled. His fingers worked quickly, unbuttoning her blouse with ease.

As he undressed her, he kissed her shoulders, her neck. When his lips reached her breasts, she sucked the air into her lungs with such a gasp he stopped to look at her. She couldn't speak but in her mind she screamed for him to continue. She smiled and stroked her fingers through his hair. He took that as a sign that she wanted more. He led her onto the bed before hurriedly undressing himself.

Once he was naked, he went to her and started at her toes and kissed up her body. When they were face to face, he spoke again, "Are you sure, Gwen? You're shaking." He rubbed her arms with his hands as if to warm her.

"Please." She couldn't say more. She wished she could tell him what he was doing to her. Her body was tingling and burning. She was afraid she would never quench her desire. She was amazed that she was restraining herself from taking control. He was taking his time. Teasing her body with his fingers, with his kisses. She wanted to scream out for him to take her. But it all felt so good she could only moan, no words could find their way out.

***

Jason took his time. He wanted to please her. He wanted to take in every inch of her body. There were moments he had to stop and get control of himself. When he was finally ready to enter her, he knew he had already pleased her. She was withering in spasms on the bed. He held his body above her only hesitating a moment while he thought he would ask her again if she was sure. At that moment Gwen reached her hands around him and as she pulled him into her, she looked deep in his eyes and sighed. They became one and rhythmically moved together. Jason worked at being gentle, but the more excited she got the harder it was. He suddenly found himself overwhelmed and he finished as she sighed his name and buried her face in his neck. She kissed him over and over as he rested his head on her shoulder careful to keep the full force of his weight off her.

They lay together recovering. Gwen was stroking his shoulders. Jason couldn't believe what had just happened. He knew he was in love with Gwen. Every night he watched her fear recede a little more even as he touched her. He hadn't realized she was ready to take another step into intimacy with him. He was watching her closely, falling more and more in love with her. But he was cautious. He knew he had to be patient.

"So, will you go away with me?" Gwen had recovered her breath.

He laughed. "You're very convincing." He raised himself off her and lay by her side pulling her onto his chest. "So where would you like me to take you?" He kissed her forehead.

"Oh, anywhere, really. This is what I had in mind so I guess we really could just stay here."

"Hmm. A weekend in bed with you sounds like paradise. We could order delivery and only leave the bed for necessities. I like the way you think."

"Do you?" Gwen started to bite his lips. "Well, I wonder if you would like what I'm thinking now."

"Please do tell." He groaned as she moved her body against his.

"I was thinking it would be great to..." She rubbed her hand down his body and placed it between them gently rubbing him until it was obvious he liked what she was doing. ~~his balls?~~

"I do indeed." He rolled over on top of her and began again. ~~too soon~~

***

Gwen went through the next weeks full of happiness. She and Jason took turns staying at each other's condos. They ate together, shared stories from their days, laughed together.

Sometimes they went out to dinner. Gwen started to think of Jason as an extension of herself. There were times a smell or sound would bring Soary's face into her mind, filling her with regret. But those moments and memories didn't overwhelm her like they once did. When she was with Jason she didn't feel broken. She was

Sounds like she long to [?] (handwritten margin note)

looking forward to meeting his friends and family. She wanted to connect their lives together. She wanted his life intertwined with hers. She recognized that her feelings for Jason weren't as overwhelming as they had been with Soary. In a way, that was a relief; she wasn't afraid she would lose herself to him.

Gwen was excited when Jason told her he had invited some of his friends for the weekend. She wanted them to like her and she wanted to like them. As the time drew near, she found she was nervous about meeting them.

They planned to meet at the local bowling alley then they were going to have dinner. She changed clothes several times trying to decide which outfit would be best. She was in the middle of pulling a purple shirt over her head when she heard Jason call out to her.

"Gwen? Are you ready? We're going to be late. Gabriel has already called me twice. They just ordered some drinks."

"Coming. I'm almost ready." Gwen yanked the shirt down and surveyed herself in the mirror. It was snug but draped nicely around her neck, showing off her collar bone. It looked good with her skinny jeans and black boots. She finished clasping her bracelet when she felt Jason wrap his arms around her waist from behind her.

"You look great." He said as he nuzzled her neck.

"I thought we were late?" Gwen asked as she wiggled free of his embrace.

"We are but you look too good to go bowling."

"Do I?" Gwen wiggled free and went back to her closet to change when she heard Jason laugh. "What are you laughing at?"

"You look great. Come on. Let's go." He reached for her hand.

"Jas, do you think they are going to like me?"

"They'll love you." He kissed her head and led her out the door.

The bowling alley was a short drive. It was located in a remodeled warehouse that also housed several restaurants, a coffee bar, and a few boutiques. The rest of the area was still undeveloped and run down. Gwen's boss was working on a financial plan for the city to redevelop the area. The plan was to bring in a developer to build condos and attract retailers.

The bowling alley was brightly lit up. Music blasted from the speakers. The sound of the bowling balls smacking into pins demanded to be the main attraction. Gwen took in the room, glancing from one group to another as Jason retrieved their shoes.

"There they are." Gwen stared in the direction he pointed and smiled.

Jason strode toward his friends with an eagerness Gwen found endearing. He talked about them often enough that she felt like she knew them a little. They were a tight group who grew up together. Her nerves fluttered as they joined them. Gwen stood back as hugs were being shared.

"Gwen, I'm Gabriel." He smiled broadly at her. Gwen stuck her hand out to shake his in greeting. But instead he reached for her and hugged her.

"Don't hog all the attention." Elizabeth shoved Gabriel and leaned in for a hug of her own. "We've been dying to meet you." She exclaimed.

"I have been looking forward to meeting you all too." She pushed her hair behind her ear. "Jason has told me many stories; I feel like I know you already."

"Don't believe everything he says about us. Unless its good." Logan stuck his hand in her direction. "I'm Logan."

"It's great to meet you, Logan." Gwen made sure her grip was firm.

"I'm going to get us some drinks." Jason told her.

"Okay."

"I got you a ball already. I use the nine-pound one so I thought you might like that one too." Gwen followed Elizabeth and settled to change into her shoes. They took turns taking practice shots as they waited for the guys to return with their drinks.

***

Gwen was enjoying herself. Although she wasn't a good bowler, she wasn't in last place so that pleased her as well. She liked Gabriel and Elizabeth but Logan was making her uncomfortable. He kept staring at her. When she would catch him he kept staring until she looked away. His stare seemed unnatural and rude. She just kept giving him a smile she hoped looked friendly and warm.

"Hey, how're you doing?" Jason leaned in and whispered in Gwen's ear as he nibbled on it a little.

"I am a horrible bowler." She laughed as she turned her face to him and let him kiss her. Without pulling away from him she asked "Jason, do you think your friends like me?"

Jason straightened up. After briefly staring at her a wide grin spread across his face. Gwen thought she glimpsed relief flash in his eyes.

"Yep. They're smitten. Gabriel just told me he thought you were gorgeous, smart, and fun. I had to kindly remind him that you were taken and to please keep his thoughts to himself. Elizabeth likes you too. She called you sweet." He handed her the water he had gotten for her and scooted next to her on the bench.

"What about Logan?" She tried to sound casual but she heard the tension in her own voice. She knew Jason and Logan had been friends since first grade and it was important for him to like her. She didn't know how much Jason had told Logan about her.

"Ah, Logan likes you too. He said I was a lucky man," he told her. "Is that what has you so tense? Logan been giving you the stare down?" He laughed as he watched a sheepish smile turn her lips up.

"I just thought he didn't like me and..."

"And?"

"Stop laughing. And I want him to because I know he's important to you."

"Okay you two. It is considered rude to hold up the game for a love fest. Besides, you're making me jealous. Logan never gazes in my eyes like that. Not sure if he ever did." Elizabeth pointed at the scoreboard. "It's your turn lover boy." She laughed as Jason smacked at her on his way by.

"I am so glad Jason met you. He's been single for far too long. Between him and Gabriel playing the field I didn't think I would ever get a female to bond with." Elizabeth remarked as she plopped down in Jason's seat.

"You never set them up with your friends?" Gwen asked trying to sound nonchalant.

"Sure sometimes. But I don't know a lot of people they don't already know. Logan and I have been together since ninth grade so we've all basically grown up together. I haven't worked since having the kids so not a lot of chances to meet single women."

"I wouldn't think they'd have any problems meeting women." Gwen looked over at Gabriel. He was handsome. His blond hair needed to be trimmed to get it out of his eyes but he was well dressed and had beautiful green eyes. He reminded her of Jason. They had a lot of the same characteristics. Both tall, blond, and handsome. Gwen noticed they were about the same build. They could pass themselves off as brothers.

"No, not for Gabriel. He's a sweet guy. He has a few girlfriends and a lot more, um, shall I say friends. Jason has always been different. There haven't been many for him. He's picky, I guess. So, you can see why I'm so pleased. I like you. Which makes me happy because we wouldn't be meeting you if he didn't really care for you. Jason hasn't been known to bring a lot of girls around." Elizabeth patted Gwen's shoulder and smiled. She noticed Gwen's quizzical look and continued. "We're like Jason's family. He isn't that close to his parents and he's an only child. For us to meet a girl is like him bringing you home. You see the fact that we're here means you're important to him."

Gwen liked Elizabeth. She liked that she was pleased to have her around but more importantly, she liked her easy manner. Her ability to talk while all Gwen had to do was smile, nod, and say uh-huh at the right times. It was nice to be here, to be getting her life back. She let what Elizabeth said about Jason's feelings for her roll around in her mind. She was pleased and a little scared. She watched him as he talked to Gabriel and Logan. They were huddled up talking about the basketball game and making plans to go the park tomorrow to play a game. She was attracted to him. The desire to touch him was strong. She smiled as she thought what touching him always led to. She didn't think she would ever get used to climbing in bed with him. After all the years of thinking she would never have feelings for anyone again, she realized she was completely smitten with Jason.

"I love this song." Elizabeth jumped up from her seat right into Gabriel's arms. He twirled her before they started dancing.

Gwen was stunned when her heart leapt into her chest. Her hands started to shake. She couldn't breathe. She tried to count but the attack came on fast. The smile she had watching Elizabeth and Gabriel was lost. She tried to steady her breathing and find her numbers. She heard Elizabeth ask her what was wrong. She stopped dancing and stood over Gwen. Her voice sounded muffled. Gwen was watching them in slow motion.

Soary's voice halted the blood in her veins.

Jason came up beside her. He took her hands and pulled her to her feet. Logan and Gabriel came into focus; they were gaping at her. She wanted to care what they thought but all her energy was focused on breathing. She needed to get out of there. It had been months since she had a panic attack; she was out of practice.

"Jason, what happened?" Elizabeth's voice broke through.

"Liz, I'm going to take Gwen outside." Jason wiped the tears off Gwen's cheeks. "You all finish the game and we'll meet you out front when you're done." Jason nodded to Logan and Gabriel. Then he led Gwen outside.

They settled on a bench outside the bowling alley. He draped her jacket over her shoulders and sat there holding her hands. He didn't speak as he rubbed her hand with his thumb. His mind was racing. He knew he was in love with her and he knew she cared for him. But the ghost they didn't talk about was too much. He couldn't help feeling hurt. He wanted her to be okay, to be over this pain that she carried around like an old worn security blanket that was no longer needed.

He tried to control his emotions but as he sat there waiting for her to recover, he found that he was angry. Jason watched for signs of anxiety in her. That's how he picked up on her doubts about whether the gang liked her. He wanted to protect her and ensure she felt happy. He wanted her to fall in love with his friends. He had looked around and saw she was happy; she liked his friends and they loved her. He let down his guard. He stopped watching her, waiting for signs of anxiety to interrupt the night. Then he heard the first chord of the song. His arm was stretched behind him holding the bowling ball high, his legs were in a long forward stride when he froze. The ball dropped from his hand and rolled into the gutter. Logan groaned. Gabriel yelled, "What the hell, man?" Elizabeth had already moved from Gabriel's embrace and was talking to Gwen when Jason got to her.

Her voice interrupted his thoughts. "I am so sorry, Jason." Gwen choked out. She had gotten control of her breathing but was still crying.

"Are you okay?" Jason felt his anger subside as he looked in her eyes. He saw her pain and was sorry he hadn't been able to make it better.

"Yes, I'm better now." She was looking back down at her hands in her lap. She was wringing her hands trying to use them to help steady her mind.

"Gwen, when are you going to tell me?" He didn't know why he asked. He didn't want to hurt her but he needed her to tell him. He needed to hear her say she wasn't still in love with Soary. That it was a habit and her body betrayed her. He needed her to comfort him. He wanted her to tell him she was in love with him too and all this would just be something they laughed about later. He needed this from her right then because although he knew he was in love withher, he hadn't realized his feelings for her were becoming his life. When he saw her in the midst of her attack he didn't want to live without her. He realized that for the first time in his life he loved someone so completely it hurt. He was afraid that without her he would lose the ability to love at all.

"Jason, I haven't had an attack in a while." She sounded weak.

"Are you ever going to tell me?" He stood and turned his back to her. He didn't want to see the pain on her face anymore. He felt horrible pushing her on this but he couldn't help it.

"Jason, it is such a long story. Such a pitiful story really." She sounded defeated; he felt the guilt creep up his spine. Yet he remained still and silent, waiting. He heard her sigh and then her voice filled the air.

"I was just a kid really. I met Soary one summer while I was home from school. We fell in love. He was my first love—my first everything. My only, until you. We made plans to be together forever. At the end of the summer I had to go back to school and he had to go to Nashville. He was planning to come visit me at school and I was going to visit him as often as I could. We had a plan." She paused to clear her throat. "I remember a strange feeling coming over me when I watched him walk away at the airport. I wanted to run after him but I held myself back. It was silly I told myself. I was going to see him in a few weeks. But I never saw him again. I called him a lot. I wrote him letters. I went to visit him once. He left me and I didn't know why." Jason had joined her on the bench as she spoke. He gazed at her feeling the emotions of her story thick in the air. "I am leaving out a lot of details," she finished.

"For me? Or because they're too hard for you to talk about?" Jason asked. He knew some of the details she was leaving out. He wanted to tell her that it was okay, she didn't have to tell him anymore but he didn't. He needed to hear it from her. He needed to know how she felt about Soary now.

Gwen thought about his question. Was she not admitting to her true feelings because she was afraid of hurting him or because she didn't want to be talking about it? She wanted to tell him because she needed to but then she wanted to forget all about it. To go back topretending she was fine. Jason's thigh warmed hers as they barely touched. She understood feeling the warmth of him that she was more afraid of admitting how much she had needed Soary and how much it hurt to lose him because she wasn't sure if she would be able to keep from falling apart. Suddenly all the happiness she had felt swelled up in her. She felt like she was going to choke on it. She didn't want to fall apart because she wanted to be with Jason. She wanted what he had been giving her to be her life. She wanted Soary and all the heartache she felt to be in the past. She wanted Jason to be her future. She just wasn't sure how to make what she wanted a reality. But she did know if she couldn't give him all of the truth, she had to give him enough of it to buy her time.

"Because I'm scared." Gwen looked at him. They sat there gazing into each other's eyes until she finally started to speak again.

"I was confused at first. I would call and Jeff, Soary's friend, would answer and tell me he would give him the message. Then one day Jeff just said, "I am sorry Gwen. Really sorry." And hung up the phone. That's when I really started to struggle. He was avoiding me. That realization weighed me down. I continued going to class and managed to keep my grades up but I stopped functioning. I wouldn't talk to anyone. I was constantly checking my phone to make sure it worked. I stayed logged into my email and I looked in the mailbox three or four times a day. My friends couldn't understand what had happened to me. Eventually they started staying away.

Even my roommate. She got used to me randomly opening the door as if miraculously someone would appear. She was a good friend though. She would talk to my mom and tell her all the wonderful things we were doing. When actually it was the wonderful things she was doing. I couldn't leave the apartment except to go to class. I kept telling myself I would snap out of the funk. That everyone got over their first love. I clung to the idea that time would heal my wounds." She looked at Jason and saw him gazing at her tenderly. He reached his arm around her waist and pulled her against his side.

"I didn't know how to find him. I went to his mom's house and stayed for two days thinking he would call her and then I could talk to him. She kept insisting he called randomly but she didn't know how to get in touch with him. I didn't believe her although I really wanted to. After two days I decided to go to Nashville. I knew the name of the studio he was recording at and I had his address. When I got there, I found out he and Jeff had moved to New York. They had gotten signed and were working with a producer there. That was the first time I had an attack. Standing there listening to his landlady talk about how wonderful they were and how lucky that they were going to be famous. On and on she talked and I panicked.

I realized he walked away from me. He left me. And I panicked."
Her voice cracked as the pain of the past roared to the surface.

"I couldn't stop crying and I couldn't breathe. I shouldn't have
been driving but I had to get away from Nashville. I was almost
home when I had the accident. When I woke up in the hospital, I
went into shock. I couldn't talk for two days. I sat in the hospital
just watching as the doctor and nurses kept coming in and running
tests on me. They kept trying to get me to talk. I just didn't want
to. I was so sad. I was overwhelmed with guilt and smothered in
loss. I finally gave one of the nurses my mom's name and number.
They called my mom. My mom and James came to the hospital to
pick me up. They wanted to take me home so they could take care
of me. I couldn't stand to be in that town for one more second so I
begged my mom to take me back to school. I haven't been back
home because I feared I would see him. James told me he talked to
Judy. She admitted that she knew how to reach Soary, of course
she did. She was sorry she played a part in hurting me but he was
her son." Gwen leaned away from Jason and looked in his eyes.

"I found ways to pretend I was alive. But I wanted to die. If it
wasn't the guilt it was grief suffocating me. Some days it was both.
It took a couple of years but I finally believed I could find joy again.
I didn't know Soary was famous because I hid from it and the
people who love me helped keep me away from it. The day I met
you was the first day I'd heard his voice in years. Oh, Jason,
tonight, I... Well I had no idea I would react that way. I am so sorry.
I don't know." She looked at him for a sign he understood what she
wasn't saying, that he could forgive her.

"I was nervous about the music. I thought you were too. Then
you asked me about Logan and I relaxed. You weren't even

thinking about it. When I heard his song and I looked at you. You were gone. I tried to get to you, Gwen. I tried to keep you from hearing him." Jason cupped her face with his hands. What she saw in his eyes made her cry.

Awww

"I love you, Gwen. I will never leave you." He leaned in and kissed her eyes, her forehead, and her cheeks. He was looking in her eyes with his lips almost on hers. He was waiting.

Gwen reached her hand into his hair and pulled him to her and kissed him. She lost herself in his mouth, kissing him deeply. When their lips parted, she looked into his eyes. "Jason, I haven't thought about love in so long. I just am not sure. I need more time." She didn't know what else to say.

RIP

"There you two are." Elizabeth walked over to them with Gabriel and Logan following behind. She was rambling about the rest of the game and how the lovebirds had run out on them. Gwen was thankful for her light chatter. She noticed the frown on his face when Jason stood and moved away from her. He busied himself straightening his sweater.

parent trope

"Logan and I don't get too many nights without the kids so we want you two to take us to the best place in town to eat." She sat beside Gwen and linked their arms and patted her hand.

"Gwen is tired. I really should take her home." Jason sounded curt causing everyone to look at him in surprise.

"I am alright actually." Gwen didn't want to ruin their night. She wanted to prove to Jason she was fine. She was worried because of the way he had moved away from her and he wasn't looking at her. "I have a great idea. Why don't we go back to my place and I cook for everyone?" She tried to make her tone match the one Elizabeth had used. She looked at her and nodded.

Whoa

She saw the pity in Elizabeth's eyes right before she hid it with a smile and said, "I think that sounds perfect."

Gwen felt relief that Elizabeth agreed so easily. She understood that a camaraderie was born in that moment. They would always unit together helping the other through any hardship.

The men had no choice but to follow as Elizabeth and Gwen walked to the car arm and arm. Elizabeth chatted endlessly, occasionally patting Gwen's hand until they reached the condos.

Gwen found it nice how everyone eased into a comfortable conversation that quickly went from one subject and on to another then back again without anyone seeming to lose track. She thought this was how she used to be with some of her friends before she met Soary. At one time she too could be easygoing instead of intense and sad. Lost in her own thoughts, she didn't notice when Gabriel came into the kitchen.

"Do you like to cook?" Gabriel had an easy manner. He was leaning against the counter smiling at her.

"Actually, I just recently started cooking. Yeah, I think I do like it. I have a lot to learn though. I thought it would be an easy compromise for tonight." She laughed nervously. "I wasn't ready for the night to end."

"Well, it smells great. May I?" He reached around her and dipped a fork in the sauce she was stirring. "Mmm. That is great."

"Thanks." She felt comfortable with him, she knew she could trust Gabriel. Jason told her about his mother's death. Gabriel had stayed by her bed holding her hand for hours as she drew her last breaths. When she passed away, he refused to leave her side until the ambulance arrived to take her body away. Jason said it took Gabriel a long time to recover.

She watched as he casually took the knife and started spreading butter on the bread loaf. "Gwen, I know tonight something happened. Some type of attack. Anyway, I wanted you to know that if you ever want to talk about it, I am available. I mean I am sure you and Jason talked about it but I can be your friend too." He shrugged and smiled at her.

"Thanks, Gabriel. I have panic attacks. They can be pretty intense." She really didn't know what else to say. It felt weird yet comforting that he just addressed the elephant in the room. He nodded, gave her hand a squeeze and then changed the subject.

She listened as Gabe started talking about a client who was opening an Italian restaurant. He relayed a funny story about his secret sauce recipe. Gwen found herself laughing. She was glad Gabriel stayed in the kitchen preparing dinner beside her.

Jason came in and watched them for a few minutes before asking. "Gwen, did I tell you Gabe is a life coach?"

"I thought he was a journalist?" Gwen glanced from Jason to Gabriel.

"I am but I moonlight as a life counselor." He gave Jason a pointed look before continuing; "My passion has always been split. Destroying people's lives by outing their secrets and putting people back together after they admit to their skeletons." Gabriel laughed and air punched Jason.

"I call it a split personality." Jason teased.

Jason took a beer from the refrigerator and left the kitchen. Gwen watched as his shadow faded from the room. She admired his retreating back as the realization that they just shared another first, Jason always kissed her before he left a room. She knew she hurt him when she couldn't tell him she loved him back. She wondered if he could feel her holding her feeling hostage. Maybe he blamed her for not letting herself enjoy what was happening between them. She wasn't ready to tell him everything that happened to her and until she could she didn't want to give too much of herself away. She knew one day she would be ready but she wasn't there yet. Turning back to the sauce on the stove she smiled for Gabriel as he continued to chat about his client all the while watching her with kind eyes.

Hours later Gwen hugged Elizabeth bye. "Now you will have to come visit us soon. Meet the kids."

"Yes, really soon." Gwen meant it too. She wanted to spend more time with them.

Imagining herself a part of their family warmed her heart. Throughout the night Logan lost the intensity behind his stare. It was as if he finally saw what he was looking for in her. As he embraced her, she focused her mind on the warmth of him through his sweater.

"We have an extra room but Gabe's got the quiet house if you want to enjoy a visit without yappy kids and dogs running around."

"Absolutely. You are welcome anytime." Gabriel came to her and held her hands. "Call me any time, Gwen. We are friends now." He brushed his lips against her cheek before turning to Jason.

Gwen watched as Jason said bye to his friends. There were hugs and kisses for Elizabeth and handshakes and back slaps for Logan. But Gabriel and Jason hugged and talked for a minute before he disappeared down the hall trailing Logan. Gwen imagined Gabriel telling Jason to call him tomorrow so he could help him figure out what is wrong with his crazy girlfriend. She found herself getting angry before suddenly remembering Jason's words. "I love you," he had said.

She had not responded with the right words. Shame and dread filled her heart. She thought she was in love with Jason but she wasn't ready to say it. She was moving out of her isolation so quickly it was hard to imagine herself as she was last year.

Jason's touch, his looks, his laugh those were the thoughts that dominated her. She couldn't wait to get home to him every day. But she also loved her friends and her work. She felt a freedom to live that was missing for the longest time. Knowing that loving him wouldn't take that away was not the same as accepting it.

"Jason..." She started when she saw he was not heading back to her condo.

"I'm tired, Gwen. Do you mind if I sleep at my place tonight?"

"No. Of course not." She wanted to tell him to stay with her but the way he was already closer to his door than hers made her hesitate. He wasn't even going to kiss her goodnight. She felt her breathe catch and was scared she was going to lose control. Silently she started to count.

"Gwen."

"Yes?"

"Are you okay?" She wasn't sure if he was asking for tonight or if he was asking in general. She wondered about it herself. Here she was about to have another panic attack because he didn't want to sleep over tonight. Not just a few months ago she would have panicked if he had made a move to touch her. What a mess she was.

Was she okay? Probably not she thought to herself. She decided then that she was crazy and probably would take Gabriel up on his offer to help her figure out how to be normal.

"Yeah. I'll be fine. Good night, Jason." Gwen went into her condo and closed the door on the unknown of her relationship with Jason.

She finished cleaning the kitchen and started a bath. She wanted to wash away as much tension as she could. She was sitting on the side of the tub testing the water when the thought came to her. She crossed through the rooms and stopped in front of the radio. She reached for the power button and pushed it quickly before she could change her mind. Music filled the condo.

She didn't hear it at first but then slowly she let the sound penetrate through her. It was a song by Prince. She smiled. She remembered dancing around her room to it song as a teenager. She found herself enjoying the sound. It had a good beat and brought a smile to her face as she started to let her body move a bit to the music. Then the song changed. Song after song she discovered she missed music. The sound filled the empty space. She felt sure of herself and less alone. When Soary's voice filled the room, the air stopped. Taking a deep breath, she calmed the butterflies in her stomach. She wanted to hear his words. His voice brought back memories. She closed her eyes and the first day they met came rushing back in full color.

Gwen was running down the bank of the lake trying not to trip over any of the kids and families. The wind had picked up and her kite was pulling fast and hard. Soon she would be at risk of getting tangled in the trees. She was laughing as she kept trying to wind the string in. She loved flying kites. When she was little her dad would bring a kite along on their fishing trips. If they were having a really bad fishing day and the wind was just right he would pull it out and they would spend the rest of their time flying it. Her favorite was when they tied the kite onto the boat as they drove across the lake. Gwen loved those morning and evenings with her dad.

Just as she thought she had the kite under control a gust of wind came pulling at it fast and hard slinging it straight into the trees. The handle fell from Gwen's hand. "Shoot." She mumbled as she lurched forward after it.

Soary had been watching the girl with the kite. He noticed her first because the sun danced in her auburn hair. As he watched the light play with the colors, some gold, some brown, some red, he saw the wind rip the kite handle out of her hand. He dropped his note pad and hurried over, stepping on the handle just as it was about to fall off the bank toward the lake water.

Laughing as she came up to him, she said, "Oh my goodness! You got it in time." She leaned down and retrieved the handle. "Thank you."

"You are very welcome." He watched as she tucked a curl behind her ear and started winding the kite string around the handle.

"It's been a while since I've flown this thing."

"Really? You were doing great until the wind picked up. I was impressed."

"Well, thank you." Gwen finally looked at the stranger who saved her kite from destruction.

Her eyes searched his face. She was staring at the most gorgeous face she had ever seen. She noticed her heart had started to beat faster and felt heat rise up her chest and neck. Afraid he could tell what she was thinking, she looked down to monitor the work her hands were doing with the kite string. Soary watched her work, realizing that he should probably move on but he was unable to make himself take the first step.

"My name is Gwen," she startled him when she looked up and extended her hand.

"Hi. I'm Soary." Hesitantly he took her hand in his. His fingers closed around hers. Her fingers were cool and delicate. He felt her watching him as he gazed at their hands. His thumb rubbed across the back of her hand, taking in the silky feel of her skin. He gazed on as if neither hand belonged to him. It felt foreign, this object at the end of his arm. Meeting her eyes, he thought he saw the same confused emotion inside her. "It's nice to meet you, Gwen." He managed to let go and take a step back.

"Soary." She said as she continued to tighten the string around the kite handle. "Why do I not know you?"

"Do you know everybody in this town?" he tried to sound flirty but instead sounded grumpy.

"Mostly. At least our age." She smiled. "You do know we only have one high school so if you went there, I would know you. And with a name like Soary I wouldn't forget you."

"Well, you caught me. My mom and I just moved here. I graduated a couple years ago, so you see I didn't go to your high school."

"Are you staying here for the summer?"

"Yes." He told his first lie to her within minutes of meeting. He had planned to head back to Nashville after getting his mom completely settled. But for some reason he didn't want to tell her that. "I'm moving to Nashville afterwards though." He paused and helped her fold the kite and slip it into a vinyl bag. Their fingers grazed each other's in the process, making him feel nervous and unsure of himself.

"Nashville, is that where you moved here from?"

"Yes, I grew up there. My mom got a job as director of nursing at Golden Age Retirement Homes. It is her dream job actually. So, we moved her here. But my future is there."

"I see." Gwen looked at Soary again. She wasn't the type of girl to be flirty or get sappy over boys. She was friendly enough but not *overly outgoing. She had no idea why she was asking him so many questions. She knew she should tell him thanks for his help and move on. She didn't though. Instead she gazed at him. Their eyes locked. A rush of adrenalin raced to her brain. Her mouth went dry and then watered. Her heart pounded in her chest. She was imagining that he was going to kiss her. What surprised her most was she wanted to be kissed by him, a total stranger.*

Soary was experiencing the same unnerving desire. His hand trembled at his side, daring him to reach out for her. Seconds, possibly minutes passed as they willed themselves to part ways.

"Gwen." He started.

"So, you have been here a matter of minutes really. You probably don't know where to get the best burger." She started to turn away from him as she spoke.

Soary took several steps toward the bench where he left his notebook and several more to come along beside her. "No, actually. I have met my mom's neighbor. But I doubt he gets out for burgers much."

"Then you're in luck. I happen to know every excellent place to eat in this town. As a thank you for saving my dad's kite and a welcome to town will you let me treat you to the best burger you will ever taste?" She kept her pace steady heading toward the parking area.

"Actually..." He hesitated. He wanted to eat with her. He wanted to stay with her all day but he promised his mom he would volunteer at the retirement home today. He was going to play some songs for the residents. But he couldn't imagine telling Gwen no. "I can't eat there. Maybe we can get them to go?" Gwen stopped walking and looked at him quizzically.

"I told my mom I would come by after lunch and volunteer at the retirement home." Glancing at his watch, "She will be expecting me soon. I have a car in the lot over there. If the burger joint isn't far

maybe we could get them to go and you could get some volunteer time in too."

Gwen studied him. *"You want me to get in the car with a man I just met and eat burgers on the drive to a retirement community in the country to volunteer?"* There was amusement in her voice. *"Okay."* She suddenly decided. *"But you have to tell me two things first."*

"Okay." He sounded bemused.

"What will we do for our volunteer work? And what do you like on your burger?" She grinned at him and realized she was flirting. She was also going to go with a guy she had just met, going against all of the self-defense tactics she learned, not to mention the proper way a lady should behave.

"Well those are easy. I will play some songs. You could play some chess or checkers. Or maybe paint. You could also dance with the residents, if you wanted. I eat my burgers all the way but with pimento cheese instead of cheddar." Soary couldn't remember ever feeling so much joy because of one other person's presence. He already knew his entire plan was changing.

Laughing, Gwen said, *"Let's go."*

They got their burgers in a big red barn that smelled of grease and meat. There was not any marketing on the building or the bags they were handed. Soary would never have known the place was a restaurant. But it was packed, every table full of happy customers. Gwen explained the owner hadn't intended to have a restaurant full time. He had opened it as a temporary shop to feed the police officers and other volunteers who came to help with desegregation in the sixties. The food was so good people never stopped coming in for more and eventually he accepted that he was a restaurant owner. But he never named the place. It was known as the Red Barn or some older people in town call it De's for de-segregation. The atmosphere was welcoming and friendly. Soary immediately liked it. They took their burgers to go and ate during the drive talking companionably.

Soary admitted it was the best burger he had ever eaten.

"I love them! I can't believe I went so long without one this year." Gwen rolled her wrapper and started gathering Soary's discarded items and stuffing them into the bag. She settled back in her seat with a satisfied look on her face.

"Why has it been so long since you had one?"

"I just got back in town from school. I went up to Tennessee to study accounting. They have some good places to eat but I haven't had a burger like this anywhere." She glanced over at him and giggled. "I'm sorry—I should've been helping you since you're driving." She reached over and wiped ketchup from the corner of his mouth. The action was both intimate and endearing. Soary looked at her, understanding something amazing was taking place between them. He felt he had known Gwen his entire life. There was such a peace inside him just being with her. Even though they had known each other only hours he knew he wanted to spend every minute he could with her. He thought about Bethany and Jeff and understood this comfort and desire to be together must be what they felt for each other. His heart fluttered in his chest.

When they arrived at Golden Age Soary took his guitar from the trunk and started guiding Gwen up the tree-lined walkway to the side entrance. The facility was surrounded by natural beauty. Dogwood trees lined the walkway. There were flower gardens on two sides of the building and in the far back there was a man-made pond with a walking path zig zagging to the green houses. It was a paradise for people who wanted to spend their last years surrounded by nature. Gwen understood why Soary's mom would consider it a dream job to work here.

As they approached the building, she noticed a woman in scrubs walking toward them. She was one of the nurses coming to tell Soary his mom had already gone to her afternoon meeting but that she would show them to the veranda to set up. Gwen took a seat among several residents and joined in their casual chatter about the card *game they just finished playing. She purposely avoided looking at Soary. She also avoided looking at her phone that was vibrating in her pocket.*

Gwen was so absorbed in her conversation with the residents she didn't notice right away the music she was hearing was coming from Soary. When his voice crooned the first lines of the song however the entire area fell quiet and all eyes turned to stare at the Greek god who was wooing them with his song. Gwen watched as his raspy voice commanded the full attention of everyone present. The nurses and other volunteers had stopped their work and were quietly listening to him. His fingers gently strummed the strings of the guitar. She watched his lips move so his voice could escape into a beautiful flurry of words. She stared at his face, watching the way the words made his features smooth and crinkly. She gasped when he lifted his eyes and stared straight into hers. Gwen was inexperienced when it came to romance and love so she didn't realize immediately that was the moment she turned her heart and soul over to Soary. She did know that she wanted to spend every minute of her summer with him.

Later after several songs and games they were saying their goodbyes and making promises to come back the next week. Both of them aware that their promises ensured they would see each other the following week. They rode for several minutes without speaking. It was the kind of silence that sparked with electricity. There was a sense they were communicating with their energy. Neither could have put into words what they were feeling.

"Thank you for coming with me." Soary started. "I really enjoyed you being there."

"I had a great time. I had no idea when you saved my kite that I was meeting a future Grammy winning artist." She teased.

"Artist?" he laughed "More like a small-town guitar picker."

"Are you kidding me? You were amazing! Your voice was mesmerizing. I mean you built whole worlds with your voice—your words. I felt what you were singing inside me." She paused feeling a

bit embarrassed by her description. "I mean, I guess, I should hear you again to be sure it wasn't a fluke. You know like first time luck."

"A fluke, huh? Okay, we'll have to make sure you get an encore."

Smiling she agreed.

Turning off the ignition he turned to her, "Let me help you get your kite out." He didn't want to say goodbye to her.

"I can manage. Thank you, though." Gwen reached over and placed her hand on his arm. "You create stories with your music the same way an author weaves a tale with words, painters create a scene with paint, photographers tell a story with a picture. You are an artist. What you did was so much more than just strumming a guitar. I will never hear music the same again." Her earnestness moved him. He felt the prickle of tears burn the back of his eyes.

"So, since you don't have friends here, want to meet me at a bonfire tomorrow? It will be a bunch of us home from college. There will be beer and hotdogs. Music too but not a live band." She pulled her hand back from his arm using it to tuck a stray curl behind her ear. She busied herself with gathering her things to exit his car to avoid eye contact.

"I would love to but can I pick you up and drive you?" he wanted to make it more of an official date not just meeting her there.

"Yes, but I must warn you my mom can be a bit tough. Are you sure you want to go through meeting the parents? We could just meet there."

"I don't mind tough. Besides, I should meet them since it will be our second date." He watched her closely.

Gwen looked up from gathering her things and looked him straight in the eyes. Her pulse was racing and her body was overheating. She contemplated the idea that what just happened was a date. And realized it was pretty much the best the date she had ever been on. "Hand me your phone."

He handed it to her wordlessly and watched as she entered her contact information. "Text me later and I'll send you my address."

She handed it back to him and hurried out of the car, not allowing him time to respond.

Opening her eyes, Gwen wiped the tears rolling down her cheeks. "Oh, Soary." Her voice sounded unusually loud in the empty room. "Why? Why did you leave me?" She lowered herself to her knees and cried. But it felt different than the other times she cried for him. This time she felt she was not in mourning. She was in control. But she was sad. She cried for the girl who was so full of life and not afraid of anything. She cried for the boy who ran away. When she stopped crying, another song was on the radio. She felt cleansed. She thought this was how she would feel if she was a flower after a nice rain. Her heart wasn't aching. She had a moment of clarity that she was alive and she didn't have to pretend to be dead anymore.

As she looked around the room, she didn't see what was in front of her. She envisioned herself and her life. She saw how sad she looked holed up in her apartment at school. She was a hollow and empty shell walking around. She saw the faces of her friends and for the first time noticed how full of pity their looks were when focused on her. She saw her mother and felt regret for causing her to feel so helpless and lost. She saw James and how he always managed a smile but his eyes were always so sad when he looked at her. And then she saw Jason. The memory of the girl she had been was drastically different from the one she became.

She knew she wanted to find that girl inside of her again. She wanted to embrace life and take advantage of every opportunity just as she once had.

She saw Jason in her mind in a way she had not before. He was life. He laughed with her and encouraged her. She saw the love in his eyes. She knew she had hurt him but she didn't care at that moment because she felt she could set it all right. And she finally saw life blow into her. She sat there on her floor and listened to the music. She tried to think of Soary again but was too tired. She couldn't conjure his face. She couldn't remember what it felt like for him to touch her. She thought about their night together but couldn't remember what his hands had felt like. She couldn't remember who she was with him. Finally, she pushed herself off the floor, turned the radio off and went to her bath. After she lowered herself in the water, she heard his voice.

"Gwen?" Jason asked as he tapped on her bathroom door.

"Jason?"

"Hey." He came in and looked down at her. "I let myself in. I couldn't sleep without you." He smiled as he lowered himself to the side of the tub.

"Jason, I am so sorry about tonight. I know I hurt you. And I never, never, never want to hurt you." She tried to keep her voice from cracking.

Jason reached his hand down and stroked her cheek. Gwen reached up to him and intertwined her fingers in his hair.

"I love you, Jason. I do. I love you so much." She pulled him down to her as she stretched up to him. When their lips met, he wrapped his arms around her and pulled up from the bath. Her body drenched him and the floor as he hugged her close.

"I'm sorry I was so distant." He mumbled into her neck.

"No, I am the sorry one." She wanted to tell him about listening to the radio. She wanted to tell him she was alive. She wanted to tell him that she was not the same sad girl anymore. She wanted him to know something changed and her past was really in the past. But she couldn't keep her thoughts clear. His breath and tongue on her neck was very distracting.

Published in Variety Magazine October 2016
Concert Review: The Deuces Bring Energy and Heart
to Pacific Stadium

The Deuces are out to prove they're ready to take the world by storm. Five years ago, they were playing small venues in some of the seediest clubs. After their debut album went platinum, though, they have been the darlings everyone wants to see.

Last night they played to a sold-out crowd at Pacific Stadium. Lead singer Soary was in perfect form. He demanded an emotional response as he sang Waiting from their second album. His falsetto swelled to the size of the stadium. If it was the eighties, I would imagine women would be throwing their underwear on stage.

As the night continued the band kept up with Soary with deep emotional cuts, a mix of songs from their first two studio albums.

They ended the night with Soary's sultry voice lifting like velvet curtains into the night. If you were at home, you missed an epic show.

Chapter 5

2016

Gwen woke with a start. She couldn't breathe. She tried to steady herself. She looked over and saw Jason asleep. A small smile tickled the corner of her lips. In an effort not to wake him she slipped from the bed. She went to the kitchen and poured herself a glass of water. She took slow, deep breaths. In and out, in and out. She talked herself through each breath reminding herself to draw the oxygen deep in her lungs and to expel each one slowly paying attention to the tension leaving her body.

She counted to ten and when she got to ten, she started again. After half an hour of the same routine she started to feel the tension fully release from her neck. She felt her lungs open and her head cleared. She realized she was crying and reached for a towel to wipe her face. As she stood there regaining her composure, she saw clearly Soary's face in her mind. Memories flooded her in a rush. She felt his hands on her face and tasted his lips as he kissed her. She inhaled and held her breath, letting the memories play in her mind like a movie. She could hear his voice as if he was standing in her kitchen. "I love you, Gwen. I will never leave you. Don't go off to school and forget me."

She heard her response. "I could never forget you."

The sound startled her. She looked around her not sure if she'd actually spoken the words. She shook her head and started counting again. But the counting didn't work this time. She was not having an actual panic attack. This time she was in complete control of her body. It was her mind that she had lost control of. She wanted to stop her mind from replaying the rest of the scene. She didn't want to remember falling in Soary's arms and making love to him. She didn't want to hear his voice telling her how beautiful she was. She thought she had moved past this feeling of being trapped in the past with him yet in reality alone.

She was tired and mad. She decided she was not going to feel this way—not today. She had to focus on something else. She turned to the refrigerator and pulled out eggs, bacon, and biscuits. She would make Jason breakfast. It would give her something to concentrate on. She felt guilt engulf her. She let the guilt guide her hands as she made an omelet, biscuits and gravy, and coffee. She loaded a TV tray and piled her masterpiece on it. By the time she walked to the bedroom she had completely regained control. One deep breath later, she was kissing Jason awake.

"Good morning." She whispered as he rolled over on his back and smiled. He had not opened his eyes but was grinning from ear to ear.

"Hmmm. I think I love you so much I could eat you. You smell like eggs and coffee. A dream come true." He laughed at his own joke as he opened his eyes to the feast before him. "What is this all about?" He pushed the pillows up behind him and sat up as Gwen settled the tray on the bed between them. She sat with her legs crossed facing him and smiled sheepishly. She hushed the voice in her head that called her a fraud and a liar. I love him. I want to make him happy. She spoke the words silently in her head and then focused all her attention on feeding Jason breakfast.

"Are you ready?" Jason let himself in her condo and was pacing outside the bathroom door. "We're going to be late."

"I'm coming." Gwen put her lip gloss in her purse and took one more look in the mirror.

She looked good. She had pulled her hair up in a high ponytail. The black dress she was wearing had a low-cut back, exposing her shoulder blades as it flowed down her backside into a fish tail. She turned and admired the way the dress made her rear look round and plush. She grinned at her own reflection.

They were meeting Logan, Elizabeth and Gabriel for a night out at a new bar and dancehall. She had been looking forward to it all week. Jenny and Becky went shopping with her for the dress. Jenny said she may catch up with them later in the evening.

She wanted to make up for her bad first impression. She wanted to have a good time and she wanted them to be happy for Jason. As she took one more look in the mirror she smiled and winked at herself. Giggling she opened the door to the bedroom.

"Finally." Jason whirled around to face her as she entered the living room. He let out a long whistle. "My goodness! If I had known this was what I was waiting for I would have been more patient."

Gwen giggled again and did a slow turn so he could take in all of her. He caught her mid turn and nuzzled the back of her neck.

"You smell heavenly." He slowly kissed her neck and was working his way down her back when she pulled away.

"Jas, we have to go. We're already late."

"They can wait." He said as he reached for her again.

"No, really, I don't want them to think I'm completely self-absorbed and inconsiderate." She reached for her purse and gave him her most dazzling smile.

"You win but only for now. I don't know how long I will make it in public so be prepared if we need to call it a short night."

"Maybe you don't have to wait until we get home." She teased.

They were both laughing as they left her condo.

***

When they arrived, Gwen wasn't surprised that Elizabeth and Logan were already at the table.

"Wow, you look great." Elizabeth moaned as they approached.

"Thank you. You look great too." Gwen took her seat next to Elizabeth.

"Ah, this old thing?" She spread her hand down the length of her red gown.

"What? You spent half a day trying on dresses." Logan moaned. The girls laughed and Jason ordered them drinks from the waitress.

"Where is Gabriel?" He asked.

"He has a new girlfriend and she needed his help reapplying her lipstick." Logan said.

Elizabeth rolled her eyes.

Jason laughed. Gwen wondered what the inside joke was all about. She glanced at each of them with a raised eyebrow.

"Gabe has a love of public places. He likes to test his dates and see how outrageous a place he can get their dresses up and panties down." Logan told her.

"Yeah, he says the first girl that puts him in his place will be the one he marries." Elizabeth added "Although we haven't known one who can say no to that boyish face and devilish smile." She looked at her watch. "He should be back in a minute. They've been gone for twenty." They all laughed at that.

Gabriel and a cute brunette arrived at the table a few minutes after the hostess delivered their drinks. He was smiling as he leaned over to kiss Elizabeth on the cheek. He looked at Gwen and leaned down and gently kissed her cheek before taking his seat next to Jason.

"Gwen, Jas, this is Candy." He smiled sweetly as he looked at his date. Jason almost spit his drink out trying not to laugh.

"Hi," Candy said as she blushed.

"Hi, Candy. It's nice to meet you. I'm Gwen." She stuck her hand out with a concealed tissue in it for Candy to take. Candy looked puzzled for a minute but saw Gwen's subtle hand movement across her own lips. Candy took the tissue and looked down at her menu as she dabbed at her smeared lipstick.

Gwen then turned to Elizabeth and started a conversation that quickly pulled them all into a relaxed back-and-forth. Gabriel studied Gwen, impressed with how she had so easily helped and welcomed Candy without anyone else noticing. He doubted he would date her much longer but he was pleased Gwen treated her kindly.

Throughout dinner they laughed as the guys shared stories and ribbed each other. Gwen learned about Jason's crush on his high school math teacher and Logan's love of home-ed. Gabriel apparently was a genius and was voted most likely to waste his God-given talent.

Elizabeth was homecoming queen and no one was surprised when she and Logan got married. They were nice stories of youths shared. Gwen enjoyed reminiscing with them and felt no jealousy to have missed so much of Jason's life. She was glad to hear how he used to play basketball for money in the park and that he was embarrassed by his first car because it was so much nicer than his friends'. She felt a kindred spirit with Gabriel as she learned he loved numbers and could spend a weekend engrossed in a good book. She liked hearing that Logan cooked Elizabeth dinner most nights although he was such a manly man. She loved the stories of how Elizabeth always takes care of them when they are sick. She was the den mother and helped keep them on the straight and narrow. She was thankful no one shared stories of old girlfriends and flings. Occasionally she would remember Candy was there and wondered if she was enjoying herself.

After dinner they moved to the lounge of the restaurant to discuss their next destination. "I think we should head to Echo. There's a great band playing and I know I can get us in." Candy said joining the conversation for the first time all night.

"Oh." Gabriel looked at her as if he had forgotten he had brought a date. "How can you get us in?" He raised an eyebrow and exchanged a look with Logan.

"I know the bouncer," she said with a shrug.

"I think a nice band sounds great," Elizabeth exclaimed clapping her hands

"Great. Let's go." Candy downed her drink and reached for Gabriel's hand pulling him toward the door.

"Someone is in a hurry," Logan grumbled as he helped Elizabeth up from her stool.

Gwen giggled as she realized that like herself, Elizabeth had a few more drinks than she needed. She slipped her hand easily into Jason's and let him lead her to the car. Once safely buckled in and on their way to the bar Jason smiled at her. "Sorry about all the stories at dinner."

"Are you kidding? I loved hearing about all of it. I think it is fabulous that you all have such a great history. It makes me happy to know so many people love you." She leaned over and kissed his cheek.

"You weren't bored?"

"No way. I'm having a great time." She smiled at him and realized that she was having a great time. She hadn't even hesitated at the mention of music. She was looking forward to the rest of the evening. After confronting Soary the morning after her dream she wasn't afraid to hear his voice. She didn't necessarily want to hear his music. But she did feel in control of her emotions.

Candy was true to her promise and got them in although the place was packed. She helped them find a table and then excused herself to go talk to the bouncer again. Gwen couldn't help but notice that Gabriel never gave her a second look as she walked away. She was intrigued by him. She wondered what made him have so many flings when he was obviously a nice guy.

"Are you comfortable?" Gabriel leaned over and asked her smiling

"Yeah." Gwen blushed realizing he had caught her staring at him.

"Good. You didn't share much about yourself at dinner." He was making light conversation as Logan, Elizabeth and Jason were in deep discussion on who first released the song playing.

"I was enjoying listening to you all. What do you want to know?"

"Okay, for starters, what were you like in school?" He asked as he handed her the drink that Jason had ordered for her.

"A little awkward. I was one of the girls who was friends with everyone but didn't really ever belong to one group. I was always on the outskirts. I did have a few best friends but they changed over the years. I loved to read and I was a nerd with numbers."

"You weren't popular?" He asked with indignation in his voice.

Gwen laughed. "No, not at all. I was a cheerleader and the editor of the school paper. Somehow, I managed to be cool and a dork at the same time. I am from a smaller town so everyone knew everyone but I wasn't popular like you mean. I had a few boyfriends for a minute but I was shy and well..." she paused as she thought of Soary. "I only lost my heart to one boy." She took a drink and hoped the interrogation was over.

Gabriel watched her thoughtfully. He smiled and Gwen was thankful when he moved from his seat.

"Jas, can I dance with your date since mine left me?" He didn't look at Gwen but held his hand out to her.

"Sure. Just don't be long. I might start to miss her." Jason winked at Gwen as she took Gabriel's hand.

Gabriel led her to the dance floor as the DJ played Sting's "When We Dance." He placed his arms around her waist. She lifted her arms and intertwined her fingers around his neck. She was aware of how close they were. He could have easily kissed her. She felt nervous and took a quick glance over at Jason. He was not looking their way. She could tell he and Logan were still engrossed in debate.

"Did you break his heart or did he break yours?" Gabriel's voice brought her attention back to him. She looked up into his eyes as she tried to figure out what he was referring to.

"What?"

"The only boy you lost your heart to?" He repeated her words back to her.

She stiffened at the mention of Soary. She tried to think of something to say. Gabriel pulled her closer. "I'm sorry." He whispered in her ear. She realized she must have looked stricken and was sorry for making him uncomfortable.

"It's okay." She shifted adding space between them. She looked up at him at the same time he looked down at her. Their eyes met. They were full of kindness and mischief. A giggle erupted from her. She shook her head resigning herself to his investigation. Maybe it was the drinks or maybe it was honest curiosity. Or possibly his investigative style. She wasn't exactly sure. All she knew is she wanted to talk to him about things.

"He broke my heart. Actually, he took it with him." As she thought about her answer, she decided she wanted to trust someone. She needed a friend. "He left me without saying goodbye. I was in college. He and I made plans to be together. Then I saw him off to the airport and I never saw him again. We had plans. And I never knew what went wrong." She thought no one could understand she lost more than her first love.

Gabriel watched her face as she spoke. "You still love him." It wasn't a question and it wasn't an accusation; it was just a statement.

"I don't think about him like I used to. I have moved on, am moving on." She found the truth refreshing. "I'm in love with Jason."

Gabriel nodded and pulled her close again. As the song ended, she felt his breath on her ear; "I know you love Jas." She shivered as chills ran down her spine. She wasn't sure why but she didn't want him to let her go. She felt comfortable in his arms; she held tight to him. He pulled her tighter and pressed the length of her body against his. There was a comfort in talking about her past without fear of hurting the listener. Gwen shivered. "Lady Marmalade" began to play, forcing Gabriel to release her. He looked deep in her eyes. Gwen was struggling to figure out the look, she knew something was being communicated. She was light-headed from the drinks and the dancing. She giggled again and wobbled toward him.

"You can always talk to me," he said barely loud enough for her to hear him. He caught her, wrapped his arm around her waist and guided her back to the table.

They interrupted a great debate on who had the better golf swing. Elizabeth dramatically yawned and made a big display of being bored.

"Gabe, why do you never sweep me away?"

"Because my dear, I am afraid I would not bring you back." He winked at Gwen. "Who thinks I should find my date?"

"What for? You know you won't call her tomorrow," Logan stated.

"Yeah, stay here with us. Let the girl have fun." As Jason finished his statement, they all looked in the same direction he was gazing toward. Laughter spread around like falling dominoes around the table as they witnessed Candy stick her tongue in the bouncer's mouth.

"Well, looks like you all are stuck with me." Gabriel was the last to laugh as he took a seat next to Jason.

Gwen didn't miss the flicker of sadness in Gabriel eyes just before he joined the debate claiming his was the best swing of all three of them.

Right on cue Gwen's friend Jenny approached the table. She wore a tiny black sequined dress that hugged every curve of her body. Her hair hung loosely down her back while tendrils curled around her face. She was glowing from the exertion of dancing. She looked messy and sexy. Gwen jumped from her seat and threw her arms around her a bit more aggressively than she intended.

"Whoa. I am a little off balance." Jenny told her as she hugged her back. Gwen stepped back and smiled at her friend.

"Hi, Jenny." Jason stood and greeted her with a quick hug.

"Guys, this is Jenny. Jenny, this is Elizabeth, her husband Logan. And Gabriel." Elizabeth and Logan greeted her with a quick hello and handshake.

Gwen watched Gabriel greet Jenny. It occurred to her that Jenny and Gabriel would be a cute couple.

"It is nice to meet you all," Jenny told the group.

"Join us." Gabriel pulled his chair out for her to take.

"Thanks. But I have a group waiting on me over there." She waved her arm. "I just wanted to come say hi to my Gwen." She squeezed Gwen's arm. "I love that dress on you." She cooed at her.

"Look at yours. You look incredible."

"Jenny works with Gwen," Jason told them.

"Really? That firm must have a monopoly on gorgeous accountants." Elizabeth laughed. "Are you sure you can't join us, Jenny?"

"Thank you but I just wanted to say hello. My date wants to head out. I think I wore him out dancing." She gave Gwen another hug. "See you Monday."

"See you Monday. Be safe."

"Always." She waved at the group and dashed off.

"She is stunning." Elizabeth watched her go.

"I know. She's funny, smart, and nice too." Gwen winked at Elizabeth. They both glanced at Gabriel who was already back in debate with Logan and Jason.

***

That evening as Gwen crawled in bed with Jason, she smiled.

"What are you smiling about?" he asked as he leaned over to nibble her ear.

"I was just thinking what a nice time tonight was. Your friends are great and I want us to see more of them. I mean, they only live a couple of hours away."

"They love you too. Gabriel gave you the very meaningful nod. And Logan asked me to bring you to stay the weekend with them. But let's not talk about them." He was kissing down her neck. "Let's not talk at all."

Gwen giggled and snuggled down in the bed with him

***

Monday morning Gwen rolled over and reached for Jason. She was disappointed when she didn't find him beside her. She raised herself up in the bed and then heard the shower. Relief washed over her. She fluffed the pillows and leaned back, mentally planning her day. She wasn't looking forward to going to work. They were engrossed in preparing financial reports for a company involved in a complicated acquisition and she had a lot of reports to present in a meeting. Public speaking was not her favorite part of the job. She preferred preparing the reports then passing them on to someone else to present. But the sooner the week got started the sooner she would get to the weekend.

James called a few weeks prior to recruit her to help him plan a surprise birthday party for her mom. She eagerly took over several tasks including the invitations and decor. There was a lot left to do this week. Jason had a busy week ahead at work to wrap up the Southside project but she convinced him to take off early Friday so they could get on the road before traffic got bad.

She decided to get out of bed and get her week started.

***

"Do you think your mom will let us share a room?" They were driving through Gwen's hometown. She was excitedly pointing out landmarks, filling Jason in on stories from her past. She noticed how happy he looked at her excitement. His question interrupted her version of her first high school dance as they passed the local school.

"Hmm. I'm not sure. I think James would have talked to her about it. He would say yes but I don't know. She'd be nervous about it."

"Well, if I have to sleep down the hall leave your door unlocked."

"Turn here." Gwen couldn't contain her excitement as they turned on her road. "I am so excited that I wouldn't mind sleeping without you for a night."

"What? Already over me?" He teased; a wide smile graced his face.

The street she grew up on was idyllic. The street was wide, sidewalks with trees framed both sides. The houses were pretty pastel colors. Each lawn was neatly manicured without being pretentious. There were bikes strewn about at various points indicating that it was a kid friendly street. All the mailboxes matched with the black iron-worked scroll and bright red flags. Gwen pointed to a blue house with knock-out roses along the front.

"Right here." She was bouncing in her seat. As soon as they turned in the driveway James and Sarah came rushing out of the house. They had obviously been watching for them. Gwen was opening the car door before Jason came to a stop. She was in her mom's arms in a second.

"Let me look at you."

"Mom. It's only been five months." Gwen whined.

"Well, a woman can change a lot in five months." As she spoke, she turned to Jason. "And look at you. So handsome." Sarah reached for him and embraced him warmly.

"Welcome. Now let's get you two settled in so you can rest before the party. I am afraid James has gone all out. He rented the clubhouse at Meadows Golf Club. He wouldn't let me help with any of the arrangements." She reached for Gwen's arm and steered her in the house.

"What party?" Gwen feigned innocence, causing her mother to laugh.

"Gwen, you know no one can keep a secret from me." Sarah winked at Jason and continued to direct them in the house.

Jason and James exchanged a handshake and gathered up the bags.

"James, I'd like a chance to talk to you and Sarah privately. If that's okay." Jason wasn't planning on asking so soon after their arrival but he realized it was going to be tough to get Sarah alone during their visit and he really wanted to ask them a question.

"Sure. We'll make time before the party. Gwen promised to help with some of the details so she will be busy." James gave him a knowing look and smiled.

"Jason, I made up the guest room for you. It is one down from Gwen's. Although you'll have to share the Jack-and-Jill bathroom with her." Sarah smiled, turned to Gwen took her arm and led her to the kitchen to get a cheese tray put together for lunch.

Jason carried their bags upstairs to the rooms Sarah had indicated. He could hear their voices floating up the stairs. There was such peace and happiness in them. He lingered in the hall looking at pictures of Gwen as a young ballet dancer. He admired one of her in a full-camouflage fishing vest. He smiled at the young Gwen. He could see her happiness in her eyes, the way she tilted her head at the person taking the picture and smiled. She did that same tilt when he was telling her a story.

He stopped on the threshold of a soft pink bedroom. He felt tears sting his eyes. This was the room she experienced loss, love, and heartache in. He imagined her sitting at the white desk in the corner writing letters. He imagined her watching Soary pull up the driveway to pick her up for a date. He imagined her comforting herself with a book in bed when she missed her dad.

He wandered around her room lightly touching the lamp on her desk, pausing to look out at the backyard through her window. He looked at several pictures and notes stuck to her bulletin board. This room was decorated by a happy girl and held the memories of her coming of age.

There was a picture of her as a teenager standing in front of Red Barn with a huge grin on her face. He felt love for her overwhelm him. Turning to her nightstand he picked up a picture of a young Gwen flying a huge kite. The wind was clearly pulling it away from her. You could see the muscles in her legs taut with the effort to brace herself. She was looking over her shoulder, grinning at a man who had his back to the camera. The man appeared to be clapping for her and she was clearly in love with him. He knew at once this was a picture of Gwen and her father. The pure love on her face was beautiful. He placed the picture back on her table and made a silent request to the man in picture.

Later that evening Gwen was on her way to the Club to check on the cake. James had told her how he wanted it situated in the middle of the room on a table filled with lilies and he was sure the caterer would stick it in a corner for fear of someone knocking it over. Gwen was excited to help and quickly checked to make certain Jason was okay arriving with her parents before heading out. They told Sarah Gwen had to run an errand before meeting them for her birthday dinner. She made it easy on them by not asking many questions.

Jason was nervous as he sat across from James and Sarah on the couch in their living room. He knew this was a family he wanted to be a part of. And he loved Gwen with all of his heart. There was no doubt he wanted to make her his wife.

"Sarah, James. I know this may seem soon. But I want to ask your permission to ask Gwen to marry me." He had planned a long speech about his love for her and how although she hadn't met his parents, he knew they would welcome her in the family and they weren't that close so even if they didn't fall in love with her, he didn't care. He wanted to tell them he would care for her and wanted to make certain they knew he wouldn't leave her. But his carefully planned out words left him when his mouth opened. Words spilled out of him in a heap.

Sarah gasped and then immediately started to cry and James took her hands in his and patted them softly.

"I'm sorry. I know this is your night and I should have waited but you see we are going on a trip next weekend to visit my friends and I had a plan to ask her then and I well, I wanted to do this right." He was so nervous he started to sweat. He knew he should proclaim his love but he was afraid to say more for fear to upset them more.

"Oh, Jason." Sarah exclaimed and moved off the couch and coming to him she knelt at his feet. She placed her hand on his knee and looked up in his eyes. "You have just given me the best present of all. I would love for you to marry Gwen."

"We are very happy. You have really made Gwen happy. Are you sure it has been enough time though?" James asked.

"I think when you know you've met the right person there's no reason to waste time. I know Gwen still has some healing to do. But I know she loves me and I love her. I can take care of her and I can make her happy." He paused. When he started speaking again his voice was musical, "Gwen doesn't need me to make her happy. She is happy. I can see her happiness growing inside her more every day. I was looking at all these pictures of her. She had such a glow in every one of them. From the moment I met her I knew she was special and beautiful. But as we have spent the last months getting to know each other and falling in love I have seen that glow return. Some may think it is being in love. And it may be some of that. But seeing her as she used to be before, well it is clear she is finding herself again. And I am privileged to be a part her life. We haven't known each other long but I can't imagine being without her. I need to make her my wife and the mother of my children."

He was so sincere Sarah started to cry again.

"Jason, can I tell you something?" He nodded. "When Gwen was in elementary school, she and her friends wrote stories of how they would get engaged. I am not sure I still have it but I remember how romantic her version of a proposal was especially compared to her friends. I don't know what you had planned but I would like to share what she dreamt of with you." Sarah paused waiting to see if he wanted to hear. He nodded again and grinned. It was so like Gwen to plan her proposal.

"Well, it is actually quite convenient you're here and we are going to the club for dinner. For a small town we don't have many private romantic places. Her description is this: dinner at the club then a moonlit walk through the west side of the golf course to the lake. Once you get there, she described white rose petals spilled over the stone bench and a table with champagne and two glasses and tiny box. You would drop to your knees and take her hands and tell her all the sweet things you feel for her and ask her to marry you. She will cry and tell you yes and you will celebrate by placing the ring on her finger and sharing champagne while sitting by the lake planning your future." She paused and looked at Jason. "I know it's a little corny. But she was a sweet little girl and I think it would be perfect. Unless of course..." She trailed off.

"Thank you for sharing but it is your night..." Jason looked back and forth between them and saw immediately the disappointment. He realized they wanted to be a part of the new beginning and he would be bringing happiness back to Gwen in her hometown. "Well, I do have the ring with me."

Sarah jumped to her feet before he could say more.

"James, can you call the florist and arrange for the rose petals and when we get to the club, we can have the manager take care of the rest. It will be perfect." She started to whistle to herself as she rushed from the room to get her purse. James laughed and slapped Jason on the back as they stood to prepare to leave.

"Don't forget the ring!" Sarah called from the back of the house. "And hurry up I don't need to be late for my surprise party."

"I didn't mean to take over the evening." Jason gave James a perplexed look. "Did she say her party?"

"I have never been able to surprise that woman. You made Sarah really happy. But if you want to stick to your original plan don't let her pressure you."

"I am ready to marry her today. I want to ask her." He grinned and followed James to the car. Sarah was already in it waiting on them with the phone pressed her ear.

*****

Sarah pulled off the perfect surprised face and "you shouldn't haves" as she greeted her guests. She kept Jason close, introducing him to all her friends. He allowed himself to be her pet for the night because it was helping him relax. But periodically he would let his eyes roam the room looking for Gwen.

He smiled when his eyes met hers across the room. She raised her glass to him and winked. She was surrounded by several women about her age. He guessed they were school friends. One of them turned to see who she was toasting. He raised his empty glass back at her just as her mom introduced him another of her friends. He watched Gwen laugh at his predicament.

After the cake had been cut and the presents opened Jason asked Gwen if she cared to take a walk. He had one of the waiters show him the way earlier so he wouldn't lead her in the wrong direction and was a little nervous about the ring not being on the table when they arrived. As they walked Gwen talked about how perfect the party was and asked Jason questions about family members he had met. She was apologized for being so preoccupied throughout the night and hoped he didn't feel neglected. When they approached the opening in the bushes and walked out into the moonlight Gwen stopped in her tracks.

"What's this?" She sounded hoarse and Jason felt himself get nervous.

He dropped to his knees at once although they were still a few feet away from the roses and table.

"Gwen, I love you more than the salt in the ocean, more than the stars in the sky, more than the grass in the fields. I can't imagine being without you for one minute of my life. I fell in love with you the first day I met you as we walked down to the river. I knew you were aching over something but I saw an amazing strength in you. I ached to touch you. I knew you were someone I could count on to be brave and kind and stand with me through the good and bad this life will offer. Whenever we're apart I feel at a loss and it's hard for me to concentrate. I dream about the life we can have together. I dream about the children we can raise. I dream about you by my side." He paused and took a deep breath. "Gwen, will you marry me?" He was looking up at her and couldn't quite make out her expression. Shadows danced across her face, hiding her expression.

"Jason, I..." She dropped to her knees and cupped his face in her hands. They sat there like that for what felt like an eternity.

She had silent tears streaming down her cheeks. Jason waited for her to gather her thoughts.

The butterflies that danced in his stomach felt more like rams trying to escape. The longer she sat quietly the worse the pressure felt. Just before he gave in and spoke, she leaned her lips close to his and whispered, "Yes. I will marry you." He crushed her lips with a deep kiss and they lost their balance and fell sideways onto the grass. He was on top of her when their lips finally parted.

"Yes?" he questioned her.

Mistaking what he was asking with his question, Gwen reached her hand between them, nodded, and moaned "Yes." There wasn't time to properly undress as the urgency to fill herself with his love overcame her. She pulled up her dress while pushing his pants down. They made love on the grass by the lake under the moonlight.

***

Afterwards Jason went to the table and poured two glasses of champagne and brought Gwen the small box from the table. He handed her a glass and sat beside her. She smiled as he opened the ring box and showed her a one carat oval shaped diamond. He lifted it from the box. As he slid it on her finger he smiled and said, "I will never leave."

"I know you won't." Gwen felt so many emotions rolling around inside of her. She had spent the evening finding old memories that she had lost after Soary left her. She was enjoying the way friends and family carelessly brought up old events and she found herself laughing along as they reminisced with story after story of a time long past. She was happy Jason was getting to share the experience with her. A whole life was lived before that summer and it felt really good to talk about those times.

She laid beside Jason letting the surprise of the evening and his proposal warm her as the stars twinkled their approval from above. She had started thinking more about her future with Jason weeks ago, she was certain she was ready to take this step into the future with him. The anxiety that threatened to take up a place between them did not belong and she longed to kick it out of this memory.

"Jason." Gwen pulled herself upright. She took a deep breath and slowly released it into the night breeze. Jason stirred beside her. "I want to tell you everything that happened after Soary left me. I want you to know all of me before you become my husband." She tried to steady her voice but it waivered at the last.

"You don't have to talk about this, Gwen. I love you. I don't need to know if it hurts to share it."

"I know. But I need you to know. I need you to know I am strong enough to let it all go and be your wife. When I walk down the aisle to marry you, I want you to know it is just you and I who are married."

Jason held her hand as she told him the missing pieces of her story.

Alice Smith was still angry at her ex-husband George for not being faithful to their marriage. She was willing to forgive his indiscretions before he decided to divorce her for a young model he met on tour with one of the bands he covered. George was a video journalist for the cable network, Bio. He spent ninety percent of his time traveling. When Alice found a box in the attic of the house they once shared, with the words Off the Record written on the lid, she considered calling George and blackmailing him for more money. After listening to the recording inside she called her attorney instead.

All the Songs= One Girl

The following is a transcript of a recording purchased by Star Magazine in December 2016. The voices on the recording are George Smith, of Bio TV, and The Deuces lead singer, Soary. The recording took place backstage after the American Music Awards in 2014. All rights to the recording and transcript are owned by Star Magazine.

George: Holy hell, man! What are you busting in like that for?

Soary: Sorry, I was, I need to get away. It's just too much.

Long pause. Rustling sounds.

George: Here. I just made this drink. You take it, I'll make another.

Soary: Thanks.

Sounds of ice hitting glass. Rustling sounds.

George: I'm waiting on the scoundrel XXX, to get back here and honor his commitment. We already paid him for the interview.

Soary: Good luck. I saw him earlier. I don't think he is capable of an interview tonight.

George: Yeah, I know.

Pause.

George: What is wrong with you? Why aren't you out celebrating?

Soary: I thought I saw someone and then when I finally found her in the crowd.... It wasn't her.

George: I don't get it, man.

Slurping sounds and long pause. More rustling sounds.

Soary: You know how everyone always asks who I write about? Hell, I think you asked me once too. It was her. I thought she was here. But then it wasn't her. Man, I am so tired of running.

George: Yeah. What are you running from?

Soary: Her. The shame. The memories. You're married, right?

George: Yep.

Soary: Do you hate your job? Being here and not at home living a normal life with your wife?

George: No. This is my normal life. Besides my wife isn't the type that wants me home.

Soary: I don't think I would mind a normal suburban life. Being home with my girl sounds like heaven right now.

George: What, can you give this all up? Man, your second album is amazing. You guys are going places. You don't have time to be at home.

Soary:	Yeah, and she isn't going with me to those places. What's the point?
George:	Who is she?
Soary:	She is my heart. Man, she's perfection. She is the one I left behind for this. I miss her.
George:	Tell her. You could have anyone you wanted tonight. If she is who you want, tell her. I bet she would be happy to have you back.
Soary:	She isn't like that.
George:	Like what?
Soary:	She is more than this. She is more than a girl who wants to be with a musician.
George:	In my experience every girl wants a musician.
Soary:	No, not her.
George:	What's the issue? I still don't get it.
Soary:	I made her promises and I left her behind. She wouldn't want this—all this. She wants normal, small town America. And I think I want that too. But I can't walk away from this. It's like, I don't know who I am without music. But I'm dying without her. The music is dying without her.
George:	Listen, fame only lasts so long for everyone. You either fall out of style or die. If this girl is your one, don't let her go. If you're in this stuffy dressing room with me whining about a girl who is, where? It doesn't matter. She isn't here. And there are a lot of girls here wanting to show you how much they love

you. The point is this, if you can't enjoy it, why do it?

Long pause

Soary: George, it was nice seeing you again. Thanks for the drink.

George: Soary, this was recorded. You remember I said I'm interviewing XXX tonight.

Soary: Can you keep it off record?

Coughing

George: Yeah, sure, why not? Good luck to you.

Rustling sound.

George: Hey, Soary. You know if being away from her is the reason you can write those songs...well, there is that.

Soary: Yeah, sure. There is that. But George, what is that?

Chapter 6

2011

Gwen knew she was the happiest girl in the world. She had no doubt about it. She had just spent the most beautiful summer falling in love with an amazing boy. She was certain as she woke the week before she was to start her sophomore year at the University that she was probably the luckiest girl in the world. Soary was perfect. He was gentle with her and he was interested in what she had to say. He sang her songs and played his guitar for her every night.

What girl wouldn't be in love with a boy who serenaded as the rule not the exception? She couldn't wait to see him that morning. They planned to stay the entire day together at an inn on the beach before she had to head back to school. Gwen hurried to the shower although it was barely six o'clock. She rushed through her morning rituals and headed down to the kitchen to leave her mom a note. She didn't want to risk having to have another conversation about virtue and how she was making a mistake to spend the night with Soary.

Gwen wanted to be with Soary. She had waited nineteen years to give herself to a boy and she knew he was the one. She quietly rushed downstairs to write her mom a quick note promising to be back in time to finish packing for school. As she fumbled in the drawer next to the stove for the pad and pen her mom always kept there, she saw James on the deck.

"Good morning." She almost whispered as she stepped outside. She could send her message through him.

"You're up early. Not waiting to talk to your mom again?" He smiled at her warmly.

James had always managed to be a father figure without being more than a friend. She smiled back at him and felt her cheeks burn as her blood rushed to them.

"I just don't want to waste one second of today arguing with her. Soary should be here any minute and I promise I'll be back in plenty of time to get ready to go back to school." She paused. "She is up too, isn't she?"

James took another sip of his coffee and grinned. "You know she is just concerned about you. It is hard for her to let go. Remember how she acted when you went off to school? But she does want you to be happy. Well, this is big step for you and for her. She is scared for you."

"I know. But she doesn't see this as more than a school crush. I waited until I found someone perfect to give my whole heart to. I can't stay untouched forever. She has to let me grow up. Heck most girls at school have more partners in one semester than I probably will ever have. She doesn't need to worry. I love him and he loves me."

Gwen was surprised at how comfortable she felt saying these things to James. She had thought when the time came for her defend her love for Soary she would feel like a child. But she didn't feel that way at all. She felt happy and confident. Soary was the person she dreamed of from the moment she decided boys weren't gross after all.

James looked at her with understanding in his eyes. And at that moment she was more thankful than ever that her mother had him. He stood, laid his hand on her shoulder and kissed the top of her head. "I will tell her you promise to return in plenty of time to get back to school. I love you, Gwen."

"I love you, too." As she said the words she heard Soary pull into the drive.

She couldn't help but grin and shiver. Just the thought of seeing him made her heart skip and her stomach flutter. She grabbed her overnight bag and left the house through the front door. She bounded down the porch steps taking them two at a time. Adrenaline coursed through her veins. The joy and excitement she felt almost blinded her vision.

She smiled at Soary who leaned casually against the car. He grinned back and walked toward her. He paused in front of her and reached for her duffel as he leaned down and kissed her gently on the cheek.

"Good morning, my love," he crooned.

"Hi." Gwen wondered if she would ever get used to his sensual voice. Or ever tire of looking at him. She watched him stroll back to the car and open her door. He was tall and lean but his shoulders and biceps were taut under his shirt. His hair was a dark chestnut, a perfect mixture of black and brown. Gwen had never seen anyone else with that exact color before. And his eyes could penetrate into her causing her both alarm and excitement. They were so deep and rich she often shivered when he gazed at her. Sometimes when he looked at her, she wondered if he could see straight through her and read her every thought. He would find mostly thoughts of himself in her head. What a lovesick fool he would think her if he knew her every thought.

"Are you coming?" She hadn't walked to the car yet.

"Of course." She laughed and rushed to get in the car.

As they drove, Gwen filled him in on her class schedule. She talked about her roommate, her professors, and her hopes to get her own apartment so when he came to visit they could be alone. She told him all about the company she was going to intern with and how nervous she was about not being ready to take on her first job. Soary asked questions when appropriate. But mostly sat and listened to her ramble on about how her life would play out in the next few years. He couldn't help but to be reminded that for most of it he wouldn't be present. But her nervousness kept her talking without noticing the tension that crept into Soary's body. Finally, her voice slowed and she asked him the question he had on his mind.

"When do you think you will come and visit me?"

"Ah. As soon as I can. Jeff finished our demo last night. He is sending it out today to several recording studios and producers. He actually thinks a producer in New York will listen to it. Hopefully, it will work out with the producer and we get some radio stations involved. But we're still going to send the demo out to as many as we can on our own." He glanced at Gwen and grinned when he saw her enthusiasm.

"We also discussed sending it straight to a few radio stations. We figure if we can get some stations to play it record labels may be more inclined to give us a shot. It's a hard industry to break into but people are getting more creative every day. We already have 52,000 followers on Instagram and our You Tube video has over 500,000 views. Jeff also mentioned a friend in England that knows an owner of a production company, so we could possibly even head over there if things don't work out here."

He reached for her hand and held it as he continued to talk about getting his music produced. He realized he avoided her question. He had actually planned to surprise her and go up with her to help her settle in but the more she talked about the future, the less certain he was that he should. He had started to feel like a summer fling. That's what his friends keep telling him was anyway. Jeff was pissed when Soary said he met someone and was staying the summer with his mom. It wasn't that he wasn't sure he was in love with Gwen. He starting to feel afraid of the depth of her love for him.

On his way to pick her up he planned to tell her that he wanted to give her forever and maybe they should promise themselves to each other. Not exactly get engaged but make the promise to wait for each other. Now that they were talking about what their lives would be like in a few short weeks that sounded silly. His forever and her forever were on two different planets. Every plan she rattled on about was evidence they weren't heading in the same direction.

Thinking of all the plans they had already discussed seemed stupid. How could they really think an accountant and a musician could build a future? How could she live out her dreams following him around on the road? The carefree girl flying the kite wasn't so free after all.

"Did you bring me a copy?" she asked grinning. He wanted her to want to listen to his music but still felt fearful she wouldn't like it. Of course, he sang to her all the time but he hadn't let her hear a recorded song.

"Of course. But you can't have it until tomorrow."

"Now that's not fair." She laughed as she leaned over and kissed him.

"Sure, it is. You get the real deal for hours to come. You can use the CD to comfort you on those lonely nights in your dorm dreaming of me." He hoped she would be in her dorm alone and not out with other guys.

"Don't tease me. I don't even want to think of being without you," she pouted.

He wondered if she knew how it really felt to feel like you couldn't live without someone.

He couldn't shake the feeling that he would have to give up everything else he wanted to be with her. What terrified him the most about the feeling was that he was afraid he would actually give it all up if she asked him to. A brief glance at her etched her beautiful profile into his mind.

As they pulled up to the Gulf Inn, Gwen felt her stomach leap. Soary squeezed her hand again, leaned over and kissed her lips gently. He looked deeply into her eyes. Gwen knew he could see how nervous she was and she hoped he could see the happiness that encompassed her heart. She never imagined that wanting someone could hurt. Her body ached for his touch.

"Let's go check in and drop our bags in the room. Then we can get you some breakfast. You must be famished." He leapt from the car and opened her door before she caught her breath. As Gwen climbed out Soary took her hands and grinned at her. She smiled up at him and knew this was going to be a perfect day. She was hungry but not for food. She was ready to lock themselves in their room and not emerge again until it was time to head back. Instead of telling him that she just smiled.

"You are beautiful."

"You're not so bad yourself." She laughed as she stretched up on her toes to kiss his jaw.

They stood there a moment looking deep into each other's eyes. Then he wrapped his arms tight around her waist and lifted her as he swung her in circles. He kissed her deeply. Gwen tilted her head back and laughed. It was a musical sound and made Soary's heart skyrocket. How could he put her laugh to music he wondered as he set her back on her feet?

They checked in with the front desk clerk and dropped their bags in their room before they went down to the small dining area to have brunch. As they ate there was an easy flow of conversation. Gwen told Soary about her roommate and how she was sure he'd like her.

"I think we should introduce Jeff and Brenda. I really think they would like each other. She is very artsy. You'll have to see her paintings. What do you think?"

"I'll bring him with me to visit. Maybe we can stop by after we leave Nashville. If things work out, we'll go on to New York. I'll have to get a job to pay for all the traveling though." He was thoughtful. It occurred to him that he may not be able to afford to visit Gwen. He felt his chest grow tight at the thought. He wasn't sure he'd be able to stay away from her.

"Gwen, how long till you get a break from school?"

"Oh, I don't know. I would normally go back home every few weekends but with the internship I don't know. You can stay with us on campus though. I could sneak you into the dorm."

"Yeah, your mom would love that."

"Soary, I am an adult. My mother doesn't get to make decisions for me anymore." She sulked as said it which made Soary laugh.

After breakfast they took a walk on the beach. They strolled hand in hand kicking sand up with their toes. Soary talked about his CD and his dreams. Jeff was more interested in producing than actually writing or playing although he would play bass on most tracks. Soary's passion was singing. He dreamed of touring and putting out a few great records then starting his own production company and finding talent to produce.

Gwen listened to his excitement over the possibilities that lay before him. She found herself caught up in his dreams. It didn't occur to her that his dreams would take him away from her for long periods of time. The fact that their dream paths were as different as night and day didn't register with her. She pictured herself sitting backstage watching him perform and snuggling with him on the tiny tour bus bed. She also saw herself building her career. The two dreams crisscrossed into a nice woven pattern in her head. They walked and talked for a couple of hours. Gwen felt her connection to Soary grow stronger; ironically, she didn't notice

Soary had grown quiet. Where she couldn't see any of the issues they would face to be together, he couldn't see past them.

Gwen turned to Soary. "Take me back to the room." She hoped her demand held some hint of sensuality. But she was sure it didn't. She surprised them both when she grabbed his hand and led him down the beach to the Inn.

***

Soary watched Gwen casually walk around the room. She ran her hand along the console that held the TV, refrigerator, and safe. Then she strolled over the small writing desk. She paused there looking out the window. Soary sensed a change in her mood.

Gwen's insecurities surfaced when they entered the room. The click of the door closing represented the finality of her youth. She knew Soary had been with others before her; she worried she would disappoint him. He didn't tell her much about his past flings but he answered her questions as well as he could.

Soary approached her from behind and placed his hand on her shoulder.

"Song for your thoughts." He whispered. She couldn't answer. "Gwen, there is no rush. We have our whole lives."

She turned to face him. She searched his eyes for an answer; a sign of some sort, she didn't know what question she wanted answered or what she wanted to find in his eyes. Her emotions were like lightening bugs flitting here and there. The light extinguished before its glow revealed any secrets.

She lifted her hand to his face; her fingers traced his lips. His eyes bored into her but he stood motionless. She removed her finger from his lips and used it to trace her own. She watched Soary lick his lips; she swallowed the lump in her throat.

Soary reached his hands and placed them on either side of her face. He gently pulled her toward him as he took a step to her. His eyes didn't leave her face as he slowly closed the distance between their mouths. When his lips finally touched hers, she moaned and stepped closer to him. His mouth left hers only to connect with her nose, her eyelids, each cheek, her forehead, and back to her mouth.

Gwen felt her knees buckle. Soary swiftly moved his hands from her face and held her at the waist steadying her as he led her to the bed.

Passion blinded Gwen.

She listened intently to Soary's voice whispering how much he loved every inch of her body. She felt beautiful and loved. She tried to whisper back to him but words would not form. Gwen surrendered herself to him as he kissed every inch of her body.

Soary took his time. Gwen's body withered and shuddered under his touches. He had to take short breaks to keep them both from going over the edge. Finally, he pushed himself into her; Gwen cried out and gripped his shoulders as her hips instinctively rose to meet him. She barely registered the sharp pain she felt as he entered her because it was mixed up with the pleasure her body was enjoying.

They made love the rest of the afternoon.

***

"You have to be hungry." Soary ran his fingers up and down Gwen's arm, admiring her smooth silky skin.

"A little but I don't want to leave this bed or you." She turned to him and started to kiss his neck and ears.

"I have created monster." He laughed and rolled on top of her. Soary began the task of kissing every part of her body as she wiggled and squirmed under his touch. He loved to hear her laugh and played with her just long enough to make her beg for release. Once she began to plead, he gave in to her and gently moved his body into hers. He noticed her body tense under him.

Gwen arched her back and dug her fingers into his shoulders. She heard herself speak as if she was floating above her body watching instead of taking part.

"Please," the request confused her. When she felt places in her body get excited and erupt in pleasure she was unaware existed she understood what she was asking him to do to her. Soon they both collapsed in exhausted satisfaction.

"I love you." He whispered in her ear. Gwen wanted to respond but she couldn't form words. She squeezed his hand as she drifted off to sleep.

Soary woke to the sound of music in his head as he often did, but the tune was so sad; it hurt to hear it. He climbed out of bed careful not to disturb Gwen and went to the desk in front of the window, desperate to write the song down before it left him. His heart thudded in his chest as he put the lyrics to paper. He heard the notes in his head that would accompany the words but he couldn't add them, not yet.

Soary read the lyrics several times before the heaviness of them settled in his heart. He folded the paper quickly and stuffed it in his bag. He paced in front of the window waiting to see the first signs of dawn breaking. He opened the windows and leaned out to feel the cool breeze on his face. He smelled the ocean in the air. He listened to the waves crash onto the shore. Silent tears ran down his cheeks drying in the breeze before they could fall to the ground.

***

He lay beside her in the bed and watched her sleep. She was so beautiful. Her auburn curls lay across her shoulder and she smiled in her sleep as if she was having the happiest dream. He knew when they parted he may never see her again. The loss was quickly building inside him. He kissed her sleeping lips aware his decision was made.

The lyrics flooded his mind again—

> *I know I will leave you but forgive my selfish heart*
> *for I must take all you got.*
>
> *I am sorry to leave you in the cold*
> *but I can't give you any more of me.*

His kisses became rougher. He needed her to wake up and chase away his thoughts. She opened her mouth to his kiss and he forgot the words. He climbed under the covers with her and held her face in his hands as he kissed her lips over and over.

"Good morning." Gwen murmured pressing her body to his.

"Well it isn't quite morning but it is good now that you are awake. I thought we could get up and run to Starbucks, have a latte and muffin before I take you home."

"Really? I was thinking we could have breakfast here." She flashed him a mischievous smile as her hand moved to caress him. All the guilt he wanted to feel vanished as the pure joy of her love engulfed him. Her body moved in rhythm with his. She watched his face her eyes gazed into his. He had to close his eyes to ensure she couldn't read the goodbye he hid from her. As their bodies began to erupt in pleasure, she sighed, "I love you." He lost all control at the sound of her whisper. Not because of the words but because he felt her passion and at that moment, he knew he would never love another in this way. He wanted to stay with her and protect her and keep her by his side forever. But he also wanted to run because wanting her so much meant giving up a part of himself he couldn't sacrifice even for her.

Chapter 7

2011

As Gwen dressed her nerves danced inside her stomach. She was excited about school. She knew this was an important year for her. But all she wanted was to stay with Soary. She half thought that if he asked her to go with him, she would. She scolded herself for such thoughts.

She knew what she wanted and always swore to be independent and take care of herself. But being with Soary made her want to be dependent. She wanted to give him everything she could. In return she only needed his love. For the first time the reality of their separation started todawn on her. She realized it may be difficult for them to find time to visit each other. The thoughts made her frown.

"What are you thinking about?" Soary sat by the window watching her, his expression unchanged since they had gotten out of the shower. It dawned on her that he had not kissed her since then either so she crossed to him and sat on his lap.

"I was thinking you sure are far away." She felt his body tense up when she bent to kiss him.

But as he wrapped his arms around her, causing her to wonder if had imagined it.

"I wish we could stay like this forever. Just you and me and this room with the sound of the ocean out the window."

"I would never get any writing done." He laughed as he nudged her from his lap and gathered their bags before heading to the door.

He loaded the car and checked out while Gwen finished getting ready.

Melancholy accompanied them on the ride back to Gwen's house. Neither knew how to say what they were thinking. Both were afraid to overthink the situation.

Gwen held his hand in her lap and Soary mindlessly kissed her fingertips every few miles. When they pulled up in front of her house Gwen made a decision, she would second guess for years.

"You're going to airport this morning?"

"Yeah, my plane leaves at ten." He smiled.

"Let me take you. I'm completely packed. I can pick you up and drive you then James and my mom can meet me at the airport to take me on to school." She saw the hesitation in his eyes so she continued, "I am not ready to say goodbye. We need a more normal bye. Not this blissful doe-eyed romantic goodbye we have going. If I don't get to leave you now and then see you one more time, I might never be able to concentrate on my work." She tried to smile and make her request seem light-hearted. But in reality, she could feel the distance building between them and she wanted more time to convince herself she was wrong.

Laughing he leaned over and kissed her. "Okay, my silly girl. Pick me up by nine."

***

Gwen knew her mother would not like this plan but she had to change to shake the gloom out of their goodbye. She rushed into the house and up to her room and hurriedly put the last of her items in her school luggage. She carried them down to be loaded into the car. James was in the kitchen when she scurried through.

"Hey, kid, what's the rush?"

"I need you to back me on this one. Mom will definitely get upset. I am going to take Soary to the airport to say goodbye. Can you meet me and we can head to campus from there? I couldn't bear to say our goodbyes in the car this morning. I wanted something..." she hesitated, not sure how to put it into words. "Something more normal. More real. You know?" She hoped he did because it was going to take his support to make it happen.

"Sure, kid." His took the bags from her hands and started toward the car. "I'll get these. Go up and talk to your mom. She didn't sleep all night. I think she thought you would run off with him and she would never see you again." He chuckled as he headed to the garage.

Gwen sighed and headed back up the stairs. When she came to her mother's room, she squared her shoulders and took a deep breath. She wondered if her mother would think she looked different. Would she be able to tell her daughter had spent the night making love to the man of her dreams? Of course, she could guess that was what happened, but would she look different?

Gwen loved her mom and wanted to please her. She knew it had been hard for her mom to accept she was in love. Sarah wanted her to wait for love until she had accomplished all her dreams. But she didn't understand that Gwen's dreams were all about love. Sure, she wanted to be successful, but she wanted someone to love her like a fairy princess. She wanted to be touched the way Soary had touched her, she wanted to be looked at the way Soary had looked at her, she wanted to be loved the way Soary loved her. She craved a man to be the man for herthat her father had been for her mom.

"Mom?" Gwen peeked her head into her mother's room. Sarah sat on the sofa facing the window. At first Gwen thought she was asleep but as she entered her mom stirred.

"Gwen, come sit with me."

Hovering near the doorway Gwen spoke, "Mom, I want to take Soary to the airport. James said you all could meet me there. I know this wasn't the plan but I really want to see him off."

Hesitantly Sarah spoke as she rose and crossed the room, "Well, I guess that will be alright. Let me look at you."

Gwen was always surprised at how beautiful her mother was. Sarah had a timeless beauty. Her skin was smooth, her hair was shiny, her poise was perfect. She looked effortlessly beautiful. She didn't look a day older than thirty-five. She was religious about her yoga and meditated daily. She held Gwen's hands and studied her face. Gwen started to squirm uncomfortably. Sarah released one of her hands and stroked her cheek.

"You look so young. You have the same expression you had the first day of school when you were determined I was going to let you walk in by yourself. So stubborn and independent." Sarah paused. "No, that's not right, is it?" Tears balanced on her eyelashes. "Oh, baby! You are loved!" she exclaimed.

"Mom!" Gwen moaned.

"I'm sorry. I just never thought about this day. My daughter is a woman in so many ways now. But you will always be my baby. How do you feel?"

"Mom." Gwen moaned again. But she decided this would go more quickly if she gave her mother some details. "He was so sweet and wonderful, Mom. I am in love. I can't imagine how we are going to make it apart for so long. Soary is off to try to get his record deal and if that works out who knows if he will be able to come visit me. And I won't have time. I mean I am going to have to work really hard on this internship. I can't bear to think of it. I really want to get to him so we can have as much time together as we can before he gets on his flight."

Sarah sighed and released Gwen's other hand. "I love you, darling girl." She leaned over and kissed Gwen's cheek. "James and I will meet you at the airport."

Gwen kissed her back and rushed from the room. Sarah sighed and went back to her seat.

She didn't hear James come in. He leaned over the back of the couch and kissed her neck. "How are you?"

"I am fine. I can't believe our baby is so grown up. I just wanted her to stay a baby forever. You don't think she will do anything stupid for this boy do you? I just don't feel good about this whole thing."

"No. She's smart girl. And he's a good kid. They both are driven and I think they'll stay on course to meet their goals. But it's the first time she's been in love so it will be dramatic for her." James moved to sit beside her and held her hand. Sarah laid her head on his shoulder and mourned for her baby.

***

Gwen couldn't wait to see Soary again when she pulled up to his house. It felt like much longer than an hour since she felt the warmth of him next to her. She wondered how she was going to get through without him with her. Her heart felt like it expanded in her chest. There was a sense of completeness that automatically filled her up when he started walking toward her car. Happiness tingled through her body, exploding like tiny firecrackers, tickling her skin from the inside out. She told herself not to smile so big. She wanted to appear grown up. But the harder she tried not to smile the bigger her grin became. He was all she had ever really wanted in a man.

Soary's mom was waving from the front porch. Love swelled in her heart as she saw Soary blow her a kiss. But the atmosphere changed from sweet to heavy as soon as Soary closed the car door. The depth of her disappointment surprised her. In an instant her happiness melted away and she couldn't pinpoint why. There was something in Soary's eyes. He seemed changed in the hour they were apart.

"Hi." Soary slipped in the passenger's seat. He leaned over and kissed her. Gwen stopped him from moving back to his seat with her hand on the back of his head, keeping his lips firmly on hers for much longer than he intended.

Gwen pushed aside her fear and savored the kiss. She wanted to burn the memory of his lips on hers into her brain to help get through the long fall and winter months without him. She wanted to remember the way his hand slowly slipped up to her hair and stroked her neck. She knew her memory could never make her feel the way his actual touch could, but she tried to imprint it deep.

She wondered how she was going to make it through the next few months. Soary caressed her neck as he kissed her cheeks, forehead, and then lips. Gwen let her mind empty of all thoughts and concentrated on his touch. She heard herself sigh as his hand slipped from her neck to her breast. Her heart began to race as her body responded in excitement at his touch.

Laughing, he gently pushed her away. She had not even realized she was trying to unbutton his shirt.

"Hey, hey. Not really an appropriate place," he whispered in her ear.

Gwen opened her eyes and realized they were still parked outside his house. The smile faded from her face when she gazed into Soary's eyes. What was it that she saw in them she wondered? Something felt wrong. The intense way he touched her and looked at her was different. She thought of something her mom said about knowing someone; when you really know someone, you don't have to talk about everything; you will just understand what they need. Gwen hoped she was understanding what Soary needed as she turned away from him and started the car.

"Shall we go?"

He leaned over and brushed his lips along her ear. She shuddered. "Do we have to?" His voice made butterflies dance in her stomach.

"Unfortunately, we do. You have a plane to catch and I have to get on the road too. You know if I thought you were going to try to seduce me, I wouldn't have offered to drive you." She grinned.

On the ride to the airport Soary traced his finger along Gwen's arm. They were quiet most of the drive, both lost in their own thoughts. Gwen was already planning Soary's first visit. She was trying to decide when she thought she would get a break and be able to fly and see him. Soary was trying not to think about Gwen. Instead he focused on the different lyrics in his head. When he allowed himself to stop the train of words, his mind went directly to imagining what a life with Gwen would be like. He couldn't see her on the road with him. He couldn't see her in the studio with him or hanging out with his friends. He just couldn't see her in his life beyond this town.

But he knew he loved her. Gwen made him feel a way he had never felt before. He didn't know someone could make your heart actually jump and your mouth water and your ears ring. The electric current that coursed through him from touching surprised him. And no one ever told him that kissing someone could take his breath away. He was sure he loved Gwen and he was sure he would never feel this way again. But as they got closer to the airport, he was also sure this was more than just see you later. This was goodbye. His heart hurt; he heard stories of people dying from broken hearts so he mouthed a quick prayer that he could survive it. In that moment he wanted to survive leaving so he could get all the music bursting inside him out.

It was a busy day at the airport. Gwen really couldn't remember any day when there was a crowd of this size. Summer vacations were over; there was work to be done, contracts to sign, papers to write. Gwen felt her heart get heavy as she realized they would have to say their goodbyes soon. With all the security measures she couldn't stay with him until it was time for him to board his plane. He would have to go through security alone. They approached the checkpoint; Soary stopped and turned to Gwen. He wiped the tear off her cheek and laced his hands over her shoulders.

"I'm going to miss you so much." She leaned her head against his chest. Soary kissed the crown of her head and rested his chin on her.

"Gwen, I'm going to really miss you, too." A thought took him by surprise. But he knew in his heart he couldn't do it. He asked anyway. "What would you say if I said we should get on a plane to the Bahamas? Runaway together. Change our destinies. We could go there and teach tourists to scuba dive or I could play music in a local bar. You could find work as a bookkeeper or make kites. We could walk away from all this and just be together: you and me." He heard the desperation in his own voice. He searched Gwen's face looking for any sign that she was buying into his suggestion.

"Soary, it's a romantic idea. But we can't do that. You can't walk out on Jeff. He trusts you and needs you. But we could plan a vacation. Maybe we can go on fall break." She reached up and tousled his hair and smiled at him.

"Gwen, I'm serious. I love you. I want to be with you. Let's just go away. We could build a life together. We could be happy. We could learn how to deep-sea fish." Soary realized his grip on her shoulders had tightened. His answer was displayed on Gwen's face. She wouldn't walk away from her life. But he wasn't ready to give it up. He knew if he left her now, he wouldn't turn back. "Gwen, babe, have you thought about what our lives will be like?"

"Of course, I have. After I graduate, I'll come to you. Before then we'll try to see each other as much as possible. I will come see you as often as I can. James already said I could use his skymiles." Her eyes searched his face needing to see he was okay. That they were okay.

"I love you, Gwen." He pulled her to him and kissed her slowly, not caring about the travelers who stopped and stared.

"I love you, too." Gwen said as she moved away from him. "Call me as soon as you land."

"I will. Bye, Gwen." He didn't look at her again before turning his back and walking away.

Gwen watched Soary juggle his guitar case and carry-on through the security checkpoint and smiled to herself. He was handsome. He stood a foot above the rest of the travelers. His dark head swayed in and out of the crowd. She watched as he stopped to help a struggling child pick up her teddy bear. The child looked up at him through her blond curls, flashed him a shy smile, and ran to catch up to her parents. Gwen imagined the child experienced her first crush. She waited until she couldn't pick Soary out in the crowd before she turned to leave.

Gwen meandered through the airport reluctant to leave. She remembered the day her dad died. She was restless; unable to concentrate. Her teacher corrected her several times and even threatened to call her mom. But no matter how hard Gwen tried, she could not sit still. Back then she didn't understand what she felt. Later she recognized it as a feeling of impending doom. Fear that something bad was going to happen. It was a feeling of helplessness; an inability to change the course of a tragedy. The exact feeling crept up inside her when she could no longer see Soary in the crowd.

Lost in the awareness that she loved him completely, she told herself she was silly for feeling sad; nothing bad was going to happen. She whispered a prayer for his well-being and the safe arrival of his flight.

***

Soary knew he was being a coward. But he didn't know how to make the feelings in his heart come out in actions or words. Every part of him knew this was the end for them but he couldn't tell her that and he sure couldn't control the urge to kiss her. He shuddered as he thought of how completely she gave herself over to him. He loved the taste of her strawberry lip gloss on his lips, the feel of her skin under his hands. He took a deep breath to steady his pulse. He had no idea these thoughts would get him so worked up. He forced himself to relax as he concentrated on what the flight attendant was saying. He probably could repeat it word for word himself as much as he had flown but he had to focus his mind on reality and calm down. He knew he would draw on his emotions soon enough to create music and write lyrics but now was not the time. He wanted to save the moment of realization for when he was alone. He wanted privacy to lose himself in his pain. The flight attendant's voice droned on about emergency exits, he leaned his head back and let exhaustion lead him to dreamland.

Soary woke to the thump of the wheels landing on the runway. He slept the entire flight. He must have been more exhausted than he realized. He shook the haze of sleep from his head. Jeff would be picking him up at the airport so they could head straight to the studio to listen to their demo. Soary wasn't sure if he would try to put his new song on the demo tonight but he was sure it was the hit single they needed to break through the record companies' red tape. He'd call Gwen and tell her about the song and let her know that she was the inspiration behind it. That settled it. He felt a weight lift from his shoulders. He always felt better after making a difficult decision.

Soary viewed decision-making as the hard part and the follow-though the easy part. He rarely reversed a decision once it was made. The fear he saw in Gwen's eyes when he asked her to walk away with him broke his heart. He knew then that he was right; they had to take different paths. No matter how much he loved her he wasn't right for her.

The guilt he felt lifted away when he saw Jeff at the baggage claim waiting for him. Certainty replaced doubt; he knew he made the best decision. He would talk to Gwen here and there and slowly end things. He knew she would be hurt, but he would be doing what was best for her, so in the long run that outweighed any of the immediate pain he was going to cause her. He knew their separate dreams would never complement each other. One of them would always sacrifice something for the other one if they were to make it work but this way they could just move on and remember the best of what they shared. He felt joyous as he slapped Jeff on the back and headed to the car.

"We'll go straight to the studio and listen to the recording. If we need to make any adjustments, we have the room until eight in the morning. We'll have to pull an all-nighter. Our flight leaves Tuesday for New York City. I don't want to waste too much time since we have a foot in the door." Jeff excitedly rambled about their schedule.

Soary settled in the front seat keeping his responses to "yes" and "uh-huh". His peace faded as he remembered kissing Gwen goodbye. He knew she had waited until he was completely out of sight before she left. He shook his head trying to free himself of the image of her face and told himself again that it would never work between them. She needed structure to be successful in her career. He could never give that to her—not with touring and recording. He was confident that if he and Jeff played their cards right, they could make enough money on a few records to start their own production company. Frank was the perfect person to help them get started. That's where he must focus his energy.

They had met Frank a few years prior while playing in a local bar. Bethany, Jeff's high school sweetheart, had brought him to hear them play one night. Frank thought they had a great sound and gave them his card. He was an up-and-coming business manager for Spirit Records in New York. Jeff insisted they keep in touch with him and after a few years Frank was confident enough to start taking risks with new musicians. His risks were paying off, giving him a reputation as a star-finder.

"What do you think?" Jeff asked. When Soary didn't answer Jeff punched him in the arm and laughed. "Missing her already? Get your head in the game."

"What? Oh. Sorry I was just thinking. What did you say?"

"Bethany wants to come to New York and thought it would be nice if you invited Gwen to meet us too. Have a nice long weekend. What do you think? Can she miss a few classes?"

"No!" Soary hadn't meant to sound so stern. He started over. "No, I don't think she will. She's doing her internship so when she isn't in class she'll be working. I doubt we'll see each other for months." He couldn't tell how his voice sounded the second time but was sure it was tense because Jeff looked at him like he had something flying out of his head. They had just reached the studio so Soary jumped out of the car and started to stretch to avoid any additional questions.

"Well, you might want to work on your delivery when you tell Bethany if you want to avoid one hundred questions. Hell, you aren't going to avoid the questions so you might want to get it out of the way early. She's bringing us dinner." Jeff slapped him on the back and walked in the studio, leaving Soary to stare after him.

Friendship with Jeff was easy. He didn't pry. If you wanted to talk to him, he would listen and give sound advice. But he didn't push. Jeff understood Soary went through dark periods when it took most of his energy just to get out of bed. He recognized that part of Soary's artistry came from those moments. Jeff also knew if left alone too long those moments would become dangerous to Soary's well-being. Many times throughout their friendship Jeff showed up at Soary's door, pretended not to see everything that was out of place as he forced Soary to the gym or the basketball court. Other times he would simply put a pen in Soary's hand, a pad in front of him then he would play video games while Soary wrote whatever ailed him out of his system.

Jeff was loyal and constant.

***

Soary felt nostalgia as they walked into the studio. Artists creating music to inspire, comfort, excite, and guide its listeners excited him. There was something spiritual about making music that warmed his heart. He had forgotten how good it felt to be there. All summer he had spent his days and nights with Gwen. He didn't remember missing being in the studio, but now that he was back all he could think about was getting in the sound booth and losing himself in the beats.

Jeff and Soary quickly fell into their old working habits. Soary would play a song using his guitar. After a time or two Jeff would join in. Notes were scribbled on sheet music then scratched out over again and again. The final result being a work of art that they agreed upon. They rearranged several tracks and had just finished arranging "Leaving Me Behind" when Bethany brought dinner in a picnic basket. It was filled with salad, chicken, baked beans, and potato salad.

"Soary, we missed you." Bethany sat the basket down and gave him a long hug. Bethany was known in their group as a hugger. She viewed hugging as an act of healing, like medicine. She would face the front of her body toward her subject, reach both arms around their neck or shoulders, pull them close and squeeze them into her. She wouldn't let go for at least fifteen seconds and when she let go she would touch their arms, their hands, still giving her physical self to the other person. It was truly artistic the way she hugged people. Bethany had always been one of Soary's favorite people to hug.

The tension from the long day eased from his shoulders. He rested his nose in her hair and smelled the sweet scent of vanilla.

"Ah, sweet Bethany. I missed you." Soary pulled back from her and kissed her on the cheek.

"How's your mom? And I want to hear all about Gwen." Without waiting for the conversation to take place Bethany began spreading the contents of her basket out on the coffee table. Soary watched her hands swiftly and carefully turn the table into a place for them to gather and share a meal.

"So?" she surprised him when her hands stopped moving and rested on her hips.

"Mom is great. She's settled into her new house. It is a cute little cottage. She has the white fence lined with wildflowers and rose bushes. It's perfect."

"That is awesome. I can't wait to go visit her." Bethany motioned for them to sit. Jeff joined her at the table.

"What about Gwen? When do I get to meet her?"

Soary felt Jeff's eyes on him. He wanted to scream at them to forget about Gwen. He wanted to ask them to never mention her again. But of course, he couldn't do that. Jeff allowed him to postpone their summer plans and schedule because he wanted time to get to know Gwen; because he proclaimed she was the one. Jeff deserved his explanation. And Bethany was an extension of their friendship. She was there to take care of the important little details for them. She had every right to ask about Gwen. He normally would have filled her in without her interrogation. Internally debating his response, he felt the tightness in his neck return.

Jeff and Bethany exchanged a look, a smile. Soary had always envied them the ease in which their relationship flourished through all the changes each day created.

Bethany turned her eyes back to Soary. He couldn't meet them. "Are you going to tell me about Gwen or am I to guess all the sordid details? Jeff said she was extremely smart. Where is she in school again?" Bethany stared at him waiting for her answers.

"She's studying finance and accounting at the University of Chattanooga."

"Wow. So she probably is smart. Maybe she can handle your finances when you two become rich and famous. Is she going to come to New York? I want to meet her."

"No. I don't think I will ask her." He tried to sound nonchalant but knew it wasn't working so he rushed on. "She has a lot going on with school and work, she will be lucky to take my phone calls." He shrugged.

"Oh. Well, tell me about her." Soary heard the change in her tone.

"Beth, we need to get this last song on the demo. Let's talk later." He saw disappointment flash across her face and felt bad but he didn't want to talk about Gwen. He was already trying to forget about her. The smell of her was clinging to him and her laugh was caught in his ears. He was doing all he could to stay focused on the reason he was here and she was there. He wanted to be able to walk away without feeling like he was giving up a part of himself. He reminded himself that it hadn't even been twenty-four hours since seeing her and kissing her. He knew she was probably worried about him because he hadn't called letting her know he arrived safely. He left his phone off so he wouldn't be distracted if she called. He wasn't ready to face his decision. Not yet. He would call her tomorrow. And with that thought he turned back to Jeff.

"Let's get this one on the demo and call it a night. I'm exhausted."

"Sure." Jeff smiled at Bethany and gave a little shrug. "Thanks for dinner." He didn't want her to feel hurt by Soary's dismissal but he could tell it was too late for that. She could tell something was wrong and he knew the look in her eyes meant she was determined to find out.

"Can I hear it?" she asked.

"Of course. You'll like it." Jeff answered her while Soary had already left the control room settled into the small isolation booth. He had settled the headphones over his ears and waited.

Soary closed his when the music swam in his head. He became the emotions his words conveyed. He wasn't in the studio with Jeff and Bethany. He was at the beach with Gwen. He could see her running through the waves and laughing. He could see the love in her eyes and he felt his chest hollow out as his heart disintegrated.

> *I know I will leave you but forgive my selfish heart*
> *for I must take all you got*
> *I am sorry to leave you in the cold*
> *but I can't give you any more of me*
>
> *I can see the questions in your eyes*
> *But can't give you answers that will break your heart*

When he finished singing the studio went quiet. Bethany wiped the tears from her eyes and waited until Soary opened his eyes and came back to the room. She watched him move over to the bookshelves and start to shuffle the pages of a music book. She wanted to give him a hug. But she had known Soary long enough to know he needed a minute. She looked at Jeff and knew by the way he avoided her eyes that something was wrong. She couldn't imagine what it was so she waited until Soary came back to the couch and took a seat before she approached the topic.

Jeff turned his attention back to the mixing console.

"That was beautiful and sad. I would think you would have written a happy love song." She knew it wasn't a great start but she was looking for a reaction.

"I don't know if things are going to work out with Gwen. We're just too different. She wants different things than I do. She will need stability and I don't have that to offer. We would end up trying to make a long-distance relationship work. It won't. We would end up trying to be friends but not really wanting to see each other again. Besides, I don't want stability. I want freedom and adventure. You don't even know her so I don't want to hear what you have to say."

Bethany closed her mouth. She crossed her arms in front of her and stared at him.

"Gwen is like a shooting star. You're lucky to see one in your life but you can't catch them and you can't hold them. Few photographers can get a clean shot of them on camera. She will be much happier this way. She'll figure out that I did what was right by her and she'll not even care why." He didn't realize he was yelling until he stopped talking and noticed the quietness of the room. He was too embarrassed to look at Bethany. She didn't deserve that reaction from him.

She was just a concerned friend. Soary knew she'd been happy for him and excited to meet Gwen. He rested his head on the back of the couch, his hands covered his face as he rubbed his eyes. Anger swelled around the three friends.

"Oh, I didn't realize you had broken up." Bethany kept her voice steady.

"It isn't done yet." Soary's voice was muffled under his hands.

"Does she know you are going to break up with her? I thought you and she spent the night together."

Shame washed over him.

"No, she doesn't know yet. She would make it too hard. I don't want to hurt Gwen. I will just slowly pull away. She won't be hurt then. We will just grow apart. She will be busy. Time will pass and one day she'll realize she hasn't talked to me in a while. She'll be fine." Soary finally looked up and met Bethany's eyes.

"I see. You have decided to end the relationship on your terms. You have this whole break-up routine and you expect her to dance along with you? I don't think it's fair to her, Soary. If you love her you should talk to her about what you are feeling. She may not want what you think. Things may work out. But even if you're sure you don't want things to work out, you should be honest with her. She deserves a chance to tell you her side."

"I can't, Beth. I love her too much to tell her I don't want her. Because I do. I have never felt so..." Soary wiped at the tears, not allowing them fall.

He looked away. "I can't tell her. I don't even know how I will talk to her again. I just can't think about this anymore."

"Soary, what is this about? It isn't like you." Bethany reached out to him and placed her hand on his arm. That gesture broke his resolve and he turned to her burying his face on her shoulder and cried.

Jeff left the room.

Bethany held him until his body stopped shaking and the last sob was silenced.

"I just don't know why you think it won't work out. Maybe you're just having jitters or something." Bethany pleaded with Soary to rethink his actions. "Soary you never make rash decisions. I have never known you to be careless with someone else's feelings. Look at me." He met her eyes. "You aren't the guy who just leaves. You have never been that guy. You are the guy who stays. You're the guy who takes care of people."

"Beth, I just don't know. Gwen is life. Do you know what I mean? I can feel life swirling around me when I am with her. It all looks different when I am with her." He paused imagining the breeze on his face the day he first saw her; from the first encounter with her he felt the world shift on its axis. A small adjustment was made to the universe.

"I tried to tell her on the way to the airport. But when I looked at her, I lost all my will. All I want is to stay with her. I feel like I could walk away from everything. I could give up music for her. If I stayed with her, I could go work in corporate America and be a soccer dad. I would probably be happy as long as I had her. I actually asked her to run away with me. But that isn't who I am. And she isn't a groupie or roadie. But I know if she thought I was leaving her she would offer to give up her world for me. How would I be able to turn her down? So, there we would be, not knowing how to compromise and both of us giving up everything but each other. It just seems like the best thing to do is to end it now. Save us both from the hurt."

Bethany waited for him to continue.

"When she looks at me I feel like she can't really see me. I can't be the guy she is looking at. She is so energetic and full of life. She looks at the world through rose colored glasses. I could write songs about her all day because of the passion she ignites in my soul. It oozes from her. She is passion and desire. She sees the good in people and never has a bad word for anyone. But she has these moments when she gets lost in thought and a look comes across her face that makes me wonder what world she entered. Although I wonder, I know I don't want to go there." He started to pace.

"I lost myself when I was with her. No, I wasn't myself. I can't imagine how I could make her happy. But that is what I promised her. That I would make her happy. Don't you see? I am not a good enough man for her. I am always thinking about stories in the form of songs. I look at the world and see what breaks it. When I listen to people talk, I hear lyrics. I don't want to live in a world where you go to work at nine and come home at five. I don't care for a wife to cook me dinner and go with the kids to the ball field. I want to travel and write and be free. And Gwen was born to live a happy small-town life. She needs to be a wife and mother. She is soothing. She is grace. She is peace. She is life. She's that white picket fence and flower garden my mom always wanted. She's safety." He stopped in front of the mixing table.

Bethany wiped the tears from her cheek.

"She has a passion for loving. It trapped me and I know I would let her trap me forever if I talk to her. If I continue to see her, I would stay the guy I pretended to be in Alabama. I would continue to live every moment only to make her smile and laugh. And she would never know she took my dreams away. She wouldn't be able to control it because she doesn't see herself the way I do. If you knew her you would love her too. Everyone falls in love with her, I watched it happen every day for three months. I have to stay away. I just can't see her again."

Bethany crossed the room to him. She rested her hand on the back of his shoulder.

"Soary, I think you may just need time. You've never been in love with someone like this and maybe you're just scared."

"No, Beth. I know who I am and I am not the man for Gwen. She's too perfect. I have to do this. She will always be with me." He placed his hand on his heart. "But I can't be with her." With his other hand he pressed a button on the table in front of him. His voice filled the room.

Bethany walked out.

Bethany found Jeff outside smoking a cigarette.

"I thought you were going to quit." She took it from his hand and took a long drag.

"I didn't know you started." He chuckled and took it back from her.

"I didn't." She pushed him over as she sat down on the bench next to him. She laid her head on his shoulder.

"Well?"

"Well, he has rationalized leaving her because he doesn't want to get married and have kids."

"Did she ask for that?"

"I don't think so. I don't know actually. He said they talked about the future and he found her dreams became his but then he realized that wasn't what he wanted." She sighed. "I don't really understand. He isn't making much sense. It would be easier if we knew what she was like. I could help him figure it out then." She took another drag from the cigarette.

Bethany did understand what Soary meant about losing himself but she didn't know how to explain it any better than he had. She understood some people deserve a bigger love than others are capable of giving.

"No." Jeff turned to face her. "You do not get to fix this. You do not get to meet her and figure this out. Let him make his own decisions."

"You mean his own mistakes."

"Fine. His own mistakes." Jeff took her hand and kissed it. "We all have to be able to make our own mistakes. And the people who love us just have to wait the storm out." Jeff let the unspoken, unanswered questions linger in the silence between them.

Bethany removed her hand from his. She looked at him a long time then sighed. "But Jeff, he won't ever be the same if he does this. He changed all our plans and stayed there with her. He stayed because he loves her. She is the one for him. He will never be the same if he leaves her."

"I know. I know."

Chapter 8

2016

Soary struggled to remember an extended period of time he was at home. The last time he remembered being in one place longer than a month was before they finished the demo that became their first album. Music and touring took over their lives forcing them to adjust to their new normal quickly. He sat at the dining table on their tour bus and looked around. It was a large space. They had a small kitchen, dining area, and sitting room with a couch, tables and TV. There was also a small writing desk in the corner beside a keyboard and guitar stand. Some sound equipment was pushed into the corner on the floor. They wrote most of their second album while they were still touring the first. It was an exhausting process but the songs and the music flowed out of them.

When Soary discussed the direction of their third album with Jeff they decided it was time to get in the studio to brainstorm. Soary had written several unfinished songs but he was stuck. He wasn't sure if it was writers block or the need for more space but he just couldn't finish any of them. He could feel the words in his head but every time he tried to write them down, he couldn't grab them. He told Jeff he was ready to take time off from touring.

They decided to buy a house in Nashville with an attached recording studio so they had flexibility in their work schedule. As usual they called up Bethany told her what they wanted and she made it happen. She found the perfect house, negotiated a much lower price than what was listed and remodeled it. After five years of near-constant travel Soary was looking forward to being home. As he looked around the tour bus, he couldn't help but think he would actually miss being cooped up with Jeff in it.

There was a prickle of fear in the prospect of making a home. No matter how amazing the house was and how settled he became he knew something would still be missing. All of the success they enjoyed didn't fill the void in his heart. Not a day passed that he didn't think of her and miss her. Thinking about settling down made him start to wonder if he should look her up. He wondered if she would be happy to see him too. His mom was scheduled to come visit, maybe he should go to her instead.

"Man, I'm tired." Jeff dropped down on the couch, interrupting his thoughts. "I can't wait to see Beth. She is so excited and said she's become the most popular teacher at school." He laughed as he pulled out the remote to the PlayStation and started up a game. "You know she said several of the students promised to help paint her room if she would get them autographs. Can you believe it? High school students want our autograph."

"Jeff, do you love Bethany?" Soary wasn't sure why he asked. But he couldn't stop thinking of Gwen and needed to hear why his friend wasn't with the girl he loved. Most people mistook Bethany and Jeff for a couple and Soary often wondered why they just didn't get back together.

"Sure." Jeff threw an interception that led to the computer team scoring a touchdown.

"No, I mean really love her."

Pausing his game Jeff sat up and looked at Soary. "Where the hell is this coming from?"

"You two are perfect together but aren't a couple. I never understood what really happened. Why are you not together?" Soary shrugged and grabbed the other remote and sat down next to him the couch.

"We are together. I mean not in the traditional sense. But we are together. You know we have a history and well, we needed a break. Beth...wanted a break. The break has lasted several years but we'll get back together. When the stars align." Jeff stretched back out on the coach. He re-started the game.

"What do you mean she needed a break? You two are always together and you talk to her daily. I mean to an outsider you appear to be a couple. I don't get it."

"We date other people you know that. Beth just wanted to be able to have her freedom while I worked on this with you." He waved his hand to indicate the tour bus and turned his attention back to the game. "Are you going to play or what?"

"No, I think I changed my mind." Soary tossed the remote on the coach and went back to the table.

"Beth broke up with me because she kissed another guy. She said it didn't mean anything but because of the fact she wanted to, she didn't think it was fair for us to be together." Jeff walked over to the refrigerator and grabbed a beer. After taking a long swallow he continued. "We knew we loved each other but she wanted to explore the feelings she had for other people. We have known each other forever and I didn't want to lose her as a friend so I accepted what she had to offer and moved on."

Sinking back on the coach he took his time before continuing. "We still have feelings for each other and I think one day when I'm ready to settle down we'll get back together but until then we're just friends."

Soary listened to him intently.

Jeff went on. "It really isn't that complicated. We were in middle school the first time we started dating. We grew up and instead of letting the growing up tear us apart we chose to be in limbo with each other. This is us in limbo." His voice was husky with frustration.

"What would happen if she meets someone and falls in love? What if she decides to get married?" Soary pressed.

"I guess I will be her best man." Jeff turned the volume up on the TV signaling he was finished with the conversation.

Soary knew Jeff wouldn't stand by and let Bethany marry someone else. He sat there staring at Jeff for a few minutes letting the lyrics take shape. He opened up his laptop and started to fill the screen with song ideas.

After a few hours he found himself tired and went to the back of the bus and climbed on the top bunk to get some rest. Sleep wouldn't come to him. He thought about Gwen. His mind was going in the same direction it usually took when he was alone and tired. He wondered where Gwen was and what she was doing. He imagined her listening to his songs and maybe even coming to his concert. Although he hadn't seen her in years, he could still recall every detail of her face. He remembered the way her eyes twinkled when he would tell her a funny story. He lay in bed letting the memories come to life. The day he walked away at the airport was the last time he freely let her ghost in the room. But this time was different; it felt good to think of her. He made the decision; he was going to look her up. He missed her and wanted to see her again. His desire to see her quickly escalated into a full-blown need. He felt his hands start to shake.

WTF

He closed his eyes to draw up the memory of the night he played a song just for her. They had gone to a bonfire with some of Gwen's friends. In the car on their way home she had turned to him and asked if he wanted to hang out a while.

"Where do you want to go?"

"Let's go the monuments." The moon glistened in her eyes. Soary knew that his path had just been altered. His plans would be changed so he could spend more time with this girl. They drove to the west side of town to a small park that housed several Civil War monuments. Soary grabbed his guitar from the car and they spread his jacket out and sat in the grass.

"What are you going to play for me?"

"A song I wrote." He was nervous, afraid she wouldn't like it. But after he finished he looked at her; tears streamed down her cheeks.

"That was so beautiful," she gushed. "You must think I'm silly but that was the most beautiful song I have ever heard." She laughed and the sound sent a shiver up his spine. He leaned towards her and cupped her face in his hands and slowly leaned in to kiss her. Electricity ran through his body before his lips touched hers. The kiss went from tender to passionate. Gwen opened up to him and ran her fingers through his hair. Her breathing became heavy and she gently nibbled on his lip. Soary pushed her on her back and leaned over her. He moved his mouth over her cheeks to her neck and back up to her ear lobe. He slowly opened the button on her blouse and ran his hands over her stomach and up to her breasts. Gwen sucked in air and pulled him on top of her. They joined their mouths together again in a deep and passionate kiss. Soary got lost in her kiss. He didn't want to stop kissing her but was afraid to take things too far.

"Gwen, we have to stop now." He gazed in her eyes and saw the desire in them. He kissed the tip of her nose and rolled off her on to his back. They lay there together for a while catching their breath.

Gwen rolled onto her elbow and leaned over to kiss him. "Will you promise to sing to me again?"

"I will sing to you every night for the rest of our lives. Gwen, I think I'm falling in love with you." The truth in his words shocked him. He had felt close to other girls, had even told one or two he loved them. At the time he thought he did. But now he understood he had never truly been in love before. He knew what he was feeling was special.

"Me too." Gwen kissed him again.

"I wrote that song the first night I met you. I haven't played it for anyone before tonight." He stared up into the stars as he spoke. "I think I will call it, My Heart."

"Soary." Gwen kissed him again.

After a while Soary pushed her away. "I should get you home now."

"I don't want to go home." She clung to him.

"But if I don't take you now, I am not sure I will ever take you back. And then how am I going to convince your mother my intentions for her daughter are forever?" He stood up and pulled her to her feet. When they were standing facing each other he leaned down and whispered in her ear. "I am in love with you, Gwen. And I will marry you some day." He kissed her again and pulled her to towards the car.

Soary opened his eyes, momentarily disoriented as he adjusted to his surroundings. He remembered the song he had played for her. He had never shared it with Jeff. He had not even finished writing the music for it. He had left the song, along with Gwen, in his past.

He laid there listening to Jeff yell at the video game and brought his mind back the present.

He reached for the last letter he had received from her. Bethany forwarded it to him seven months ago. Like all the others he never opened it. He stuffed it under his stack of notebooks until he could put it away with the rest. Along with the decision he wanted to see her again came an overwhelming desire to read her words.

Soary,

This will be the last time I attempt to contact you. I'm not sure if this will even make it to you. But I will send it anyway. I miss you terribly. It seems crazy to me that I could really love you in such a short time. But I do. There is no other explanation for these feelings. And I know you loved me too. I saw it in your eyes when you held me. I felt it in your touch. I don't know what changed for you but I'm not angry. Not anymore. I wish you could tell me what went wrong with us. I used to wonder about you. But it became too hard to let you in. I've spent a lot of time and effort getting over you. I can't say that I am over you now or that I ever will be, but I am able to let you go, finally. I don't know if I will ever hear from you again. I know in my heart you'll be successful. I only wish I could share it with you. I am so sad. But for reasons unknown to me we can't be together. But I will not wait for an answer anymore. I won't sit and wonder if you'll come back for me. I'm letting you go—not that you gave me a choice. I know my heart will never be the same. I know I will love you forever. Always. But I hope saying goodbye will help mend the frayed edges of my heart enough so I can live again. I am sorry we never got to talk. I did have so much to share with you.

Goodbye.
Gwen

letter from CI
before Gwen moved

Soary laid the letter aside and began to shake with sobs. He didn't know how to make this right. He broke her heart and he was sorry. He cried for the mistake he had made. He never thought he would still want her after so long. No matter what he accomplished or who he met he couldn't get her out of his mind. She was constantly with him. She was always there in his heart. After a while he picked up the envelope and looked at the post mark. She had sent the letter in May. Hope sprung up inside him. What if it really wasn't too late? What words could he use to explain why he left? How can he make her understand he feared losing his music if she was with him? He needed to love her as deeply as he did so he could leave her. He had to feel the pain and loss to get the emotion out of his soul and into music.

What a fool! He couldn't look her up. He couldn't just walk back into her life. He crumpled the letter and cried himself to sleep.

When he woke they were back in Nashville. The bus was parked in the Westbound Studio's parking garage. Soary climbed out of the bunk. His body ached and his head throbbed. He felt hung over but didn't remember drinking. He went into the living area and opened a cabinet looking for Tylenol. He got a glass of water and sat down at the table to take his medicine. He slumped his head in his hands and was rubbing his temples when he noticed the neatly folded paper lying on the table. He recognized the note Gwen had sent him. Jeff had found it, smoothed it out, and placed it for Soary to find. Soary realized Jeff must have heard his sobs last night. He touched the edges of the paper hesitantly as if it would burst into flames at his touch. He was debating reading it again when Jeff emerged.

"Good morning." He poured himself a cup of coffee and slid into a chair across from Soary. "You ready to go home?"

Soary looked up from the paper and back again. Home. Would he ever have a home, he wondered? He thought of Gwen's words, I am so sad. Yes, he thought, me too.

"Sure." He got up to exit the bus leaving the letter on the table.

Chapter 9

2016

Bethany met Jeff and Soary at their house. "I can't believe you two are finally home!" Bethany exclaimed as she hugged each of them. "I never thought I would say I missed two messy guys always being around." She laughed as she linked one arm through each of theirs.

Soary noticed the look exchanged between Jeff and Bethany. He couldn't help but feel jealous that Jeff had someone to come home to. He couldn't get Gwen's face out of his mind. He wondered how he had convinced himself she wouldn't get hurt if he walked away. It occurred to him he hadn't thought about what he would feel if he never saw her again. It was a mystery to him how he had completely ignored reality. His focus was on making the decision, not on living with the outcome. Nothing about leaving her made sense to him anymore.

"The devil is in the details and I am walking in hell," he thought.

It never occurred to him she would grow and change. He put her in his memory box and went about his life pretending she was safe and sound there until he wanted to take her out again.

"I thought you two could take me out to dinner. I also have a friend I wanted to introduce you to." Bethany noticed Soary's scowl. "What in the world is wrong with you?" She tousled his hair and looked between him and Jeff.

"Just tired. Where do you want to go?" Soary flashed her his camera-ready smile. He repressed a laugh as it worked its magic on Bethany as well as it did on all the screaming fans.

"Well, I was thinking Sambuca's. And I really think you're going to like Amy. She likes your music but she isn't going to be stargazing. She is a real down-to-earth girl and I think it's about time you started dating."

"Who says I haven't been? You do realize Jeff and I are big stars now, right?" He teased.

"Ah, yes. Two big stars who fall asleep in their tour bus together every night. Don't try to play me Soary. I know you didn't even look at one of those girls on the road. Besides Jeff called me every night and you weren't in one city long enough to date anyone!"

Soary playfully punched Jeff in the arm. "So, is that the story you're telling?" He laughed. "I'm going to unwind, see you two later." Soary strode off towards his room. Travel fatigue weighed on him. He looked forward to a few hours of rest. After showering he lay down for a bit.

Bethany had the house cleaned and decorated while they were on the road. She had created a Pinterest board and taught them how to pin images of furniture that they liked. The house turned out great. His room was located on the back side. The French doors opened to a patio that stretched across the length of the house. There was an outdoor kitchen close to the pool on the west side. He liked that his room was on the east side so he could watch the sunrise over the small pond at the end of the property. From his patio, the forest of trees seemed to sprout directly out of the pond. The sun's morning glow of reds and pinks made it a calming scene to take in.

The room was large but he decided not to over-decorate it. He had a large gray bed with white comforter and two bedside tables. Warm taupe paint covered the walls. A bench sat at the end of it and candles decorated the mantel over the fireplace. His old writing table and chair were situated in the corner near the patio doors so he could gaze outside when he was writing. He walked over and ran his hand along the top, thinking about all the sleepless nights scribbling lyrics there. Reminiscing about the teenage years he spent at this table writing and dreaming gave Soary a sense of pride. They had worked hard and their dreams had come true. Their music was on the radio, people were singing their songs, people were paying to hear them play. They were signing autographs. In some cities, paparazzi followed them. They weren't as famous as some artists but their star was rising.

He expected to see the notebooks he used to keep stacked in the drawer when he pulled it open. Instead Gwen's neat print glared up at him, daring him to read what lay inside. His knees buckled and he almost lost his balance. Bethany had stacked the letters neatly in the drawer, tied together with a piece of twine. He picked them up and sat on the bed. The top bunch were all addressed to his old apartment while a later bunch had the same original address but had been forwarded to his new house. He thought about throwing them out without reading them but he didn't make the effort to move. He could hear Bethany and Jeff talking somewhere else in the house. He almost called out to them as a distraction but he didn't. His thumb rubbed the paper under the old twine. Each stroke of his thumb added more pressure to the twine until eventually it snapped and fell away. He closed his eyes and imagined Gwen's curls falling into her eyes while she wrote them. He wanted to know what she had shared with him. He needed to know. Soary slowly opened the very first letter and began to read.

My Love,

I just arrived at school and oh how I miss you. My roommate is great. Her name is Skye. I first met her last year. She's easy to be around and very clean. She came back early to get ahead on some reading. I'm afraid I've bored her to death already with stories of you and how famous you'll be one day. She doesn't quite believe me but I know you will be. Brenda has moved into an apartment complex across town. I told her about Jeff and she thinks it would be great if you two came for a visit. That is if he and Bethany aren't together yet. I miss you. I think of you all day and even though we've only been apart for less than two days I find myself wondering how long till I see you. I do want to know you are settling in alright. I tried to call but Bethany said you were out. She seemed so nice. We talked for a while. You described her and Jeff so well I feel like she's an old friend. Anyway, call me and write to me soon. I miss you. I love you.

Your Biggest Fan,
Gwen

He folded the letter and put it back in the envelope remembering her easy manner of talking. Gwen never met a stranger. She shared every detail of her day with whomever she was talking to. Everyone they encountered smiled a little brighter when Gwen was around. Day two since he left and she wasn't even mad he hadn't called. He tried to remember if Beth had mentioned the phone conversation. He was sure she had but he didn't remember. He randomly pulled out another letter and opened it. She didn't date her letters so he had to look at the postmark to know when they had arrived. It arrived about two months after he left.

Soary,

I miss you terribly and am starting to feel like a hanger-on. I haven't heard from you in weeks. I know you're busy but I need to talk to you. I miss you and have so much to say. I wondered if you were getting my messages and letters so today, I called and Jeff answered. He assured me you were given my messages and he would tell you I called again. He was really nice and caught me up on all that's been going on. I know you just got back from New York and that all is going well. He said you would only be back for a few days. I asked for a new number and he wasn't sure what it would be. Of course, you still have your cell but I guess it doesn't get good reception.

I would tell you about me but I am not sure you want to know. Please call me. I miss you.

I love you.
Gwen

He tossed the letter to the side and opened a later one.

My dearest Soary,

Why have you left me? I can't listen to music anymore. I can't even turn on the TV. Everything reminds me of you and how I don't have you. I know you are alive and doing well. Jeff just hung up the phone with me. He just said he was sorry. Sorry for what? I wanted to scream but I didn't. I wanted to ask why he always answers your cell. Are you sitting there with him? I wish I knew. I had something to tell you but... I miss you so much. I have left my number at school. I am going home this week. I may visit your mom. I need to talk to you.

Gwen

Soary remembered his mother calling him to say Gwen was over for a visit. It was Thanksgiving week. His mom wanted him to come home but they were deep into recording the album. There was a lot of buzz about going on tour. He asked his mom to say as little about him as possible. He was busy. Besides, he was sure Gwen would move on soon. He remembered the disappointed tone in his mom's voice. She told him she didn't agree with how he was handling things. He also remembered that later that night he went to a party and drank too much in an effort to not imagine being at home with Gwen. Had he even felt bad for what he was doing to Gwen at the time? He couldn't remember.

He pulled out the next letter. It was post marked December 2011, four months after he left her.

Soary,

I don't know where to begin. I have called and written. Maybe you aren't getting my messages. Maybe you haven't received my letters. Those are the lies I tell myself to get through my days. But I know the answers. You are getting my messages and my letters. I don't know what has happened to you. I miss you. I love you and I want you to talk to me. What happened with us? What did I do to make you leave me? I can't think straight. I can't concentrate on anything. I am so lonely. My friends say forget you. But how can I forget you? You are my heart. I can't breathe without you. I find myself gasping for air even though I'm outside. Nothing looks the same without you. There's this haze around my eyes. I am so sad, Soary. I am so sad. Please call me. Please come visit me. Please forgive me for whatever I did or said that pushed you away.

I have lost something so much bigger than a summer fling. You're the only person I want to talk to about what happened. I want to let go but I can't. You are a part of me, a part I desperately need. I really need to talk to you. Please, Soary. I need you to be my friend. I am back at school. Call me, please.

All my love,
Gwen

Soary picked the letters up and stuffed them back in the drawer. He knew what the rest would say. It would be more of the same. He wondered what she wanted to tell him. Why had he refused to even talk to her? Shame washed over him. All he knew for sure was that she was the best thing to happen to him and he had lost her. He didn't want to feel like a scum ball but he did. He lay back on the bed and closed his eyes. The exhaustion set in and he was asleep in minutes.

Her hair was blowing in the wind as they were running on the beach. He called her name but she kept running. She would glance over her shoulder and smile at him every few feet. He wanted her to stop. He wanted to sit with her but she didn't stop when he called her name. Panic gripped his heart as he noticed the cliff she was running towards. He tried to yell for her to watch where she was going. But she kept running straight to the cliff. He finally found his voice and he screamed for her.

Come back, come back, Gwen, come back!

***

"Soary!" Jeff banged the door open to see his friend drenched in sweat and hunched over with his head in his hands. "What happened?" He stood in the doorway, not sure if he should enter.

"It was a dream." Soary looked up at him. He looked ghastly. His face was pale. He was sweating. "Did you ever tell me you talked to Gwen on several occasions?"

"What?" Jeff was taken aback. He wasn't sure what Soary was asking him and he was startled to hear Gwen's name leave Soary's lips. They had an unspoken rule not to talk about Gwen. He couldn't remember the last he heard Soary speak her name. He looked at his friend and felt sympathy wash over him as it dawned on him why Soary was asking strange questions. Slowing down, taking this break meant Soary couldn't run from the fact he was still in love with Gwen. Jeff moved into the room and closed the door behind him. Beth was in the kitchen making a snack tray and some drinks.

"She called a lot in the first few months. Beth and I both talked to her. But you didn't want to hear about it. I stopped telling you when she called after a while because I was mad at you." Jeff sat in the chair across from Soary. "I thought you were a jerk for what you were doing to her."

Jeff had seen the letter crumpled on the floor in the bus. He had wondered why it was out. He knew Soary carried the last letter received with him everywhere he went like a talisman. When a new one arrived, he would replace the previous one. Then after about a year there were fewer letters. The last two years no letters at all arrived.

Out of the blue Bethany called and told Jeff another letter arrived. They discussed whether to send it to Soary or just throw it out. Jeff remembered how angry Bethany became. She yelled at Jeff that enough was enough. She accused Jeff of using Gwen's pain to make money. It took him a while to calm her down enough to respond. In the end they decided to send Soary the letter. When it arrived, Soary placed the previous one in an envelope and sent it back to Bethany. Jeff never asked Bethany what she did when she received the letters back from Soary.

Jeff never read the letters from Gwen. But when he picked the last one up from the bus floor he read it and was reminded of how sad she was when he had talked to her on telephone. Even through her pain she was nice and pleasant. She always asked after him and asked about Beth. It wasn't like she was fishing for information on Soary either. She was just a kind person. She had the sweetest voice he had ever heard. He remembered in the beginning when he thought Soary would come to his senses he thought about asking Soary if Gwen could sing. The last time he talked to her he knew he had been the one to pierce her heart with the knife Soary had designed and he was mad at his friend for putting him in that position. But he got over it, after all he had never met her and Soary was his friend.

He and Bethany had talked about her a few times. Neither could understand why she didn't question them about why Soary was ignoring her. She seemed happy to have any connection to him at all. She only asked after his wellbeing but nothing more. She never demanded to know where he was or why he wasn't calling. She never asked if there was someone else in his life.

Although both Bethany and Jeff thought they were prepared for those questions they never offered more information than she asked for and they stopped telling Soary about her calls.

"Last night was the first time I read any of her letters. Then today, I opened that drawer to look for my notebooks and there they were. Bethany had them neatly stacked in that drawer to accuse me. I read some of them." Soary's voice was weak. "I can't remember why I left her. I mean I know what my reasons were but I can't remember why I thought I could get away with it. For the longest time I have been able to keep her on the outskirts of my mind. But I have never really gotten away from her. Then I read the letters and it all became overwhelmingly clear. I love her, Jeff. Oh God, I love her. What have I done?" He lowered his head in his hands again.

Tears refused to grant him peace.

Jeff didn't know what he should do. He searched his mind trying to find the right words to comfort his friend. This is the breakdown he had stopped waiting for. He wasn't prepared to help his friend. Bethany had asked him to keep a close eye on Soary. She had been convinced he would realize his mistake and break down and she was worried Jeff wouldn't be there for him.

But Soary never seemed sad. They moved from one venue to another and there was little indication he ever thought about Gwen. Soary had immersed himself in the music. Jeff had stopped looking for signs of grief and over time he rarely thought about Gwen himself. He supposed he would have noticed that Soary always went home alone if he had been taking the company of ladies himself. But it never occurred to him that Soary should have been dating because he wasn't dating. He just hadn't thought about it.

There were times he would feel guilt when interviewers asked questions about who the songs were about. Most of the first album was about Gwen. The second had Gwen in the songs too but in a more remote way. When they were pressured to talk about who wrote the songs and who they were singing about Jeff would answer with jokes. He couldn't look at Soary directly during those interviews.

"You could call her. You could explain that you got spooked and you ran away. She would want to hear from you." He offered.

"Would she? How can I call her now?" Soary stood and walked across the room to look out the window.

"Soary, I am sure she would want to talk to you. There was a lot left unsaid. I mean, man, you just disappeared from her life. I am sure she has a few questions you could answer for her." Jeff sank deeper in the chair. He wasn't sure why he was trying to provoke his friend. Jeff was a matter-of-fact person. Bethany was right to be concerned, he wouldn't know how to comfort Soary because the facts were Soary made a horrible decision that broke two hearts and wasted a lot of time.

"You think I was wrong?" Soary looked at Jeff.

Jeff looked at his hands trying to decide if he should lie. He looked up and met Soary's dark stare. "Yes, isn't it obvious you made a mistake?" Soary flinched. "Beth and I tried to tell you at the time you should talk to her. But you were too stubborn. You thought you knew best. But you were wrong."

"Who the hell are you to tell me I made a mistake. I made the only decision could. I couldn't give it up and she couldn't share this with me. Hell, Jeff, you live in a relationship that doesn't exist. Bethany dumped you years ago and you still follow her around like a lost puppy. What the hell do you know about mistakes?" Soary yelled and shook with fury. He stomped around the room.

Jeff stood. "I am living my life, Soary. I can come home and relax. I can enjoy a nice phone call with the girl I care about. I can hold her and talk to her and even kiss her. And what can you do?" He paced the room away from Soary. "Wish you could escape her memory? Drive yourself crazy for a mistake—and yes you screwed up by walking away! You were selfish, Soary! You were scared and you messed up! And you've been running away from it for years. Now that you've finally slowed down you realize you can't keep hiding." He took a deep breath and let the anger out in an exhale. Deciding there was more he wanted to say he went to stand beside Soary and placed his hand on his shoulder in solidarity.

"Now you'll have to find a way to deal with what you did and process how you feel. The road, the party, the gigs have all quieted down and you're being forced to face yourself. And the best way I can think for you to do it is to talk to her. Let her ask questions. Let her yell at you. But don't keep acting like she doesn't exist. Don't keep acting like you made the best decision for her. And don't keep acting like you aren't an ass for the way you handled things." Jeff strode to the door and opened it.

He turned back to Soary. "I'm your friend. I'm here for you but I can't go on letting you lie to yourself. It's time to heal this wound. You need to forgive yourself and I'm afraid the only way you can do that is if she forgives you first." When Jeff opened the door, Bethany was striding down the hall her face serene. She was completely unaware that the dam had broken.

"There you two are. Soary you aren't ready. Amy is here." Bethany grabbed Jeff's hand. "Come on. Let Soary get ready. We're going to miss our reservation." She pulled him out of the room, leaving Soary to get ready.

***

Soary was shocked by what Jeff had said. He hadn't realized he was running and hiding. He thought he was just living his dream. He sunk down to the floor and stared. He tried to remember Gwen's face when he had asked her to go away with him. She had looked surprised and completely happy. He realized he had overlooked her happiness at the time. He hadn't given thought to how his decision would affect them. It hadn't occurred to him that by leaving her he changed them both. He had only thought about what they would have to sacrifice to be together.

He hadn't realized that relationships were work. No matter how you lived, if you were going to live with someone else you were going to have to work at it. He leaned his head back on the bed and tried to clear his head of all the cobwebs.

The laughter of a stranger brought him back to reality. Soary didn't want to meet Amy. He didn't want to leave his room but he saw no other alternative. He couldn't imagine sitting in his room crying over his past mistakes all evening. And he didn't want to talk to Bethany about Gwen either. The only choice he had was to go and try to enjoy dinner with friends. Soary managed to pull some clothes on and go meet his guest.

When he entered the living room, he found Bethany, Jeff, and pretty petite redhead flipping through a photo album. He stretched out a hand to Amy, "Hi, I'm Soary." He smiled, thankful she didn't have any similarities to Gwen.

"Hi. I'm Amy. It's so nice to meet you. Jeff was just telling me that you all only got home this morning. If you want to reschedule dinner I completely understand." She had a pretty smile and brilliant blue eyes.

Soary quickly considered telling her that was a good idea but a quick glance at Beth stopped him. "No, we have to eat. Besides Jeff shouldn't be making you feel bad."

He exchanged a scolding look with Jeff and walked to the chair where Amy had laid her jacket. He held it open to her and asked, "So are we ready?" He wanted to get the evening over as quick as possible. Amy shrugged into her jacket and led the way out.

Bethany was nonstop with her barrage of questions. She wanted to hear in detail all the stories she had heard tiny pieces about from her daily conversations with Jeff. She asked about the different cities they visited, different people they met. She wanted to know what Ellen was really like. Was she as funny in person as she was on TV? The questions went on through the appetizers. Soary tried to stay involved in the conversation. He wanted to share his experiences with Bethany and a part of him wanted to get to know Amy but he just didn't have his heart in it and he was so tired. Bethany was interested in one particular story that had made the front page of several major tabloids. It had actually helped their second record climb the charts. Jeff and Soary had laughed over it multiple nights.

"I want to know Soary, did you or did you not hookup with ten strippers? Now I imagine that if you had ten you had to get some help and I think it was probably Jeff here who helped you." Bethany ordered her third drink and Soary could tell she was going to dig deeper into the rumor than was necessary. In an effort to save his friend the grief he decided he would join the conversation.

"Well, you have to admit I have been known to be quite selfish. I didn't share." He grinned and winked at Amy hoping she would realize he was kidding. Bethany tossed her napkin at him. Amy laughed.

"Seriously, we all saw the pictures." Amy took a sip of her wine.

Starting slowly, "Well...the truth is that our tour bus passed a broken-down van and a few yards up from where it was parked on the side of the road we saw several women walking. It was late and they were a mile or more form the next exit. What were we supposed do?"

Jeff added, "The driver asked if he could stop and help. Of course, thinking the women were stranded from the van we agreed. It was after they boarded the bus that we realized they probably didn't mind walking."

"Jeff! That is horrible!" Bethany tried not to laugh. "So, what did ya'll do?"

"What any respectable men would do, we took them with us to the hotel." Soary and Jeff laughed at the horror on their faces.

"I called Frank from the bus and let him know we had a bus full of hookers. We were trying to be gentlemen. The ladies were nice. And even knew our music. But we realized that it could look bad. Especially when we pulled up and saw the paparazzi." Jeff remembered how panicked Frank was on the phone. He told them to keep the doors closed until he talked to the hotel to figure out how to get them off the bus without being seen.

"Frank wanted us to keep them on the bus. But there was only one way they were staying locked away on a Saturday night." They all laughed at the face Soary made. "Seriously, Gwen, it was hilarious how they talked the driver into letting them off the bus." As soon as he said her name Soary's voice slowed. He saw Bethany glare at him but he kept talking until he reached the end of his sentence. Amy smiled at him warmly as she leaned back in her chair. The slight was made. Jeff picked up the story for him.

"They talked—or rather scared—the bus driver into opening the doors. The photographers didn't get pictures of us but they had plenty of the bus and the women getting off in front of our hotel. The story was printed in all the tabloids along with several different pictures of us and the band getting on and off the same bus. The story was picked up by a lot of the morning news shows." He paused for a swallow of his beer then continued.

"We weren't happy with the story, Beth. You remember how upset I was about it. But after it was out the album started rising in the charts. And Frank changed his tune. He wanted us to be coy about it and not tell what really happened." Jeff winked at Bethany. She grinned at him and reached for his hand.

"Well, I guess I will have to hope if I am ever dressed in high heels and stranded on the side of the highway, you all are going to be passing me in your tour bus." Amy stated ironically and they all laughed.

The conversation was then taken over by Amy and Bethany. They discussed some of the students and a community project they were involved in. Soary was finally able to check out of the conversation and relax. The adrenaline he'd been running on was well on its way to depletion. He had barely looked at Jeff since he left his room and only spoke to him enough to keep the conversation comfortable.

He sat back in his chair, sipped his drink and looked around the restaurant. It was a small cozy place. Dark panel-lined walls, white table clothes hugged the tables, rich brown leather chairs adorned the bar and tables. Candles were placed throughout the room creating a soft glow for ambiance. The food was delicious as well.

A disruption behind their table brought his attention back to the group. A fan recognized them. She was stopped by the manager who had been staying close by for just that reason. She asked if they would take a picture and sign an autograph.

Soary and Jeff exchanged a look of surprise. On the road they had signed a lot of autographs. They usually held a VIP session before each show where they would take pictures and sign autographs for an hour. Often after the show they spent time backstage or behind the venue signing more autographs. But this was the first time they were being approached during their private time. It was a bit uncomfortable to be approached while out to dinner.

"Should we sign them?" Soary heard Jeff ask as he watched a crowd form around the girl. The manager looked over to them with a questioning look. It hadn't occurred to them to hire a security team while at home. They assumed they'd carry on as they always had. The realization that it may not be safe for their friends and family to be with them without some type of planning was unsettling.

"I guess we should be accommodating so we don't incite a scene." Soary waved the manager over and told him they would agree to sign several autographs and take a few pictures if there was somewhere more private to do so. He didn't want to disrupt the entire dining area.

The manager escorted them to a private party room near the hostess area, where another employee helped manage the crowd. They spent the next hour talking to fans, taking pictures, and signing autographs. Finally, the manager shut it down and allowed them to leave the restaurant through the kitchen door where Bethany and Amy met them.

"Wow, that was weird." Bethany looked from Jeff to Soary. "Are you two used to that?"

"No. I'm not sure if I'll ever get used to it." Jeff looked at Soary to see what he thought.

"Yeah. I guess I just never expected to have people here ask for our autograph. I thought that would only happen on the road." He smiled at Jeff. "Pretty crazy, huh?"

"A little," Amy said. "But I've seen crazier."

"Well, it's strange to see you two getting the star treatment." Bethany laughed.

The conversation resumed in a relaxed manner as they drove back to the house. Bethany mentioned a night cap at a local bar but Jeff stepped in and saved them by claiming to be too tired.

When they arrived back at the house Soary walked Amy to her car. He wondered briefly if she had wanted to come in but he pushed the thought aside. He wasn't ready. He shuffled his feet as she unlocked her door. His hand brushed hers as he reached around to open it for her. He had an urge to take her hand, to kiss her, to let her clear his mind of all the memories swimming around. All things considered he enjoyed the evening with her. He liked her.

"I had a wonderful time." She smiled at him.

"It was a great night. I enjoyed it a lot." He gave her his winning smile and watched her smile widen into laughter.

This surprised Soary and he watched her until she quieted herself.

"I'm sorry. You're just so polite." Another giggle slipped out. "You were a million miles away most of the night. Polite and a gentleman. But a million miles away. I guess you have a lot on your mind." She touched his arm. He grimaced as he realized she was right.

"I would like to see you again. Maybe when you have some time to settle in and aren't so distracted." She paused watching his reaction. "I like you, Soary. I like your music. I liked how you were with your fans. I want to know you better." She leaned in and kissed him on the cheek without waiting for his response.

"I would like that." He responded and found it to be true.

He watched her drive away until her taillights were tiny sparkles in the distance before returning to the house.

Chapter 10

2017

Gwen packed the last of her dishes in boxes. She looked around the kitchen with a pang of sadness. She would miss her condo. It was the first home she had created all on her own and she was proud of it. It was also the place she met and fell in love with Jason. She was glad she had made Jason take pictures in all the rooms, snapshots designed to spark memories of their time here.

Gabriel came in as she wiped an unwanted tear from her eye.

"Gwen, between you and Jason it's going to take the movers a week to get all this stuff loaded and delivered. Do you think you need all of it? Did you all consolidate anything?" He noticed her eyes were wet. In an attempt to give her a moment to gain her composure he reached in the fridge and grabbed a beer.

"Yes and no. We decided to wait until we unpack everything together to make decisions on what we want to keep. Then we'll give the rest to a charity."

"It's hard to believe that you're moving to Atlanta. And we're going to be in the same building. I'm actually looking forward to seeing you all more. And maybe get some homecooked meals out of it too," he teased. "I do think you two are going to wish you waited a few more weeks though. The construction has been noisy and messy." He walked over and leaned on the counter beside her.

"Yeah, I know. But it's only a few weeks and then the building will be complete—at least that's what our realtor told us. It is hard to believe I don't have a job, though. Jason is so excited about his promotion. I think I'll get used to being free to do whatever I want. Maybe Liz and I can spend our days at the spa. And if you ever settle down, I'll have another playmate."

She leaned against the counter beside him and took the beer from his hands. She wiped her mouth after taking a drink and handed it back to him. His hand grazed hers as he reached for it. He paused and looked at her.

"I've already told you I'll be your boyfriend. All women need a boyfriend around to ward off the husbands." He laughed as she nudged her shoulder into him. He was aware his voice sounded more intense than intended. "Seriously, I'm perfectly happy the way my life is for now. Besides, I don't have to work as much as Jas. I can take you around the city and help you get to know the area. I can be your playmate."

Gwen placed her hand on his arm and continued. "I would like that. You can show me some of the art galleries. I promised Jason

I'd get some good pieces to impress his mom." Her voice sounded wistful and a bit sad.

He took her hand in his and pulled her around so she faced him. "Are you okay with this? The move I mean. I know change is hard." He tucked a piece of hair that had fallen out of her ponytail behind her ear.

She smiled at him, thankful he was her friend. Over the past few months they had spent many hours together and on the phone. Gabriel always knew what to say to make her laugh and exactly when to ask her to open up. He was patient and kind and tender. She adored him and often feared that when he did find the right woman her relationship with him would change.

Jason had told her she was silly. Gabriel would always be her friend. But she wasn't sure if Jason understood how much she needed Gabriel.

After Jason had asked her to marry him things happened quickly. She had known all along that his goal was to move back to Atlanta. He never planned to make his career in Chattanooga. She was proud of him but she was also sad to give up the life she built. She was scared of the unknown. She was giving up a job she worked hard to get. She was leaving behind some great work friends too. Atlanta was a big city and she had no connections to it or any one in it other than Jason and Gabriel. She was nervous about finding her place in her new life. Yet, the anxiety wasn't crippling her.

"I'm sad to leave this place. It has been a big part of me. This was my refuge. The place where I found myself again. I started living my life here." She smiled at him weakly. "You know this is where I met Jason."

She looked around the empty condo and felt the tears well up in her eyes again. "It actually looked a lot like this the day we met, boxes everywhere." She paused, "Gabe, I am scared I won't find my balance there. I don't want to be dependent on Jason for my happiness. What if Jason and I realize—I don't know? What if this is where I'm meant to live and not there?" She looked at her hands trying to calm her fears.

"Gwen, here is what I know about life; nothing is guaranteed. Nothing. Here is what I know about careers; you need them to pay the bills and feel like you contributed to society. Here is what I know about love; it forces you out of your comfort zone and puts decisions in your way to force you to give more than you want to give." He smiled at her before finishing his thought.

"And Gwen, here is what I have learned about hearts. They are resilient and strong. They don't actually break. Pieces of them break off. And with those pieces we lose a part of ourselves. But our heart remains. It bends and molds itself into a new shape. Our hearts provide us with the electricity to live. Our hearts drive our souls to feed our humanity. And every time the shape changes because of loss we grow stronger than we were before." He let go of her hands and wrapped his arms around her.

"When will you finally let go completely?" He whispered in her hair. Although she had only talked to Jason about how bad things were for her, Gabriel seemed to know more about how she felt than she did. She found it easy to open up to him without having to say too much.

"Oh, Gabe. I have let go. I love Jason so much. I want to be happy with him and only him." She rested her head on his chest.

"It's just that I feel like I'm missing something but I can't figure out what it is."

Gwen pulled back from Gabriel and looked up into his eyes. She found herself frozen. Gabriel had his hands resting on her arms and pierced her with a deep stare that spoke words that would be left unsaid. The tension between them wasn't uncomfortable. It was intoxicating yet at the same time safe.

Gabriel tilted his head down closer to her without breaking their gaze. She could feel his breath gently blowing on her lips. She shivered. Every cell in her body propelled her closer to him although she knew she needed to pull away. Just as his lips were close enough to touch hers, he sighed and pulled away. He dropped his arms from her and leaned further into the counter creating space between their bodies. Gwen shivered as a rush of cool air filled the space between them. Finally breaking eye contact, Gabe turned from her and drank the last of his beer.

When he spoke again he was surprised how calm he sounded, "You'll find a job quickly. Get your resume updated and I'll float it out to a few people I know. You'll see, you'll settle in no time at all." Without making eye contact he handed her one of the two beers he retrieved from the refrigerator while he spoke.

"What are you two up to?" Jason came in the kitchen. "Is everything packed up?" He had the clipboard he was using to carry his to-do list around on. "Why are you drinking a beer? We still have..." He paused as he looked at his list.

"Nothing. We have nothing left to do. We're all packed up and ready to hit the road." Gabriel laughed as he reached in the refrigerator for a third beer and handed it to Jason.

"Wow. You're right." Jason took the beer, tilted it back and swallowed. "Gwen, honey, are you ready?" He saw her balk. "I was thinking it would be romantic if we stayed the night here in the dark." He winked at her.

"We can't; Liz will be so disappointed. She really is looking forward to hosting us." Gwen laughed, leaned over, and kissed him.

"Yeah, but I bet Logan wouldn't mind." Jason said as he swung his arm around her shoulder. "Then I take it we're ready to head home."

"Yes, we're ready to head home." Gwen agreed.

"Alright, I'll meet you two in the truck." Gabriel grabbed his jacket and headed down to the street. Gwen frowned at the hunch of his shoulders as he hurried away.

"I am going to run down to my condo and take a last look." Jason kissed the top of head.

"I will do the same here." She flashed him a quick smile before turning toward the living room.

Gwen walked around the condo filled with boxes and said her mental goodbyes. She was excited about her new place and couldn't wait to get it all set up and settled. But she would miss her first real home. After several minutes she heard Jason return. He waited for her in the doorway giving her time.

Jason knew this was a hard move for Gwen. She was leaving everything behind for him. He loved her more for her strength in moving than he had the day she said yes to marry him. This was a true display of her commitment to him. He was tense because he was afraid her fears of leaving would tear her apart. But as he watched her walk around the room, he knew she was ready to leave it behind. He was confident she was ready to move on with her life with him as her husband.

Jason smiled, happy he had decided to knock on her door with a casserole dish. "Are you ready, babe?"

"I'm ready." She responded. She flipped off the lights as she took his hand to leave.

***

"What do you think? Gwen stood off to side as she waited for Gabriel and Elizabeth's opinion on the painting she purchased. She bought it from a small art gallery she found while roaming around the city. The gallery owner volunteered at several metal health facilities teaching patients art therapy. The artist was a hospitalized mental patient who had tried to kill himself several times before finally seeking help for his depression. His story touched Gwen. The painting was full of rich colors, thrown together in the middle of a dark outline. The outline looked like a tree standing alone in a forest. Gwen had thought it was perfect for the entryway of the new condo. It brought warmth and vibrancy and it was mystical. Where she saw a tree, Jason had seen a heart. She had laughed at him as he took her in his arms and swept her off to their bedroom. But she wanted to know what her friends thought. She waited as Gabriel and Elizabeth stared at it, anxious to hear how the painting spoke to them. After several minutes, her patience wore thin.

"So?"

"Well, it is interesting." Elizabeth spoke slowly as she turned to Gwen. "I'm just not sure what it is. I do like the colors, though."

"I think it is brilliant." Gabriel said. "It's a tree alone in an empty forest. It represents how we all feel in society. We are a part of the forest yet we isolated lost in our own heads. It's full of hope, sadness, joy, relief, fear, anxiety, passion, the colors of life." He continued to gaze at the painting appreciatively.

"Exactly." Gwen clapped her hands in excitement. "That is what I tried to tell Jason. Of course, he thought it looked like a heart."

"Well, leave it to you two to have the same opinion," Elizabeth said as she waved her hand at Gwen and Gabriel. "So are we going to lunch or are we going to stay here and gaze at your tree all day. I have to pick the kids up from the sitters in two hours."

"Yes, let's go. Gabe are you ready?" Gwen walked to the study and picked up her purse and met them back in the foyer.

"I actually can't make it. I have to finish an article and then meet with a contractor. I just came by to see your new purchase and let you know I had to skip lunch." He leaned over and kissed Elizabeth on the cheek as he turned to go.

"Well, good luck on your article." Gwen tried to hide her disappointment. Gabriel had been careful not to touch her or spend time alone with her since the incident in the kitchen. That was how she had come to think of it. They had been close to kissing. She had admitted to herself later that night while she lay next to Jason that she had wanted him to kiss her. She felt guilt about her desire. After mulling it over for several days she understood her desire came from the nostalgia of moving and not any real desire to be with him. Gabriel was sensitive to her moods so it made sense he got caught up in the moment too. Plus their conversation about love and hearts, it was easy to see how they forgot themselves for minute. She loved Gabe and she knew he loved her but it was a friendship love. Not romantic love. She just wished Gabe would stop avoiding her.

Elizabeth walked out the door behind Gabriel and pushed the button for the elevator. As the doors opened Gwen said, "Liz, I'll be right down." She turned as if she was going back to her condo. When the door to the elevator closed, she circled back to where Gabriel was waiting for the return elevator to head up this condo. She reached for his hand. He wearily watched their hands connect but he didn't pull away.

"Gabe, why are mad at me?"

"I am not mad at you, Gwen. I just have things to do today." Desire stirred in him as he stood there alone with her. He could smell her perfume and the warmth of her hand made his skin prickle.

"Then you're not avoiding me?" She asked, the hurt in her eyes not veiled in the slightest. She had come to need his friendship and the thought that she had lost it scared her. She loved Elizabeth but she needed Gabriel.

Gabriel sighed, trying to focus his thoughts. "No, I'm not avoiding you." He couldn't stand to be the reason she was hurting. This was his best friend's fiancée and she was his friend. He couldn't punish her for his feelings. "I promise." He leaned over and kissed her cheek just as he had Elizabeth's and felt his heart leap as his lips came in contact with the heat of her skin. "I will see you later." He pushed the down button for her and when the elevator doors opened, he handed her into it. She smiled at him as the doors closed.

204 | *Lacey Furr*

Gabe headed for the stairs. He had to get away from the lingering smell of her perfume.

Back in his condo he tried to work on his article but all he could think was how ironic life could be. Pushing his laptop away, giving up on getting any work done, he cursed himself.

Feelings he had never felt before stirred inside; for the first time in his life Gabriel had fallen with a woman he could never have.

Chapter 11

2017

Soary paced the studio. He had been working with the sound engineer for hours and the song still sounded off. They were getting close to finishing the album but Soary kept stalling on a few of the songs.

"What do you think? Did we get the change you were asking for right?" his sound engineer asked.

"No. It's good." Soary hated to be difficult. "But it's still missing something. You know, it's missing its soul. The song needs to make the listener feel. Not because of the lyrics but because of the music. It needs to be alive." His phone buzzed in his pocket.

"Hello."

"Hi." Amy voice answered his.

"Hi. How are you?"

"I'm good. I miss you though. Can you take a break night?"

Soary wistfully looked around the studio. He wanted to keep working but decided maybe a break would be helpful. "That is a fantastic idea! I could use a break and I could use some time with you." He heard her release the breath she held. "Want to stay in though? We could cook together and watch a movie." He suggested.

"I think that sounds like the perfect night." She paused. "Will Jeff be there?"

"No, he went to visit his brother for a few days. I can't get this one song right and he was tired of me."

"Well, I'm sure it will be perfect when you're finished."

"Yeah." Soary felt a little guilty talking to Amy about a song he wrote while thinking of Gwen.

"I'll see you later this evening, about seven?"

"Sounds perfect." Soary shoved the phone back in his pocket. "Let's take the rest of the night off. I'll work on it some in the morning."

Soary left the studio and jogged across the lawn to the house. He wanted to shower and run to the store for dinner supplies before Amy arrived.

***

"What do you think of this one?" Amy came out of the dressing room wearing a short, tight red dress. It hugged her curves in all the right places.

"You look amazing!" Bethany exclaimed. "Wow!" She went over to Amy and ran her hand along the fabric. "It's perfect."

"You don't think it's too much for the benefit concert?"

"No, not all." Bethany pulled her phone from her purse distractedly.

"What's going on?" Amy asked. She went back in the dressing room to change into her jeans.

"Nothing. Well, it's Jeff. He's been acting weird lately. I think he's fighting with Soary over some changes on the new album and he's taking it out on me."

"How so?"

"Well... He hasn't been answering my calls and waits hours to get back to me." Bethany knew she sounded pathetic.

"Beth, do you think you two should have the talk?" Amy used her fingers to indicate quotation marks around the words "the talk" above the dressing room door.

"What? No! Our relationship has been the same for years now. Six to be exact." Sighing, she dropped her phone back in her purse.

"Do you want it to be the same?" Amy questioned as she pushed the curtain aside.

Bethany blindly gazed at Amy, thinking about the question. Her fingers mindlessly rubbed the button on her sweater. She wanted their relationship to change.

"No, I don't want it to be the same. I want us to be a couple again. I want to get engaged and plan a wedding and have amazing sex with him everywhere he tours." Taken aback by her own words Bethany started laughing.

Amy laughed too. "Well, okay, then. I think you need to talk to him about these feelings." She paused searching for the best words. "Soary mentioned the benefit concert was a tester for some of their new music. He said they would probably be hitting the road again later this year."

"Yeah, Jeff mentioned Frank set the release date for May and they'll start promoting it in June." She sunk back on the bench. "I should just wait until they get back home."

"Okay, first, I'm not one who has a right to be too harsh. Soary and I have been dating for a couple of months and I know he's not even close to committing to me. We avoid the topic of commitment completely. But I enjoy being with him. I actually don't mind that I may be his distraction sometimes. He's kind to me. He's a great kisser." At this she grinned. "My point is, I get that my relationship is a bit odd. But you need to talk to Jeff and fix yours."

"So... what else is he good at other than kissing?" Bethany teased.

Blushing, "Lots of things. But we're talking about you and Jeff. Don't you miss the intimacy of being with him?"

"I do. Oh, my goodness, I do. You're right. It's been long enough. I'm going to talk to him tonight." Butterflies danced in her stomach.

"Good." Amy felt pleased with herself and couldn't wait to tell Soary.

***

Jeff was tired of Soary delaying the album. He understood that some of the songs were about Gwen and that was tougher on him this go round but they were good songs—no they were great songs. Soary knew they were great but was still holding back his approval to release the album to Frank. It was infuriating.

"Hey, Jeff. I think I know how we can change the melody on Never Forget." Soary stated as Jeff walked into the studio.

"Let's hear it." Soary glanced up at Jeff's curt tone.

Without speaking again Soary turned his attention to playing the song. Jeff heard right away the changes Soary had made and it sounded wonderful. The song was ready. It was perfect.

"It sounds amazing. Frank will be excited we may actually release on time." Jeff hoped Soary would agree.

"Well, it may need a bit more fine-tuning."

"No." Jeff rarely fought with Soary but since they had been back home the frustrations of Soary's procrastination had become too much.

Soary paused the song. Without looking at Jeff he questioned., "No, what?"

Jeff took a deep breath. "No more fine-tuning. It's ready. The album is ready. It's a great album. Our best yet. It's time to release it and move on to promoting it." Jeff sighed. "Look, I know we toured a lot the last five years and getting back on the road is a big commitment.But we need to get back out there with this album. We can take a break with the next one. But this one we need to tour."

Soary understood Jeff's fear of them losing relevance with their fans. They played pop music; new artists came along every day releasing great songs and albums. Some had sticking power and some were one album wonders. Regardless, the competition could be fierce within Spirit Records for funding. But he honestly didn't feel that the album was ready. It was still lacking that one song that drew the audience in and kept them listening.

"I hear you, I know we're close. But it's still missing something." He paused. "Jeff, I have the song. I just can't play it yet."

Jeff stared at Soary. Understanding dawned on him. Once again it was about Gwen. He knew Soary had a song only Gwen had heard from their summer together. He remembered Soary calling him excited about finishing it. Soary hadn't played it for him though. As far as he knew Soary hadn't played it since that summer.

"Are you going to record it?"

"Yes." Soary hoped Jeff would let the subject drop.

"Then get it recorded, Soary. Stop delaying this album for her." Jeff was tired. He was tired of Soary and his brokenness over Gwen. He was tired of Bethany and her 'let's be friends' attitude. He was tired of being nice and caring and going to bed alone. He was tired of being stationary. He was ready to get back on the road.

"I'll record it this week." Soary felt the tension oozing off Jeff. He knew him well enough to proceed with caution.

"Good." Jeff stormed out of the studio.

***

Bethany found Jeff in the kitchen. She had practiced her speech all the way over to his house. But seeing him standing at the sink washing vegetables melted her. He was such a strong, sexy, kind man. And she had spent too many years risking the loss of his love. Without delay she rushed over to him. "Jeff."

He turned to her. "Beth, I wasn't expecting you."

Wordlessly she touched his arm, holding it for balance. She stood on the tips of her toes and kissed him. Seconds passed as she pressed her lips to his before she felt his arms draw her to him. He crushed her body to his as he lifted her off her feet and carried her to his room.

***

Soary spent the rest of the week in the studio alone. He asked his sound engineer to listen to the track after he left each day and suggest changes. But he didn't allow anyone in the studio while he recorded. It was a surreal experience. Each time he sang the song he was transported back to that night with Gwen in the park.

He was angry with himself every time he imagined her face. That was the night he told her he loved her. He remembered clearly the love he felt that made him promise to marry her. Yet, within weeks he left her. The anger and grief overwhelmed him. He tried to shake the sadness.

He hit record, sat on the stool, pulled the microphone to his mouth, closing his eyes he started singing. He sang to Gwen, just as he had that night. The stars were overhead. The cicadas were chirping. She was sitting beside him with tears streaming down her cheeks. Every word, every tone was just as it had been that night. When he finished the song, he dropped his head, rested it on his guitar. He knew this was a hit. He knew he had to hand it over or he risked losing Jeff's respect. He prayed Gwen would hear it and remember how much she once loved him. He needed her forgiveness.

Chapter 12

2017

Gwen started to feel exhausted in the afternoons. She would often find herself resting on the patio and some days she would have to go lay down in bed to take a nap. She became concerned when the exhaustion was accompanied by nausea. After several weeks of her feeling unlike herself she called Elizabeth to get a recommendation for a doctor.

"Gwen, you may not want to hear this but I think you're pregnant." Elizabeth practically whispered through the phone lines. Her words sounded a bit foreign. It took several seconds for Gwen to let out the breath she held.

"Oh." Was all she managed to say. Her mind backtracked to her last cycle. She realized with a shock it had been almost two months ago. Tears burned her eyes and she couldn't speak. Her emotions were in a battle: excitement, surprise, horror, fear. An image of a tiny baby face filled her mind. The tears spilled down her cheeks. She started to hyperventilate.

"I'm coming over." Elizabeth hung up the phone before Gwen could tell her to not to come. Thirty minutes later Elizabeth let herself in Gwen's condo. She brought ice cream and two pregnancy tests with her.

"Okay, do you want me to tell you how to take this or do you want to read the instructions?" She held the pregnancy test out to Gwen.

Gwen looked at Elizabeth with a blank stare. She was grateful and terrified at the same time.

There was a secret she shared with Jason that taunted her now. She wondered about telling Elizabeth. Gabriel had become her best friend but there were topics she couldn't share with him.

"Liz." The one word expressed more than one hundred others.

Elizabeth looked at Gwen when she spoke. She saw fear on her face. Elizabeth suppressed the excitement building inside at the thought of a baby.

The first time she met Gwen she knew there was a sad story behind her sweet smile. She wasn't one to pry. She didn't mention it to Logan. She watched as Gwen and Gabriel grew close. One day curiosity got the best of her and she asked Gabriel about Gwen's past. He was his typical charming self but had revealed nothing. She never determined whether he knew anything or not.

"Gwen, do you want to talk before you take it?"

Gwen stood in the living room of her condo holding the test Liz handed her. She stared at it as if it was a foreign object. The past swam around her. She heard the squeal of the brakes. The thuds from heavy rain on the windshield. There was a flash followed by the sound of metal crunching. And a scream. The scream haunted her dreams for years afterwards. Then complete silence.

"Hey, are you alright?" Elizabeth felt her mouth go dry.

Gwen shook her head from side to side, the panic attack she expected to come stayed away. "I'm okay." She looked at the pregnancy test and then at Elizabeth. "I'm good. I'll be back."

Alone in the bathroom Gwen sunk to the floor. "Oh, baby, I miss you so much. I am so sad I never got to hold you." Her hand cradled her stomach. But she didn't cry. After several minutes she rose from the floor and took the test.

The instructions stated the results would take three minutes. She sat on the side of bathtub wringing her hands and forcing slow steady breathes in and out. She refused to wonder about any what ifs. She didn't allow her mind to imagine how Jason would feel. She willed herself to enter a meditative state. She waited calmly and quietly, eyes closed, air flowing in and out of her lungs. When the alarm sounded on her phone she took a deep breath and opened her eyes.

She studied both sticks, comparing the color and quality of the lines to each other while overwhelming joy filled her. She was going to be a mother. Jason was going to be a father. A level of happiness she could recall feeling when she sat on the side of the river fishing with her dad filled her with warmth. She took the evidence of the tests and hid it in the bottom of the garbage can. Elizabeth had been pacing outside the bathroom door. She stopped when Gwen came out. Seconds passed as they stood and stared at each other.

"Gweny! You are going to be a mother." Elizabeth squealed and gave her a big hug, "I can't believe it."

Gwen laughed.

"I will get you an appointment with my doctor." Elizabeth had pulled her phone out and dialed the number. Minutes later her appointment was confirmed.

"I want to wait to tell Jason after the doctor confirms it."

"Of course. Gwen he is going to be so over the moon."

Gwen smiled. Yes, she thought, they were all going to be happy after all.

***

With her pregnancy confirmed she spent a lot of time trying to decide how to tell Jason. Finally, she decided to fill the guestroom with images of nursery options. She bought several magazines and hung images of baby beds, strollers, and rocking chairs on the walls. She bought several different color paint swatches and painted samples on the walls. She had blues, pale pinks, yellow, grey, purple, teal. She bought a teddy bear and put a onesie on it that said "My Dad is the Best Dad". She placed her pregnancy test along with the test results from the doctor and their next appointment card in a gift box. She had just finished writing a letter to Jason when he had arrived home from work. She quietly closed the door and rushed to get ready. Her excitement caused her to smile without ceasing.

She had spent too much time preparing her surprise so she was running late. Gwen felt a mixture of excitement and anxiety.

Logan had gotten them tickets to a VIP concert at The Mansion. It was a fundraiser event for a local children's hospital. There was a golf tournament the next day that the guys were playing in as well. Gwen was excited to dress up and have a night out with Jason and their friends. Jason had been busy at work while she spent most of the past month unpacking and decorating their condo. They managed to eat dinner together and go to bed together each night but they were both exhausted. The wedding was less than a month away and Gwen wanted everything perfect beforehand. She debated telling Jason about the baby until their honeymoon but knew she couldn't keep the secret from him for a month.

Jason and Gabriel kept yelling for her to hurry or they would miss the concert which they were certain would be the best part of the event. Gwen was trying to hurry but she kept getting sidetracked by her thoughts. She couldn't help but touch her belly and smile, and then she would realize she was daydreaming and shake her head and continue getting ready.

"Are you decent, I've been sent to hurry you along." Gabriel came in the room and handed her a glass of wine. Gwen took it and sat it down as she handed him her necklace.

"I am ready. Where's Jas?"

"He took a call on the patio. He said to get you." Gabriel sat his drink down next to hers and took the necklace from her. "You know these charity events can be really boring."

Gwen laughed. "Logan is pretty excited about it. He said the band was going to be amazing. He seemed surprised he was able to book them at all."

"Yeah, because Logan is known to be the fun guy." He said sarcastically as he clasped her necklace. Her back was to him, the nape of her neck was smooth and tanned. She had applied a subtle shimmer lotion that smelled like freesia. It intoxicated him.

Gwen turned to face him. "So how do I look?' She gave him a big smile and wink.

"Amazing. I'm jealous as always." Hoping he sounded playful he bowed to her before taking his drink and leaving the room.

Jason gave a long whistle as Gwen stepped out on the patio. "I've got to go." He said into the phone. He dropped it on the table as he took her into his arms.

"Leave it at home tonight." Gwen said as she stepped into his arms. They kissed and Jason nodded his consent.

Gabriel stood to the side trying not to notice the electricity in the air. He was truly happy for his friends. He loved Jason like a brother and his feelings for Gwen overwhelmed him at times but their happiness was important to him. His time with Jason and Logan was important to him. And he enjoyed spending time with Gwen so he placed his effort on ignoring his other feelings for her and hoped they would go away completely one day.

"Gabe, is Ashley meeting you there?" Jason asked as he gave Gwen one last kiss and took her hand and led them to the door. "You are glowing tonight." He whispered as she stepped past him into the waiting elevator.

"Yep. Apparently, she had a case that was keeping her late at the office so she said she would change there and meet us later." Gabriel had been dating Ashley for a few months. It was the longest relationship he'd been in since Gwen had known him. He had met Ashley in college and they'd hooked up a few times. He ran into her during a lunch interview. He was working on an article about a set of foster parents who were fighting to adopt three children.

Ashley was representing them in the case. He'd been stunned to see her and had asked her to meet him for drinks later to catch up. Drinks led to them going back to her place. He was different with Ashley than the other women he hooked up with. He knew he wasn't in love with her but he cared about her and enjoyed her company. He wanted her around in the morning, afternoon, and evening, which was a big change for him.

***

They hired a car to take them to The Mansion. On the ride over Jason and Gabriel discussed the current rankings of the Falcons. Gwen wasn't too interested although she did enjoy going to the games. Her mind had its own agenda tonight. She wasn't sure if she would be able to keep the news from Jason all night. Already she wished they were on their way home.

When they arrived, Gwen spotted Elizabeth right away at a table front row center stage. She tapped Jason on the arm in parting and headed in that direction as he waited with Gabriel for Ashley.

"Gwen." Logan called to her. He stood by the bar talking to a tall guy Gwen hadn't met before.

"Logan. Hey. I just spotted Elizabeth." She leaned in and kissed him on the cheek. "I'm getting her a glass of wine. What are you having tonight?"

"I think I'll stick to water for now." She smiled at the guy with Logan.

"Coming up." He ordered her water. "Gwen, this is Jeff. Jeff is in the band."

Gwen stuck her hand out and smiled. "It is so nice to meet you. Logan has told us how great your band is. I'm sorry to say I don't know much about today's music, but I'm looking forward to hearing you play."

Jeff stared at her in stunned silence.

Gwen was starting to think he was a rude celebrity when he finally smiled and took her hand.

Logan saved him from speaking, "She wouldn't know your music. She barely knows the classics. Gwen didn't listen to music until the gang invaded her life. Heck, Jas, said she wouldn't even turn the TV on as background noise. Our Gwen is more of a reader and a thinker. But we are bringing her around, or down." He chuckled. Gwen flinched at his words. She sounded like some strange freak.

"It's nice to meet you." Jeff remembered the sweet tone of her angelic voice. He told Bethany that he was certain she would sound polite even if she was yelling at you. But more than her voice it was the electricity he felt. As a musician he had become accustomed to following his instincts and listening to his feelings. He learned to read people and situations, looking for the hook. And every part of him knew this was Gwen. Soary's Gwen. But he had no idea what he should do.

"Gwen, where are you from that you didn't listen to music growing up?" He smiled and tried to make his tone sound casual.

"Small-town Alabama. But not so small we didn't have music. I just, well, I guess I was just easy to over-stimulate. Sound-sensitive, maybe." She shrugged her shoulders. He noticed the cloud of unhappiness sweep through her eyes and regretted asking. The energy around her shifted slightly.

She wrapped her arms around her waist. "But I'm sure your band is great. And that I'll be a big fan by the end of the night." She managed a radiant smile.

Jeff wanted to tell her she would hate it and should just go ahead and leave. Her innocence awoke the chivalry in him. She was even more beautiful than he had imagined. Her long auburn hair was swept up in a loose bun with tendrils framing her face. Her eyes were big and wide.

When she gazed out of them, she bared her soul. She was average height and average weight. She was slender yet curvy. Extremely sexy although she didn't carry herself as if she knew it. She was possibly the most beautiful woman he had ever seen. She made him want to wrap her up and protect her like an expensive and breakable porcelain doll. But there was also strength about her. A fearlessness. She seemed electric; he was drawn to her. Even though he knew he should walk away and find Soary to warn him, he wanted to stay at the bar and chat with her.

"Well, it's okay if you're not. Actually, we're not that great." He sounded lame even to his own ears.

Logan handed her the glass of water. Gwen reached for Elizabeth's wine glass, blushing as she noticed Jeff was intensely watching her. "I'll take Liz her drink so you can finish your conversation. It was nice to meet you. Good luck tonight." She smiled at Jeff, nodded to Logan and walked toward the front table.

Jeff couldn't concentrate on what Logan was saying. Since Logan was an executive at the advertising company Frank hired, he had to pretend to care what the guy said. Frank made it clear he wanted to ramp up their marketing differently with this record. He was looking to grow their audience base. He thought Logan's firm would be a good fit for them. It was important he not offend him. He tried to nod in the right places and respond to Logan's questions. When another friend of Logan's interrupted, he jumped at the opportunity to excuse himself.

He scanned the room seeking out Bethany and noticed she was seated three tables to the left of Gwen. He caught Gwen's eye as he passed her table and noticed again how beautiful she was. She smiled up at him as he walked by. There was a warmth in her interaction with the woman at her table. They clearly adored each other. It dawned on him that the woman she was with was married to Logan. He groaned. 'This is not going to end well,' he mumbled under his breath as he tapped Bethany on the arm and motioned for her to stand so he could get her full attention and whisper in her ear.

"Where is Soary?" He hissed.

"I think he's in the back. I saw Amy head back there about ten minutes ago." She looked at him and saw the flicker of his eye towards Gwen's table. "What is going on?" She hissed back.

"Gwen is here." He looked toward her table again and then back to Bethany just in time to see her jaw drop open as she stared. "Quit staring."

"My God, she is magnificent." Bethany was one of those rare women who didn't have to be the best-looking woman in the room. She could admire the beauty of others confidently. "How do you know it's her?" From Soary's many descriptions that summer, Bethany knew which lady he thought was Gwen. She was glowing, clearly happy.

"I talked to her. She's friends with Logan, he works with Frank, for the marketing firm. His firm is one of the primary sponsors tonight," he explained quickly when she looked at him questioningly. "Anyway, I don't think she knew who I was. I recognized her voice. She has no idea Soary is here, well at least she didn't seem to know who I was or the band. Hell, she may not even know anything about him." Jeff felt nervous energy crawling around in his stomach.

"Jeff, she called and wrote for months. You don't think she kept up with him?" Bethany tried not to look at Gwen again but the urge was overwhelming. She glanced over just as three guys and another girl arrived at the table. She saw one of the tall handsome blond men lean down and kiss Gwen and watched her face light up in a smile. If she knew Soary was in the band she wasn't fazed by him.

Bethany also noticed the other man watch the exchange and hide sad eyes behind a smile as he turned to the pretty redhead. From her perspective it appeared that there was an interesting dynamic with the group. Although they appeared to get on well; they were all smiling and talking, each of them interacting with one another at the table. Bethany felt anger rise in her. If Soary had handled things differently Gwen could be sitting with her. She knew it was irrational but she felt sad at losing Gwen as a friend.

"I think you're right. It would be strange for her to know Soary's band and not recognize your name as part of it. Plus look how happy she seems." They exchanged a look of disbelief.

"What should we do?" Jeff was nervous this night wouldn't end well.

"I don't know. Maybe we should just let the cards fall where they may." She couldn't think of a way for them to cancel the show at this point.

Bethany felt bad thinking she wanted to see an exchange between the lovely brunette and Soary. But she wanted it. She had spent a long time wondering why Soary hid behind his stubborn pride instead of making his relationship with Gwen work. Jeff told her about how Soary reacted after finally reading the letters she'd sent. There was no doubt he was still in love with Gwen, although he and Amy were enjoying a nice romance. They were spending more time together and Amy was already planning on meeting him on tour during her breaks from school. Bethany sensed Amy would get hurt tonight.

Amy approached the table with a wide smile, forcing them to finalize their decision to do nothing.

"Hey, you two. Soary wanted some time by himself to prepare for the show. What are we drinking?" Amy was easy on Soary. She didn't demand too much of his attention or his time and in return he pampered her. He gave her everything except his heart which he kept neatly tucked away in the desk drawer in his bedroom.

Bethany gave Jeff a quick kiss then sat back down at the table beside Amy. She stole one more glance at Gwen. She was laughing at something the guy with sad eyes had said. Watching the way they leaned toward each other and smiled convinced Bethany there was a secret between them.

***

"I can't believe she said that!" Gwen exclaimed. As she leaned in a little closer to hear his next comment she noticed the woman a few tables over looking at her.

"She did. I swear it." He held his right hand up and Gwen doubled over with laughter. "Can you share the joke with the rest of us?" Ashley gave her sweetest smile and Elizabeth hid her laughter behind her napkin.

Elizabeth nudged Gwen and whispered, "She is so controlling of his attention. If she isn't the center of it, she puts that fake smile on. It's just infuriating. I wish she would relax with us. You know, just be who she is when it's just them. I know she has to have a good side or he wouldn't have kept her around this long."

Gwen smiled. "Be nice! He really likes her and she isn't comfortable with us all yet. She will be one day, though. I really think he'll commit to her."

"How do you know he really likes her? Did he talk to you about her?" Gabriel rarely opened up about the women he dated. He preferred to hide his feelings in jokes and teasing comments. "You know we used to hang out with her in college. She was a bit more laid back but only a bit."

"No, I didn't know. And he hasn't actually told me he was ready to settle down with her. You know Gabe doesn't really talk about himself. I can just tell. Besides, he's been with her longer than anyone else." Gwen sighed. "Seriously, Liz, we need to be inclusive with her."

"Okay. Okay, you're right. I will be sweet." Liz flashed a big smile. "How are you feeling by the way?"

"Good, tonight. I was sick this morning though. I was afraid I wasn't going to get over it. But it passed around lunchtime."

"Is the surprise ready?" Gwen nodded and smiled.

They turned their attention to Gabriel. He had engaged Ashley in conversation. Gwen noticed his smile stopped before it crinkled his eyes. He was smiling but he wasn't feeling it. She wanted Gabe to find someone he could fall in love with. He was good at making everyone else happy; she wanted that for him too. Her mind turned to planning a dinner party and inviting Becky. It had been a while since they'd seen each other and she missed her friend. Plus, she wondered if Gabe and Becky would hit it off.

"Are you having fun?" Jason tapped Gwen's water glass. "Let me get you something more relaxing to drink. The band will be out soon." Gwen loved how he took care of her.

"No, I'm good. I think coming was a great idea. I am having so much fun. But since I'm feeling better I don't want to risk the alcohol upsetting my stomach tonight." She hoped he wouldn't guess her real reason for skipping a drink.

"Okay. But you let me know as soon as you're ready to leave."

"I will." Gwen touched his hand and smiled.

Encouraged by her touch Jason leaned over, pressed his lips to hers, ignoring the rest of the table.

Logan interrupted the group to let them know it was time for the band to come on. He was as excited as a little boy. He had landed the band's production company as an account a few months ago. It was a big win for him as he would be responsible for marketing several of their bands' tours and album releases. Elizabeth laughed and slung her arm over Logan's shoulder.

Gabriel and Ashley turned their attention to the stage.

Jason kissed the tip of Gwen's nose. "I love you."

"I love you, too."

"Who is playing again?" Jason asked her.

"I don't know. But I met one of them earlier." She flashed him a teasing smile.

"Really? Are you going to run off and become a groupie?" he teased back.

"Never. You can't get rid of me that easy!" As she spoke the event host took the stage and introduced the band.

***

Soary felt butterflies dancing around in his stomach. This was the first show they had performed since the tour ended. He knew it was important for them to perform well since Frank was romancing a new PR firm the label hired to handle some of its business. They had been successful for the last several years by building a fan base and touring. The idea with the third album was to think bigger. Frank wanted to get them on *Good Morning America*, *SNL*, *Kelly and Ryan*, and *Ellen* again. His goal was to limit their tour dates but book larger stadiums. The reason they booked this benefit concert was to impress one of the marketing execs so he would be encouraged to use his connections to help secure a few of the stadiums on his wish list.

Although he always got a little nervous before a performance, he never felt stage fright like some entertainers he knew. He took a drink of his water and tried to calm his stomach. He briefly wondered if he was going to be sick. He motioned for one of the stagehands to give him another water and watched as Jeff and the rest of the band took their places on stage. He noticed Jeff gaze toward the audience. Jeff was agitated about the table set up. He told Frank they were too close to the stage. They would be able to see a quarter of the room's faces from the stage even in the dim lighting. Soary didn't mind seeing the faces gazing up at them. It helped him get in character; he imagined he was acting as a musician. Their reactions were fuel for his stageego.

When he lost himself on a dark stage while singing, he felt too vulnerable. He took anothergulp of water to finish the bottle. The band was settling in, a signal to him that it was time to take the stage.

The crowd was cheering and he could see many were standing and clapping. He made his usual greetings around the stage to each band member. When he got to Jeff he noticed something was not quite right with him, he looked pale. Soary's stomach fluttered and he wondered if he was going to be sick again. Maybe he was coming down with something. Jeff managed to give Soary his standard nod and 'let's do this' look.

Soary continued on to center stage. Just as his hand hovered over the microphone, his mouth open, ready to greet the crowd, he saw her. She was directly in front of him. She stood between two men, one had his arm around her waist and she was leaning into the curve of him. Her hands were clapping but she was gazing up at the man she was with. She hadn't noticed him on stage. Soary felt his stomach flip-flop. He was probably going to throw up for sure. It dawned on him Jeff knew she was there. He glanced over his shoulder; confirmation that Jeff had seen her was written in the anxiety on his face.

Soary had little choice but to turn back to the microphone. "Good evening." He watched her. "Thank you all for coming out to support such an awesome cause tonight." Time seemed to slow down. He noticed the second her body tightened. He saw her hand jerk off the guys arm, it was suspended in the air on the way to her mouth, frozen. He watched the slow movement of her disappearing smile. Then time sped back up. She turned to face the stage, fully aware of who she was going to find there. Their eyes locked. He felt the rush of love and pain, sorrow and regret, disappointment and sadness escape her and capture him. Her eyes began to glisten.

"I am so sorry." He mouthed.

His silence was noticeable. The clapping from the crowd had quieted down, they were waiting on him to speak. Still he stood staring at her and she at him. The memories flowing between them. Emotions tore at his composure. Out of the corner of his eye he saw her date turn to her. Soary watched as he put his hand on her lower back. She didn't look away from the stage. Soary loved her even more for that. He watched her mouth move as she inhaled a deep breath.

He saw her say his name. The microphone was in his hand, his mouth answered hers, "Gwen." His voice filled the eerily quiet banquet hall. The audience was still standing, no longer clapping, looking curiously toward the stage and around the room. Confusion filled the air. He started talking, he listened to his words echo back at him.

"I want to start tonight off with a song from our new album. It's actually an old song I wrote one summer years ago. Tonight, I want to sing it for you." He watched her standing there with all his memories circling her. Her laugh, her fighting with the kite, the way she chewed her food, the way she watched him when he played. Similar to the way she watched him now.

"It's called My Heart. He took a seat on the stool that a stagehand had brought out for him. He adjusted his guitar and met her eyes again. She was still staring at him. "I wrote it for a girl I gave my whole heart to; the only woman I have ever loved, the one I still love." She stood completely still, captivated. "That girl was the best person I have met. I don't deserve her, never did. But I will love her for the rest of my life. She is My Heart."

***

Gwen was shocked to hear his voice. Physically she recognized his voice before her mind could process it. She turned from Jason, looked directly at Soary, and the earth stopped circling the sun.

He was the exact same boy she had loved all these years. A little age showed around his eyes but otherwise he was unchanged. He stood there in front of this crowd and talked to her as if the past five years had not passed in silence. She watched him sit down with his guitar. She watched his fingers start moving across the strings. She heard his eerie falsetto fill the room. It was the same voice that had the ability to make her weep; and still could.

***

Bethany watched the scene unfold before her as if in a movie. Gwen watched Soary without blinking as he started to sing. Jeff seemed catatonic. The rest of the band looked confused. She wasn't sure if they knew the song or not but a few lines into it Jeff started playing along with Soary. The crowd began to settle down from the unusual start to the show. Amy sat and watched Soary sing to another woman. Tears glistened in her eyes. Bethany saw Gwen's date lean down and whisper to her. Gwen looked away from Soary and cupped his face with her hand. Gwen's back was to her so she could not tell if she spoke. She stared as the other blond man pulled her chair back making room for her to leave. Logan, who she recalled meeting at another business function, said something to the other woman at the table. Their happy group appeared to be in chaos. Bethany felt guilty, wondering how she could have stopped this whole scene from unfolding. She turned back to Soary and watched him sing with his entire heart exposed.

***

Soary opened his eyes just as Gwen turned to weave her way out of the ballroom. He leapt from the stool and in a one swift movement jumped from the stage, only to find himself face to face with the table of people Gwen had just left. Jason moved around the table, facing Soary. Gabriel and Logan moved to flank him on either side.

"Excuse me." Soary started forward as if he was just casually passing through. The crowd seemed to buzz with anticipation. Jeff watched intently as he made his way to the front of the stage.

"I'm Jason. Gwen's fiancé." Jason extended his hand toward Soary. Soary took his hand and shook it.

"I don't intend to let you follow Gwen until I know she wants to talk to you." His voice was surprisingly strong. Jason turned and spoke to Gabriel. Gabriel slid past Jason and followed Gwen.

As Bethany watched from a distance the scene reminded her of a snow globe. The world, once so peaceful and beautiful, all of a sudden was shaken up. Nothing was as it should be. She hoped it all settled back peacefully.

Soary and Jason remained facing each other. Soary was trying to process that the man in front of him was Gwen's fiancé. His emotions were out of control. The fact that she had a fiancé meant she loved another man. Nausea returned to his stomach.

Jeff knew it was up to him to salvage the concert. Frank was frantically talking to the venue manager on the side of the stage. Jeff motioned to the band to start playing. He moved Soary's stool to the side and began playing one of their more upbeat songs. The crowd toward the back of the room immediately started to enjoy the music and some were getting up to dance. The crowd closest to the action were still curious about what was going on. They were watchful and patient.

***

Logan moved closer to Jason. Ashley and Elizabeth stayed back.

"I just want to talk to her. It has been a long time. I just..." Soary let his words trail off.

Anger welled up inside of him. He didn't like being detained from going after Gwen. He didn't want to cause any more trouble but he didn't like the feeling they were protecting her from him.

"Yes, you should talk to her. There doesn't need to be any more words left unsaid. You left too many unanswered questions for her already."

Soary flinched and took a step back. He didn't like that Gwen had talked to this man about their relationship. He felt violated and ashamed. Of course, Gwen would talk to her fiancé about him. She wouldn't go into a relationship with secrets.

"It's time to close the vault on that chapter." Jason's words sounded more confident than he felt. His hands were shaking at his side.

Fear welled up in Soary. Jason's confidence startled him. Awareness dawned on him that he may have waited too long to win Gwen back. He spent the last few months working on the album and enjoying time with Amy, biding his time to making a decision on how best to reach out to Gwen. Now it looked like he may be too late.

Before Soary could say anything in response, Gabriel returned. He took his place by Jason. He glanced around at each face and made a mental note of the situation. He leaned near Jason and whispered, "Gwen is ready to talk to Soary. She's waiting in the park across the street." And because he felt Jason stiffen, he added, "It's okay. She is strong. I think she's ready to say goodbye to him."

Jason studied Gabriel's face, his eyes. Gabriel had been his best friend for most of his life. He'd always been able to read what Gabe was thinking and feeling in his eyes. He knew Gabriel loved Gwen and he trusted Gabriel completely. Reassured, Jason nodded, squared his shoulders and took a step towards Soary. The movement resulted in four men in black that had thus far gone undetected moving toward them. Soary raised his hand as if he was a king halting his soldiers. In response, Gabriel and Logan stepped in line with Jason.

Bethany held her breath from where she watched. She knew this could get bad fast. Jeff played on, focused on winning the crowds attention.

"Soary. Gwen is ready to talk to you." Jason had a vile taste in his mouth. As Soary processed the words and turned to go, Jason grabbed his arm. Both men stared into the others' eyes. "I will give you fifteen minutes alone. Then if Gwen wants more time, I will respect her wishes."

Soary nodded at Jason, glanced over his shoulder at Jeff before heading to the exit. He blinked back tears as he pushed the door open and felt the air rush past his nostrils and fill his lungs. He inhaled a bated breath and continued to her.

Chapter 13

2017

She sat on a bench in the park. Her back was straight, so still, she appeared to be deep in thought. He noticed as he got close she had her arms wrapped tightly across her waist and her lips were moving. He heard her voice, softer than a whisper, counting. When she got to ten, she started over. He almost dropped to his knees and begged forgiveness right then but he didn't. The memory of when they met entered his mind. Gwen was carefree and unaware of herself. She was enjoying the activity of flying her kite. She was serene. Seeing her working so hard for control filled him with renewed guilt. He sat down beside her leaving a few inches of space between them.

Soary ran through the different scenarios he had played out in his mind. He had imagined her showing up at his concerts. In those daydreams she was always alone. She would seek him out and fall into his arms as he told her he was sorry. Lately his daydreams evolved into him finding her. He would deliver a romantic speech and she would fall back into his arms. Once he imagined that he stood up to object at her wedding. He knew that was cheesy but he it was his daydream and in the end she fell into his arms. In all his imaginings Gwen was the exact same. And they always picked up right where they left off.

Yet here he was, sitting next to her after all this time, and he had no idea what he wanted to say. All he wanted was to touch her and pull her into his arms. He wanted to simply grab her and kiss her until the years passed between them and they were caught up in the present together. Her voice shocked him to attention.

"Soary." She spoke quietly. He turned toward her and started to speak but she stopped him. "I'm getting married in a month." She paused letting her words fill the space. "Jason is a wonderful man. He loves me and I love him. I have hurt him tonight and I will spend the rest of my life making it up to him. But I have to know why."

She turned toward him. "I waited for you a long time. I tried to contact you. I left so many messages and sent letters. You never sent a word to me. You ignored my pleas. You even had your friends and mom lie to me. I know they knew where you were and yet you asked them to lie. What did I do, Soary? How did I scare you away? Why did you leave me?"

"Gwen, no, it wasn't you. You didn't do anything. You were perfect." He fought back the tears. "Gwen, I don't know. I got scared. I thought you deserved better." The bitterness of her statements hit him. "I thought someone like Josh would be better for you." He hissed. He felt defeated. He realized the depth of the pain he had caused her. Reality seeped through the cracks of his hope; only in his fantasies would her forgiveness be thinkable.

The pain he caused her was too great. The time he allowed to pass was too long.

"Jason. His name is Jason. And you don't get to bring him into this." She snapped and pulled her arms tighter around herself.

Silently she started to cry. Soary couldn't stand to see her cry. Instinctively he reached for her and pulled her into his arms. She let him hold her close. The familiar warmth of him as she fit into his arms, cradled perfectly into his chest, brought her soul the peace she sought. She felt at home in his arms. It had taken her a long time to push the memory of being held by him to the back of her mind. She worked hard forbidding it to creep in on her daily life. The comfort being held by him offered confirmed what she already knew, she would always love him. He was as much a part of her as the color of her eyes were.

As she rested her head on his chest, she thought of the night they spent together and how gentle he had been with her. She remembered how he touched her cheek and made her weak with one look. She thought about how she felt like a princess when he sang to her. And she remembered how his voice would lift like a velvet curtain revealing the pageantry on stage. Briefly she wondered how she had moved on without him. She was drawn to him. She wanted to touch him, to explore his face with her fingers. She wanted to sear the feel of him into her heart forever. She needed him for her survival. She took a deep breath thinking this is what it feels like to breathe.

She heard his voice softly singing the song he had written for her years ago, the one he started to sing onstage tonight. As he sang Gwen settled in his arms. The lyrics were about the girl she had been and the boy who was going to give her the world. He sang about lovers who would perish apart from each other. But they hadn't perished. They both not only survived, they thrived. Gwen spent five years wanting to be that girl but she knew she wasn't. And the day Soary left her he stopped being that boy. Listening to him sing, she understood this would be the very last time he would hold her. And for the first time since she met Soary she wasn't sorry about losing him.

Soary finished the song, cleared his throat before he tried to explain the unexplainable. "I couldn't think straight. During the drive to the beach I began to get this feeling that I was losing you. It was irrational, I know. I tried to shake it off and I did eventually."

He squeezed her closer. "I had a beautiful time with you."

The memories swirled all around them. "Later that night I woke up and was overwhelmed with...I don't know how to describe what I was feeling. A foreboding, maybe. The saddest music filled my head. I got up and started scribbling lyrics, the words just flew onto the page. I knew we couldn't stay together the way we planned. I saw us falling apart. I wrote that song telling you goodbye." A sob escaped his mouth. Gwen lifted her face and looked into his eyes.

"God, Gwen, I still love you. I have never stopped. I didn't open your letters until this past December when the tour ended. I read the last one you sent me. When did you send it, May of last year?" He saw her flinch and understood how painful writing those letters were for her. "I couldn't bear it. I couldn't tell you I didn't want to see you anymore because it was a lie. Do you remember, we promised to never lie to each other? I couldn't talk to you because I knew I wouldn't let you go if I did. Those letters, they broke my heart. They destroyed me. The pain I caused you tore me to pieces. I am sorry. I want to make it up to you." He pressed his lips to her forehead and let the smell of her skin fill his nostrils. I must remember this, he thought.

"I thought of looking you up after I read the letters but I was afraid you would hate me. And well, I couldn't bear that." He wasn't explaining himself very well. He couldn't find the words to make sense of his actions. He needed her to understand. He wanted her to grasp his love for her had grown daily since he left her. He searched for the words that would change the past but being here with her was making coherent thought difficult. All he wanted to do was touch her and kiss her.

He gazed longingly into her eyes, "I'm sorry I broke your heart, Gwen."

"Hearts don't break." She returned his gaze for several minutes. She saw the pain he was feeling in his eyes, she opened her arms. He fell into her and received the comfort she offered with her embrace. She buried her face in the back of his neck and took in the sweet smell of his soap and sweat. He always had smelled good. They sat there for a while holding each other.

"I forgive you." Her voice was barely above a whisper as she released him.

He cupped her face in his hands and searched her face, looking for the details of all the missing years. He felt her draw him in. He lost himself in her eyes. He saw that the girl she had been was now a strong and kind woman. Slowly he leaned forward and watched in wonder as her lips parted. His heart thudded loudly. Desire sparked between them. Just as his lips were about to graze hers, she interrupted him.

"I loved you the moment you stepped on the handle of my kite." She smiled at the memory. "I would have waited for you to sort things out if you had talked to me. I needed you to be honest with me. I believed in you. I knew all your dreams were going to come true. I believed in us. I would have found a way to make us work. But you...you didn't believe in me. You threw our relationship away simply because you were scared." She wiped fresh tears from her cheeks. "I gave you my soul and I have spent a long time mourning the loss of it. But I am fine now. More than fine. I am happy." She pulled back slightly.

"That November when I went to your mom's house, I desperately needed to talk to you. Do you remember? I do—it was the day before Thanksgiving. I remembered you never missed a holiday with your mom. I knew you would be by or at least call her. You had been gone almost four months. I felt shame and embarrassment invading her space for a chance to just talk to you." She paused to get her voice controlled. "Just as you can't really put words together to describe why you left me, I can't find them to explain the depth of the pain I felt when even then you refused me." Sighing she let the silence speak for her.

"After I left your mom's, I had a car accident. I was sick, really sick." Tears pooled in her eyes as she remembered the loss she experienced. "It took a long time for me to heal. But I did. I worked hard and I got better. I still loved you though. I continued to wait for you to come back to me." Gwen decided to leave out the worst of it. Their grief would push them toward each other, but she didn't need him to experience that loss with her, she didn't want to bond over shared regret.

"I still love you. But we are not those two kids anymore. Jason knows everything about that summer and the years following it." She gave him a tender look. Soary felt his hope dissipate. "I heard you on the radio for the first time the day I met him. I didn't respond very well. Soary, I was still broken. In a way I still am. But for some reason Jason stuck around and saw past my broken pieces. He loves me even though he knows I still love you. He asked me to marry him knowing you still had a room in my heart. And he was willing to allow you to be a third wheel in our marriage because he understood how much I ached for you." She took his face in her hands again. A part of her wanted to kiss him and pretend their summer just ended, this was that first goodbye all over again. A part of her thought it would be the perfect love story if she just fell into his arms and let him whisk her into the life they had planned. But she already knew how their story ended.

"We recently moved here. Jason got a promotion. I quit my job to be here with him because that is the decision he allowed me to make. I could have made that decision for you if you had given me the opportunity, if you had trusted us enough to talk to me about what you were feeling."

Soary tried to process what she was saying. He had hoped there was something for them. He wanted a chance to prove he deserved her. Gwen startled him with her sudden movement. She was standing before he had chance to register that she was not still beside him. He gasped, choked by grief. He felt the tears well in his eyes as he looked up at her, not waiting to hear what she had to say. He stood and grabbed her arm.

"Gwen, I love you. I want to find a way to make you understand and maybe we can make it right. Maybe we can be together. Now that we have found each other. We can take things slow, get to know each other again. I want to hear all about you and..." He pleaded. Gwen removed his hand from her arm and walked away. She flagged a passing cab. Soary strode toward her, closing the distance.

Her words halted him.

"I can't, Soary. Those days are someone else's life now. But I would live every second of it over and over again even if it ended the same every time. I will always cherish those memories of us. I don't want to understand any more about why you left me. No words can change how we ended. And I don't want to hurt you by describing what I went through when you left. I just want to cherish the amazing love we shared that summer. I want to go into my marriage knowing that my past is in the past. Jason is my future." She paused letting the night breeze blow through the sadness.

"Will you tell Jason I went home? Goodbye, Soary. I wish for you to find happiness. I will always love you." She turned, climbed into a cab and was gone.

***

Soary sat on the bench for a several minutes trying to understand what just happened. He analyzed every word, look, and movement that passed between them. She had given him some hope when she was in his arms. He knew she wanted an explanation and he was slow in coming up with one. He had spent so much of the last few years ignoring what had happened that he couldn't find the words he needed.

Something she said kept rolling around in his ears. It suddenly became important he know exactly what happened to her after he left. He needed to know about her accident. He wanted to know everything she held back. Then, if he knew, he could start to make it right between them. He gathered his strength and started back to the hotel. When he looked up, he recognized the guy who followed Gwen out and the others from her table. He saw Jason at the back of the group. He intended to walk past them. He had no intention to talk to them. He just needed to get his things so he could leave. His only goal was to figure out where Gwen went and talk to her again.

"Where is Gwen?" Elizabeth asked glaring at him.

Soary looked at her. He realized this person would always hate him without ever knowing him. He thought that would be fitting since so many would love him without ever knowing him. He noticed for the first time that the press was also there snapping pictures. He tried to remember if they had been there when he was talking to Gwen but he couldn't remember. This was his life now, no more privacy, no more secrets. This is why he left her in the first place. This is what he wanted for himself. He knew she wouldn't be happy with it, wasn't that his reasoning? But she was right—he should have trusted her to decide for herself. And now he was going to ask her what he should have asked her years ago. And what he failed to ask her in the park.

"She went home." As he said the words, it dawned on him she may live with Jason. He knew he shouldn't go after her but he couldn't shake the thought that if he didn't go to her tonight he would never see her again. Soary turned from the crowd. He wanted to find Jeff or Bethany or Frank. He needed to get out of here.

Jason stepped to the front of the group. "Did she tell you what you did to her?" He asked. His voice was deeper than normal, harsh. Anger replaced the relief he felt when Soary returned without Gwen. He hated the man standing before him and wasn't ready to watch him walk away without inflicting some pain on him.

"No. Listen, we talked but we have more to talk about." Soary could not face them. He didn't want to waste time talking to them. Now that he knew what he needed to say he wanted to go to Gwen. He had to get to her. He had no idea what they knew of him or how they felt about him. He had no idea what they meant to her. All he knew is he had to get to her before it was too late. Without turning back to Jason, he continued to push through the crowd.

"Well, I will tell you." Jason found his voice had gotten heated. He couldn't believe the gall of this man to tell him he had more to talk to Gwen about. This man who destroyed years of her life thought he could walk back into her world. And by accident not by choice. That was unacceptable to Jason. Soary had to know what he did to her. His body trembled with rage. He wasn't a violent man but he wanted to hit Soary. He needed to see him in pain. As he heard himself speak he didn't recognize his own voice.

"She couldn't function after you left. The first days that you didn't call her back she worried if you were okay. But your friends told her you were fine. The first month she failed every test because she couldn't concentrate. She became agitated and moody.

Her friends stopped inviting her out. They didn't understand why she couldn't get over a summer fling." He took a breath then continued.

"She waited by the phone every night. She got in the habit of opening the door just to check to see if you were there and she had not heard you knock and she would pick up the phone to hear the dial tone. She was afraid she would miss you when you came back for her. She even convinced herself you had called when she was in class." He saw the pain in Soary's eyes.

Instead of comforting him it fueled his anger. The raw emotion in Soary's eyes were on display because he loved her. A flash of confusion passed through Jason. It never occurred to him Soary loved Gwen. He hesitated for a moment.

Gabriel put his hand on Jason's arm but Jason flung it off and screeched "Don't. He needs to know." He glared at Gabriel. The look Gabriel returned made him pause, ashamed he was telling her darkest secrets to her friends and strangers, but he had to go on.

He had lived with helping her heal and now he wanted to tell the man who caused it what he had done. He ignored the crowd, the photographers. He stepped closer to Soary.

Soary's bodyguards watched intently for their signal.

Bethany and Jeff arrived on the scene and pushed through the crowd trying to get closer to Soary.

"She went to find you. But your mother hid you and your friends hid you. When she got to Nashville you had gone. She didn't know what she was going to do but her decision was made for her." He swallowed and lowered his voice. He used his words as daggers to rip through Soary's heart. "She was pregnant with your child. She miscarried alone on the road looking for you. All she wanted from you was to tell you. She had decided to keep the baby and raise him with the help of her parents. She just wanted to tell you." Jason's hatred boiled over, seeping from every pore. He didn't notice the intake of air from Soary. He felt nothing when Soary fell to his knees.

Elizabeth started to cry and looked to Logan to do something.

Gabriel tried again to pull Jason back, but was once again pushed away. He was in shock at what Jason had shared. His heart broke for Gwen.

Bethany knelt beside Soary. She was too scared to touch him. She looked up at Jason. "Please, stop." She pleaded as tears ran down her face.

"Oh, that surprised you? Well that isn't the worst part. She had to stay in the hospital for two days alone. Not only was she physically sick she was in shock. She was devastated and catatonic. She felt guilt and shame that she had not protected your child. The only reason she was out on the road was because you wouldn't take her calls. And even though you were the guilty one, she told me her worst fear was that you would blame her—that you would hate her for losing the baby. As if you had a right to blame anyone but yourself for the destruction your cowardice caused. The nurses were finally able to get a phone number from her to call her parents. When she was released from the hospital she forced her mother to take her back to school." Jason took a deep breath to push back the tears that were threatening.

"When she finished school, she knew she wanted to focus on her career. She wanted to get over you. She spent a lot of time healing and learning how to live with the anxiety and depression. She made the best decision of her life—she decided to leave it all behind hoping your memory would not follow her. But you did. She didn't return home for years. The memories were too unbearable for her. She saw you everywhere in her mind. She couldn't listen to the radio or watch TV because everything reminded her of you. She held herself together by wrapping her arms around herself and squeezing tight. How pathetic, her only solace was her own arms. She does it still when she is upset. She is so afraid she will fall apart again."

He took a deep breath then knelt down beside Soary. "You changed her. She isn't who she was before you ripped her apart. She is stronger than she gives herself credit for though. She went to a grief therapist, she started to use meditation and yoga and breathing techniques. She learned how to control her panic triggers. And now she's a volunteer at a crisis center for teens. She is not the girl you destroyed. She is a survivor. She is strong and brave. She is still full of love and light. She built herself up into a better woman."

"I didn't know. I didn't know about the baby." Soary said more to himself than to anyone else. He raised his face and looked at Jason. Their eyes locked in shared pain and love. Jason felt his anger subside but he wasn't done. There was more he had to say.

"How could you? You disappeared. You took her virginity and snuck off like a pirate with his loot. Got you a hit song out of it too!" With that Jason stood and stormed off.

The silent crowd parted to let him pass. Some people were crying. Some of the paparazzi were anxiously snapping pictures and calling in on their cell phones wanting to be the first to break the story. This story was made of the stuff that sold magazines, made some careers, and destroyed others.

Soary looked at Bethany with tears streaming down his face. "I didn't know." He cried.

"I know. I know." She said and put her arms around him. She looked for Jeff to help her.

She had to get him out of here. Jeff rushed over with the help of a few their bodyguards. They hefted him to his feet. Soary steadied himself. Jeff kept his hand tightly under his arm to ensure he wouldn't lose balance and motioned for the others to back away.

Soary looked up to see Gwen's friends staring at him. "I love her. I have always loved her. I need to talk to her."

"Never." Gabriel told him then turned and followed Jason.

Amy had watched the entire scene from the back of the crowd; she also turned and walked away.

Logan tuned to Elizabeth, "I have to go to talk to the event manager. Maybe Frank can keep the band playing for the night." He shrugged. "I know it's messed up. But I have to do something here first. You go to Jason and I will join ya'll as soon as I do some damage control."

Elizabeth nodded, wiped a tear from Logan's cheek, gave him a quick kiss and followed after Gabriel and Jason.

Chapter 14

2017

Gwen started to shake after getting in the cab. As soon as she climbed in the panic attack started. It was mild but she couldn't remember her address. The cab driver was kind. He drove in silence circling within several blocks of the hotel waiting for her to tell him where they were headed. He only spoke to tell her he thought they were being followed. Gwen had sat silently at that comment. After a few quick turns the driver spoke again.

"I think I got rid of them. You can tell me where you want to go now, ma'am." The cab driver watched her in the rearview mirror. Finally, able to remember, she gave him her address.

"Here we go." He began to smile at her but stopped before his lips stretched across hisface.

Gwen realized as soon as they arrived, she didn't have any money. The condos were so new the door man took the evenings off. Jason had been uncomfortable with them moving in before the building was complete but Gwen had loved it and wanted to get their home put together and teased him that they weren't royalty—they didn't need a doorman twenty-four seven. Now she regretted that she won that argument.

"Sir, I uh. I don't have any money. I am so sorry. I didn't even think about it before. But if you come by tomorrow, I promise I will pay you." She looked at him full of embarrassed regret.

"Well, I guess." He looked at the building and thought about his decision for several seconds. "You going to be alright?" He gave her a sympathetic look.

"Yes. Thank you." She tried to smile but found it difficult.

He studied her a few more seconds. "Okay. I will come by tomorrow. Who should I ask to see?" He had kind eyes.

"Jason or Gwen from 501." She started to climb out of the car. "Thank you." She said as she closed the door.

The night air was cool and crisp. Taking several deep breaths, she felt a calmness start to settle inside her. Her hand instinctively went to her belly. Cradling her babe, she smiled. But she couldn't get her mind to move past Soary's face. She was surprised at how she felt. She had thought that if she ever saw him again, she would fall in his arms and live happily ever after with him. When she had accepted Jason's proposal, she still worried what would happen if Soary came back into her life. That fear had been gnawing at her heart for months. She knew she loved Jason, but what she didn't know was how she would react to Soary.

Instead of desperately wanting to see him, she had started to pray she never would. She didn't know what would happen in her heart if she saw him again but she was certain what she didn't want to lose. She wanted her life with Jason. She wanted to wake up with him every day and know that she was building a life that would make her happy. Sure, there were a lot of things she was afraid she was compromising. Her career for one. But she thought the sacrifices were worth every smile he gave her and every touch of his lips on hers. She knew she didn't want to lose those. Besides, she knew he would support her career decisions. The only true compromise was location. She also couldn't remember laughing with Soary the way she laughed with Jason. And laughter had become a very important requirement to her life. She couldn't think of a day spent with Jason when they didn't laugh. Looking back, she couldn't ever remember being so full of joy. She had been happy with Soary and he too had made her laugh, but it was different.

He ignited so much passion in her she was never at peace. She was never content on being without him. She was driven to be with him. Whenever they parted for the day or even for an hour, she was consumed with desire to be with him again.

How ironic! she thought. When she finally didn't want to see him, there he was. And what was this she was feeling? She needed to figure it out before she could talk to Jason. He deserved her honesty and immediate assessment of tonight's events. She knew he must be worried about her. With this final thought she decided to take a walk.

Instead of heading into her building when the cab dropped her off, she headed south toward the city. The street was darker than most city streets since it was still located in an area under construction. She remembered the first time she and Jason had looked at the building. It was an empty shell with dirt piles and rubble everywhere. She was not enthusiastic about it then. But when the contractor had shown them the plans for the building and the block, she had changed her mind. It would be perfect for a young couple and family. There were shops that were planned and a park with a play area. The Atlanta Council for Central Arts was working on a campaign to bring a children's museum to the area. There would be coffee shops, boutiques, a bookshop, a few pubs, and restaurants. Gwen found the plans quaint and knew they would thrive there.

She headed towards the park that was nearly complete. The landscapers did a nice job on the flowers and bushes that surrounded the park. It was peaceful and welcoming. She could smell the fresh mulch in the flower beds. As she approached the park she turned left toward the playground. When she reached its center, she looked back toward her building. She could still see it even in the dark. Smiling, she thought it would be a great place to bring the baby.

Jason had been less excited about the building than she was at first. He wasn't sure it was a nice enough neighborhood. He had read the research from the urban developers. He looked at the area real estate comparisons but still had reservations. The deciding factor had been when Gabriel said he was going to buy a condo here too. The plan was for this to be a younger version of Park Avenue. The developers wanted to attract young professionals. They wanted it to be swanky yet family friendly. The park was going to be central to the surrounding four blocks and the developer was organizing a neighborhood watch program. All the condo buildings were working together to contract a local security firm to patrol the area and position twenty-four-hour surveillance around each condo building. They idea was to create a community that felt safe roaming about night or day.

As she walked, she became engrossed in her thoughts. She did still love Soary. She had wanted to kiss him. Gwen shook her head and tried to ignore that truth. She placed her hand on her belly. For the first time since meeting Soary she didn't want to love him, she didn't want to feel anything for him. All she wanted was her life with Jason. This thought caused her to laugh out loud. There were so many years she craved the dream of being rescued by Soary. Now she realized she had rescued herself years ago and all she truly wanted was to share her life with a man who was her best friend and lover and to raise children together.

She remembered her surprise for Jason. She had left it all out in the spare room. She had planned on showing him tonight when they got home. She felt such disappointment and frustration that her plans were ruined.

She decided to go back the condo to put it away. She didn't want to tell Jason about the baby tonight. She wanted to make the news of the baby a joyous occasion. She didn't want him to doubt she chose him for any reason other than she wanted to choose him. She began to walk faster afraid he would get home before she had a chance to put everything away.

***

Bethany was relieved when they finally approached Soary's dressing room. He appeared to be in shock. Jeff went to get him some water as Bethany tried to soothe him.

"We are getting the bus pulled around. We'll be home in no time." She told him.

"No!" His voice was harsh, his eyes were frantic. "No, Beth. I need to see Gwen. Find Frank, I need to know where she lives."

"Soary, I think you need to give her a little time. Tonight was..." she paused. "Tonight, was more than you both expected."

"I can't give it time. I gave it too much time already." He stood and started to pace. "I have something I need to ask her."

"Soary, you need to slow down," Jeff told him as he handed him the water.

"Jeff, I know I screwed this up. But I know how I can fix it. Gwen and I were meant to be a family. She is my family. I need to go to her now. Please, Jeff, help me find out where she lives."

A knock at the door interrupted them. Frank slowly pushed open the door. He entered followed by Logan. Soary visibly stiffened.

"Okay, so this is a messed-up situation. Damn, guys." Frank scratched his head and leaned against the wall. "Logan has talked to the event organizers. They are fine with the band playing out the rest of the night. They aren't going to pay though. But they aren't going to sue for breach of contract. Which would be really bad for the album release."

"Frank, I couldn't care less about the album release." Jeff grabbed Soary's arm and pulled him back as he lurched toward Frank.

"Sorry. I know, I know. This is just so messed up." Frank was at a loss.

Logan cleared his throat. "Look I have a job to do here. I have several associates on the phone handling the media. You will need to release a statement of some sort. Someone in my office will write one up for your approval. Then you need to go home and lay low for a while. Let this blow over. We aren't sure yet but I've assigned a group to monitor the media outlets the next few days until we know how big this thing is going to be."

"No way! You don't get to come in here and tell me to go home. I'm going to talk to Gwen."

"Listen, you hired my company to market your band. Trust me I would rather be punching you in the face than helping you get out of this mess. I don't like you at all." He towered over Soary. "But I signed up to do a job and I will do my job. Do you understand me?" Logan glanced around the room at all their faces.

"We understand. And we're thankful. Soary doesn't want bad publicity to hurt Gwen either." Bethany wanted Logan to leave without further incident.

"Okay, I'll go see if the bus is out back yet." Frank left the room followed by Logan.

"I'm not going home. I can't leave without talking to her again." Soary slumped onto the coach.

"Okay, I'll get us a hotel. But no more bulldozing. Logan is apparently going to see you onto the bus heading home. Let's just give the appearance we're giving him what he wants." Bethany reasoned.

***

"Drink this." Gabriel handed Jason a whiskey shot.

"I need to get home." Jason coughed after drinking the whiskey.

"I know, we're going to head there." Gabriel pushed the hair from his forehead.

They were regrouping in the lounge of the hotel bar. Elizabeth sat on the small couch beside Jason. She was rubbing his arm offering little comfort. Jason seemed to be calming down.

Gabriel was reeling. He was concerned about all the information Jason had shared. Elizabeth said Logan was going to make some calls to work on damage control. His main goal was to keep Gwen and Jason's names out of the press. But Gabriel was more concerned with how Jason was going to forgive himself for sharing Gwen's secrets with the world. A sob brought his mind back to the present. Elizabeth was holding Jason as he cried. His body rocked with the sobs. Gabriel hated to see his friend in so much pain, he had to turn away. After several minutes Jason quieted down.

"I am so ashamed of myself. Gwen trusted me." He was wiping his face with the back of his hand.

"You just need to be honest with her and tell her what happened. She will understand. She'll forgive you." Elizabeth sounded confident.

"Gabriel, was she okay when you talked to her?" without waiting for a response Jason continued, "We were having a great time. She was so relaxed tonight. The look on her face when she heard his voice." Jason swallowed back another sob. "She looked terrified. And, and in love."

"No. You're wrong." Gabriel went over to Jason and knelt down in front of him. "No, she was surprised. Anxious, unprepared for the encounter. But she had no intention of being with him. You saw that for yourself when he came back alone." Gabriel leaned a little closer. "You asked what she said? She took some time to calm her nerves. She wanted to ask him why. And she said she loved you. Jas, Gwen chose you."

Jason took a deep breath and nodded. He knew Gabriel was right. Gwen left and went home.

It was time for him to get home to her and make sure she was okay.

Logan walked in and went straight to Elizabeth. He held her in an embrace. "The car will be outside these doors in about five minutes." He nodded his head toward the doors leading out of the empty hotel bar.

***

Gwen walked quickly with her face turned down. She didn't notice that two guys followed her. She didn't hear their footsteps or see their shadows fall across hers. Her thoughts were scattered. She wasn't focused on her surroundings. She entered the code to the building doors and immediately felt a hand on her shoulder. She turned, expecting to see Jason, but instead faced a stranger.

Something cold and hard pressed into her ribs.

"Excuse me, miss." A gruff voice filled in the space between her and him. The sudden sound penetrated through her thoughts and caused her to scream.

The other man clasped his hand across her mouth. "Not another sound!" he hissed pushing the cold, hard object harder against her ribs.

Gwen nodded her assent.

"Good. Is anyone home in your condo?" The man asked as he pushed her through the lobby doors.

Gwen couldn't find her voice so she shook her head no.

"Take us there and be quick about it." He turned her toward the elevators and pressed the gun into her back. "We aren't going to hurt you. We just want all the money you have. Okay?"

He was close enough to her neck she felt his spit splatter on her skin. Chills rushed through her. Again, she nodded. She pushed the button to their floor and prayed Jason wouldn't come home and get hurt. She knew he didn't keep a gun in the condo. She was standing close enough to one of the men that the sweet smell of gin burned her nostrils. When the elevator arrived, they pushed her forward, each man holding an arm.

Each floor had two units and shared a lobby space outside the elevators. Gwen had convinced the contractor to comp the furniture for their lobby space. She had several bags full of small decorations to place around on the tables once the construction was finished. She went with neutral blues and beiges hoping it would complement the style of whomever bought the condo across the way. She pressed the passcode to open the door and escorted the strangers into her home.

One of the men went straight in and started rummaging through drawers. "Where do you keep the money and jewelry?"

"In here." Gwen led them into the master suite and into the walk-in closet to the floor safe. She opened it and handed them the little cash they kept and some of her jewelry. They tossed the credit cards aside.

"Is this all you have?" The second man asked scornfully. "Yes." Gwen stated calmly hoping they would leave.

He jerked her to her feet and dragged her from the room. He pulled her down the hall opening doors as they went. Most of the rooms were barely furnished. When they got to the end of the hall, they entered the room Gwen planned on make the nursery. A small table held the onesie that read *Daddy's Biggest Fan* and the gift box. She had written a note to Jason from their unborn child and placed it in an envelope on top of the popular book *What to Expect When You're Expecting*.

Gwen started to cry when she saw her surprise in the bright light of the room. She saw the bag full of candles to her left. She knew then that she had been right to think the room would feel magical in candlelight instead of using the overhead light. She almost laughed at the direction her thoughts had taken.

One of the men pushed her to the ground, pulling her from her reverie. She lay with her back to them in the fetal position. Fear gripped her replacing the calm, as she realized the severity of her situation. She started praying they would leave now that they had what they wanted. As she prayed, she focused on her breathing. She wanted to control herself and keep a clear head. She had to find a way to save her baby. She tried to think of something she could do to get them to leave. She heard them arguing but couldn't make out their words. She held her breath to keep her sobs under control. She lay as still as possible; she didn't want to draw more attention to herself.

They stopped talking, and in the silence. Gwen thought they left. She steadied her nerves and turned to look.

Gwen heard the click of the gun.

"You've seen our faces. We can't risk you turning us in." He gave her an anguished look and she heard the fire of the gun and her lungs began to burn. Stunned she looked down. Blood ran from her chest. Her hand instinctively rested on her stomach.

"My baby," She cried and then lost consciousness.

***

Jason, Gabriel, Logan, and Elizabeth arrived at the condo to blue and red lights. Police cars and an ambulance blocked the street in front of their building. Logan told the driver to stop and let them out. Before the car stopped rolling Jason was out the door sprinting toward the building. Gabriel was close behind.

"Halt." An older policeman blocked their path to the door. "Where are you two headed?"

"We live here. My fiancée is in there." Jason tried to go around him.

"I can't let you in, yet. There's been an incident and we need to cheek everyone out first."

Jason pushed the policeman aside, leapt over the yellow crime scene tape blocking the elevator, and disappeared behind the doors.

Gabriel cursed under his breath as he followed him by taking the stairs. He could hear the policeman yelling and cursing behind him.

Jason reached the lobby outside his condo first, Gabriel reached him a few minutes later but not before he was knocked to the floor and handcuffed.

"What the hell?" Gabriel went to Jason. "Are you alright?"

"She wasn't in there. They wouldn't tell me anything."

"Okay. Okay, let me talk to someone."

Gabriel approached a young officer standing outside Jason and Gwen's condo. "Excuse me, officer. Can you tell me where the woman who lives here is? Did something happen to her?"

"Who are you?"

"I'm a friend. I live in the building. That's her fiancé." He motioned over toward Jason.

The officer nodded. "I see. Listen, I'm not in charge. You'll have to wait for Officer Jacobs to finish up inside."

"With all due respect, sir. Can you ask Officer Jacobs to come speak to us?"

The officer looked at Gabriel then at Jason and without any indication of what he thought he walked inside the condo.

***

The waiting room lights were harsh, the chairs were dirty, and the TV was loud. Logan couldn't believe the night had taken the turn it had. He started off in the dressing room of the hottest band of the year and ended up in an ER waiting room. They were all in a state of shock. Jason called Gwen's parents and then disappeared to sit in the chapel. Gabriel took it upon himself to pace between the chapel and the ER ready to deliver Jason to the doctors or the news to Jason.

Logan was torn between shock, sadness, and fear. Jason, Gabriel, and Logan had been friends most of their lives. They went through grade school, middle school, high school, and college with only a few broken bones between them. Logan's grandfather died when they were in high school. Jason and his high school sweetheart called off their engagement the year they graduated college. The only real tragedy they survived together was the death of Gabriel's mom to due to cancer.

Logan watched Elizabeth talk to one of the nurses. She was trying to get some information on Gwen. Logan prayed Gwen was alive. He knew without a doubt she was hurt. He just needed her to survive. They all needed her survive.

***

Frank hesitated outside the hotel room door. He knew Soary was on the other side waiting for him. Bethany had tried to get Soary to go home and regroup. Frank had tried, too, but when Jeff waved his hand in defeat, they both knew it was useless. Instead of going home they holed up in a Marriott. Frank left them in order to discover as much information as he could regarding where Gwen may live. Soary was determined to talk to her again against all their better judgement.

After several calls Frank found the information he wanted. He also received information he had not wanted. In a million lifetimes Frank never dreamed he would be in a situation such as this one.

The first time he heard The Deuces' debut album he knew there was more hurt in the songs than he ever wanted to feel. But that's what made them rise quickly. People relate to pain and heartache. People need to know they're not the only ones. It gives them hope to believe the beautiful rock star survived his heartbreak so they could, too.

The problem Frank saw in front of him as he slipped the key card into its slot was that he wasn't sure his beautiful rock star could survive the heartbreak he was about to be given.

Chapter 15

2017

Elizabeth put the kids down for their nap and closed the door. She had made some food to take over to Gabriel's and needed to get there in time to lay everything out. Once that was finished, she and Logan would join Jason and Gabriel at the funeral home.

Downstairs, her mother was packing her cooler. "Are you sure you don't want me to go over and handle the food?"

"No. I appreciate the offer but I want to keep the kids here. I don't want them to see everyone so upset." She wiped the tears from her eyes. She hadn't been able to stop crying in a week. Her mother hugged her and patted her back.

"Liz, you need to remember to take care of yourself. I know you want to be there for Jason but you lost her, too."

"I'll be okay, mom." Elizabeth kissed her mother on the cheek and picked up her cooler. "Thank you for staying with the kids. I don't know how long we'll be."

"No rush. I brought movies and an overnight bag. Don't worry about us."

***

Gabriel paced the viewing room at the funeral home. He had been over the arrangements with the funeral director many times but when he arrived there was music playing. He had just finished having a heated discussion with the manager. There was not to be any music. Gabriel was trying to make the day as smooth as possible for Jason. As he paced, he pushed memories of the night Gwen died out of his mind. It was too painful to remember. He shook his head and left the room. He couldn't give in to his own grief. He needed to be strong for Jason. He could feel sorry for himself later.

He found Jason sitting at the kitchen table where he'd left him. He watched as Jason twirled the spoon in his coffee. He had dark circles under his eyes and sunken cheeks. He hadn't eaten in days. Gabriel didn't know what to say or do to help him. He sat down beside him and laid his hand on Jason's. Jason met his eyes with a vacant stare.

Gabriel knew that sometimes the only thing you can do for people is to be present. He silently sat with Jason as the seconds passed into minutes.

When Elizabeth arrived with Logan she immediately went to Jason. She kneeled beside his chair. Jason turned to her as she straightened his tie. She brushed his hair from his face. Jason sat like a child as she made him presentable. "Jason, have you eaten anything?" She asked.

"I'm not hungry."

"I know, but if I get you something will you try to eat it for me?" She glanced around the kitchen looking for something to feed him.

Jason nodded.

Logan helped her to her feet. She decided on a pack of crackers. She opened them and instead of waiting for Jason to feed himself she put one to his lips, prompting him to open his mouth.

"Logan, you and Gabriel need to go out and start greeting everyone. Jason and I will be there soon." She instructed.

Logan was happy to be assigned something to do, although he didn't want to socialize. He thought funerals were horrible. People gathered together to watch as others struggled to deal with loss. Everyone had the same things to say, "How tragic. She was so young. What a shame." He couldn't stand pretending he cared what everyone thought and felt. But he couldn't stand by and watch his friend retreat so far he wouldn't even feed himself. As they walked out of the kitchen, he noticed for the first time how awful Gabriel looked.

"How are you holding up?" he asked.

Gabriel shrugged in answer.

"Look I know you loved her too," Logan stated as he stopped walking. Logan knew Gabe had fallen in love with Gwen. The look on his friends' face as he followed her from the ballroom confirmed every concern Logan had about his feelings. Logan also knew Gabriel was struggling with being the last of them to talk to her.

Gabriel stopped and turned to him. For the first time since meeting Gwen he was able to be honest about his feelings. He let his pain out of the bottom of his heart where he had locked it away. The tears began to flow and his body rocked with sobs. His knees buckled as his sight went black. Logan reached for him with strong hands and pulled him into an embrace and let him cry.

"You know?" He sobbed. "I never meant to feel this way. Oh, Logan. I loved her so much. She was amazing. But I love Jas, too. I never let anything happen, you know that, right? I never acted on my feelings. And if I thought I would, I would put a lot of distance between us."

"Of course, I know. I'm your best friend, I know you. It's okay." Logan patted him on the back in the same manner he did his son when he cried.

"I tried to deny it even to myself. She was the person I was looking for. Jason just found her first. There were times we didn't even have to speak to communicate. She thought of me as her best friend and I was. I was her friend." Gabriel pulled back. "When they moved to Atlanta my feelings did shift. I was secure in our friendship. When I started dating Ashley...I became more aware of what I want in my life."

"It's okay you loved her. Jason and you always did have similar taste in women." Logan wasn't good at talking about emotions. He wondered why he even said anything. Maybe he thought Gabriel deserved to mourn for her too.

Gabriel wasn't used to letting his guard down so he quickly replaced it. He wanted to be alone with his memories of Gwen before telling her goodbye.

"Thank you," He stated, wiping his eyes with the back of his hand.

Gabriel straightened his tie and wiped the last of his tears from his face as they continued toward the viewing room. He wasn't surprised by all the people who were there. Although Gwen wasn't overly social, people who met her seemed to like her immediately. He recognized several people from Jason's office and there were a few neighbors from their previous condo building.

Even though he never met them in person, Gwen had told him many stories about the group of women huddled in the corner. They were her friends from the CPA firm she worked for before moving to Atlanta. One of the women left the group and walked toward him.

"Gabriel?" Her voice was shaky.

"Yes, Hi." He extended his hand to shake hers.

Instead she wrapped her arms around his neck and hugged him tightly. After a few minutes she released him.

"Sorry. I'm Becky. I worked with Gwen." She blushed and looked down at her feet before glancing back up at him.

Gabriel remembered Gwen talking about Becky. He smiled remembering her telling him she knew a woman he should meet.

"Gwen talked about you."

"She talked about you, too. I miss her." Her voice cracked.

"Yeah, me too."

"I know she was happy to have your friendship. She told me you were someone she could count on. It can't be easy, what you're going through. I wanted to tell you that I know you were a comfort to her; being that you were one of the last friends she talked to that night; I know you were a comfort to her."

Gabriel stared at Becky. "Thank you for saying that." It was odd that the words of a stranger could provide the strength to carry on.

"We will be heading back home after the funeral. But if you need anything..." her voice trailed off.

"Thank you, Becky." Gabriel watched her walk back to her friends.

The strength he had pulled from her comments vanished when he saw Jeff and Bethany. He immediately looked around for Soary but didn't see him. Until that moment it hadn't occurred to him Soary would be here. He wasn't sure if Jason could handle a confrontation with him today.

Logan was greeting people and telling them Jason was holding it together. Gabriel listened for a moment then moved through the crowd. He stopped to shake a few hands and hug a few people. He saw Gwen's mom and stepdad sitting in the corner. They were surrounded by several friends and family. He was starting in their direction when Jason and Elizabeth entered the room.

He felt a wave of sorrow for Jason when all eyes turned in his direction. Elizabeth held tight to his arm and guided him through the room. She slowed, letting several people offer their condolences, but kept him moving so he didn't have to mutter responses. She finally walked him to Gwen's parents where she stepped back and let Sarah embrace Jason. James joined in on the hug and the three of them stayed that way for a long time. Logan found his way over to Elizabeth. He pulled her to him and held her to his chest. To all onlookers it was obvious this was a family in crisis. Without each other to lean on they would crumble.

Gabriel headed toward the door to get some air. He sat on the front steps of the building and rested his head in his hands. He thought of Gwen. He remembered how beautiful she looked the night she died. He remembered thinking that she glowed. When she had asked him how she looked he had almost given himself away. He'd had to get away from her then. His mind wandered back to the night she died and their conversation.

Gabriel caught up to Gwen just as she reached the ballroom doors. "Hey, slow down." He placed his hand on the small of her back and guided her through the crowd in the lounge area. He could feel the tension in her back, hear her erratic breathing. Finally, they reached the exit door. Gabriel pushed it open and waited for Gwen to pass through. The crisp night air rushed into their faces. Gwen took a deep breath and bent over at her waist as a sob escaped.

"Hold on, babe. Hold on." Gabriel wanted to get her further away from the hotel. He wrapped his arm around her waist. Gwen straightened and leaned into him. "Gabriel."

"Shhh." He soothed her and guided her across the street to the hotel gardens. He settled Gwen on a bench secluded behind a few bushes. Instead of sitting beside her Gabriel knelt in front of her. Their hands were clasped together on her knees. He searched her for signs of shock. He released one of his hands from her grasp and felt her forehead. He then smoothed her hair back. Taking both her hands to his lips he kissed them gently while making shushing noises. His heart raced. He didn't know what to do but he knew he needed to make sure she was alright. He wasn't sure exactly what he had just witnessed. Guilt played inside as he realized in his effort to protect Gwen, he left Jason.

"Gabriel." Her voice was still shaky.

"I'm here."

"That's him. That's Soary."

"Yes, I guess it had to be."

"Oh, my goodness!" She squeezed his hands and pulled him closer. Losing his balance, he rose to sit next to her on the bench.

"Gabriel, what do I do?" She looked at him pleadingly. "Should I talk to him?"

Gabriel let all he remembered of Gwen's past run through his mind. He knew she was stronger than the girl whose heart was broken by the first boy she loved. He knew too that she wouldn't be able to see she didn't love the man the boy became until she said goodbye to the boy. He gently wiped the tears from her eyes and waited for her to come to her own conclusion. Her eyes searched his, looking for the answers she already held.

Nodding her head, she told him, "I want to talk to him." Pausing she gazed at the hotel.

From their vantage point there was no indication anything had gone awry. A few groups of people were walking through the front doors dressed for the benefit. He wondered briefly if they knew the headliner was off-stage.

"I don't want to hurt Jason. I never want to be the reason he feels pain. I love him, Gabe. He is my life now. But I have to talk to Soary. There is so much I need…" she trailed off.

"I know. Will you be okay here while I go get him?"

Gwen nodded. Gabriel leaned towards her. His breath warmed the side of her cheek. Then he whispered, "You are stronger than the girl you once were." He let his lips lightly touch her jaw below her ear in a soft kiss. She leaned into him briefly. When she pulled away she squared her shoulders and nodded as a signal she was ready.

"Gabriel." He had just arrived to the street crossing. As he turned, she continued, "I am happy you're in my life. You are my best friend, my person." He smiled, dipped his head in a mock bow and continued toward the hotel leaving her to gather her thoughts and emotions.

He wondered how events would have changed if he had done what he had wanted to and pulled her in his arms and kissed her.

He was so caught up in his own head he didn't hear anyone sit down beside him. He felt a soft hand rest on his shoulder and gently pull him into an embrace. He let himself relax to her touch and spoke the name that was on his lips.

"Gwen." The sound of his voice released him from his trancelike state. He looked up into Bethany's eyes and jerked back, startled.

"I am so sorry for your loss. I know it's a very difficult time for you and your friends." She didn't remove her hand from his shoulder as she spoke.

"You're Bethany," he stated. She didn't respond. "Is he here?" he looked around as he asked.

"I don't know." She removed her hand from his shoulder. "He loved her deeply. I know it is hard for you to understand but he did. He never stopped loving her. If he had known what he was doing to her, he never would have left her. He just thought she would be happier without him. He wanted her to find someone like Jason and have the life they were planning." She spoke softly.

Gabriel believed her, but knowing Soary didn't mean to hurt Gwen didn't change the fact that he had.

"He shouldn't come here." He stood. Bethany stood with him.

"He loved her just like you. He needs his closure too." She said the words gently but she might as well have smacked him. For the second time today, he was ousted for his feelings. He briefly wondered if his grief made him transparent.

"I knew you loved her when I first saw you with her at the concert. I didn't know Gwen but I wish I had. She seemed to capture everyone's heart. I think she was a generous person and I believe she would want Soary here today." Bethany spoke in a calm voice, trying not to antagonize him. She didn't want to cause him pain. She could see he was in need of a friend.

He shook his head. "You didn't know her. But you are right, she was a loving and kind woman. If she thought Soary being here helped him in some way she would want him to be allowed to come in. I won't keep him out." Gabriel turned and climbed the steps. When he got to the top he turned back to Bethany and asked, "You say you knew I loved her from the first time you saw me with her." He paused not sure if he really wanted to ask her. "Did she know?" He tried to control his voice but it broke as he pictured her in his arms the night they went out dancing.

"I think so. I think she loved you too." Bethany watched as he nodded and turned to go back inside.

Instead of climbing the stairs she turned to the parking lot and walked to where Soary was parked.

***

Jason sat between Sarah and Elizabeth for the service. Each of them held one of his hands. He was shaking and trying to control his tears. He didn't want to be here. He wanted to be anywhere else as long as Gwen was alive and with him. He was unaware when the preacher had finished praying. He saw James stand and go up the podium to talk about Gwen. He told funny stories of her growing up. He told sweet stories of her falling in love with Jason. He talked about how excited she was about her new life in Atlanta and how she was looking forward to her pending nuptials. Jason was overwhelmed with Gwen's presence. He felt her with him.

He imagined her squeezing his hand and smiling at him. He wondered how he was going to live without her. He choked back sobs.

Several more friends and family shared their stories but Jason didn't hear any of them. He couldn't concentrate on what was happening around him. He knew he was expected to say something but he wasn't able to find the strength. Instead he sat there and let his mind wander through his time with Gwen. He smiled as he thought about the night he proposed. Gwen was so surprised. He remembered how her smile had melted his heart. He loved her more in that moment than he thought possible. Her smile was capable of bringing him joy even on the worst days. His eyes automatically followed her when she entered a room. She liked to tease him about it.

The months they spent engaged were the best days of his life. Although they didn't move in together until they moved to Atlanta it became normal for him to stay at her place. She surprised him for his birthday by staging his condo with Paris scenes so they could pretend they had gone away. The kitchen became a French bistro, the living room became city streets with a large cardboard Eifel Tower in front of the window. She staged the bedroom as if it was a hidden room at The Moulin Rouge cabaret. They didn't leave his condo the entire weekend. That was the Gwen he would miss the most. The carefree woman who only wanted to be with him, who laughed and teased, and loved life.

The doctors tried to save her and their baby. She was in surgery several hours but in the end she had lost too much blood. Gabriel held him in the floor of the hospital chapel until no more tears would fall. Then he silently cleaned up the mess Jason had made of the room, straightening chairs and picking up books. He moved into Gabriel's condo. It occurred to him he would need to figure out where he was going to live. There was no way he could stay in his condo where Gwen was shot.

Elizabeth squeezed his hand. It was time to go to the cemetery. Jason felt sick to his stomach. He couldn't stand the thought of Gwen being lowered into the ground. But he let Elizabeth lead him to the hearse and he climbed in. Sarah and James were already buckled in. 'What would happen if I just walk away?' he wondered.

"Do you want me to ride with you?" Elizabeth asked.

"No, it's okay. I'll see you there." He leaned out as she started to walk away. "Liz. Check on Gabe. He's hurting too."

Elizabeth nodded and turned quickly so Jason couldn't see her tears. Gabriel had been taking care of Jason. He had been trying to get him to eat. He had answered all Jason's mail and phone calls. He had arranged the entire funeral and delegated responsibilities to her and Logan. He sat up through the night watching over Jason as he had nightmare after nightmare. And he ensured Jason took his anxiety medicine. He was being stoic. But they all knew how much he loved Gwen; how important she was to him. She and Logan had been concerned about Gabriel for several months, they were afraid he would pull away from the group after the wedding. When he started seeing Ashley on a regular basis their worries decreased, except Elizabeth knew Ashley preferred to keep her distance, making it hard for them all to connect. Now none of it mattered.

She noticed Ashley standing beside Gabriel waiting to see which car she was going to ride in. Elizabeth smiled as she remembered her last conversation with Gwen. Gwen told

Elizabeth it was up to them to include Ashley; that she was good person and seemed to really care about Gabe. Elizabeth had to admit that Ashley had been hovering close by ready to take on any task to support Gabriel while not intruding.

She whispered under her breathe, "You may have been right about her, Gwen." Then she hurried over to Ashley and wrapped an arm around her waist.

"Ash, how are you?" she asked.

"I am managing. I wish I could do more. Gabe seems so lost and I don't know how to help him. He's rushing around trying to make sure Jason is okay. I don't know what to do." She held back tears but her voice cracked.

Elizabeth saw that Ashley had deep feelings for Gabriel. "Maybe after the funeral, when things settle down, you should suggest taking him away. A nice long weekend would do him good. He needs to grieve. He needs time to let her go in his own way."

"I think you're right. But I am not sure he wants me around right now. I think he needs time to process his feelings alone." She followed Gabriel to the car he picked and climbed in.

***

The funeral procession meandered through the tiny town streets. Passing cars pulled off to the side of the road. Some people exited their cars and stood with their heads bowed. Pedestrians in the town also stopped and bowed their heads. Men who wore hats removed them and held them low behind their backs. It was a sign of respect but Jason wasn't if it was respect for the survivors or the deceased. He was unaccustomed to it.

The hearse pulled to a stop. Jason gazed out the window and the rolling green hills of the cemetery. If he hadn't known better, he would think it was a garden. The lanes were lined with evergreen trees and bushes. Rows of annuals filled the mulch flowerbeds. The grass around the tombstones was manicured. The sky beyond the hills was a pale blue. Large, white, fluffy clouds floated high in the sky. The wind stirred the trees.

"She would love this day." Sarah read his mind.

"Yes." He stared out the car window.

"Jason, look at me." Sarah commanded him.

He didn't want to look at her; just as he had avoided looking anyone in the face since that night. It angered him to see his suffering mirrored in other faces.

Sarah repeated her command. He saw Gwen in her eyes.

"Listen to me and believe me. I know what you are going through. Not exactly, because we aren't the same people. But I know what it feels like for your mate to die, to suddenly be taken from you. All your plans, all your dreams, all your problems all the sudden became yours alone." She reached for his hand.

"You are not alone. We are your family, James and I. We love you. I know Gwen would want you to survive this. She would tell you to take your time, learn to breathe deeply, let the breeze catch your kite, and find peace by the water." Her hand reached up and cradled his cheek. "You will survive this. I know you don't want to but you will. And when you come out the other side you will still love her and you will still miss her; probably until you die. But you will love again and you will find joy again."

Jason stared at her. He knew what she was true for her. For that matter he knew it was true for many people. He just couldn't fathom how it could be true for him. He didn't have the energy to debate it. "Okay."

Sarah glanced at James and then back to Jason. "Okay."

***

At the cemetery Gabriel waited outside the hearse for the door to open. He knew this part would be harder for Jason because he wasn't sure how he was surviving it himself. He didn't want to leave Gwen out here in the cold earth alone. He took Jason's arm; they leaned on each other until they made it to the graveside.

A hush fell over the crowd as they approached. Jason sat as Gabriel stood behind him.

Elizabeth and Logan stood on either side of Gabriel offering physical support. Sarah and James sat beside Jason. The graveside ceremony was short; the pastor said a brief prayer then played Gwen's favorite gospel song, Let's Go Down to the River and Pray. It was a beautiful song that fit her perfectly. Jason didn't bother to wipe the tears from his face. He just let them fall.

At the conclusion of the song the family stood, approached the grave and dropped roses on the lowered coffin as their final goodbye. James held Sarah upright as he escorted away from the graveside.

Jason sat motionless. He didn't think he could do it.

Gabriel asked if he wanted his help. Jason couldn't respond.

Several minutes passed before Jason moved toward the coffin. He sank to his knees at the grave. The pain was unbearable. A loud scream startled the crowd. He sounded like a trapped lion preparing for escape. The raw pain he displayed was startling.

He leaned towards the opening in the ground and screamed Gwen's name. His heart felt as if it leaped from his chest. After what seemed like minutes, he felt the wind leave his lungs. He wondered briefly if it was possible for him to suffocate from screaming. If he continued, although his lungs were burning for air, would he die? And just as the thought seemed to make sense and he prayed for God to take him, his voice was silenced and oxygen assaulted his lungs. He leaned back on his heels, dropped his chin to his chest and sobbed. He gave in to the grief.

Gabriel, Logan, and Elizabeth began to move forward to wrap themselves around Jason. But another figure reached him first.

Soary moved through the mourners stopping beside Jason. He lowered himself to his knees slowly as if he was trying not to startle Jason. Without looking away from the coffin in the ground he draped one arm around Jason's shoulder and waited for Jason to regain control.

When the tears stopped flowing from Jason's eyes, he looked toward Soary. Their glares turned into stares until they simply sat studying each other.

The crowd knew they were watching two stories merge together over love.

Jason handed Soary the rose he had brought to place on Gwen's coffin. As Soary reached for the rose Jason felt a breeze brush his cheek. He imagined it was Gwen. He knew she wouldn't have left him for Soary. Just as he knew she would never stop loving Soary.

"She was pregnant." He stated looking back at the coffin. "I lost my entire family. I don't think I can live without them." His voice sounded weak even to his own ears.

Soary started to cry. "Unfortunately, you will." The look Jason saw on his face told the story of another man who lost his entire family and lived anyway.

Yes, Jason would survive losing Gwen and his child.

Soary was the first to speak again. "I am truly sorry. I wish I could change what happened that night. I wish I could have found the right words."

"Seeing you caused her pain but I also know she wanted to see you. She needed to say goodbye."

Both knew the outcome the other wanted was different only if Gwen was still with them; without her none of the past hurts mattered.

Soary looked at the rose Jason had handed him. He understood Jason was right; no matter what words he had spoken, Gwen would always have said goodbye.

He stretched his hand over her coffin and looked to Jason. "Shall we?" He asked.

Jason nodded and placed his hand over Soary's.

"We'll never stop loving you." Soary spoke the words with a teary voice. "You have our hearts."

"Forever." Jason added.

Together they released the rose.

Afterwards they walked away from each other.

Acknowledgements

Years ago, I finished the first draft of *Come Back* snuggled in bed next to my husband. I must thank him first. He was my first reader. He was my cheerleader. He was the reason I thought I could do it. Thank you, Lennie, for encouraging me, for finishing that first draft.

Then life took over. I focused on a career in banking. He focused on building his own business. We entered the world of infertility as we prayed our daughter would be our blessing. There were a lot of distractions. There was no time for a hobby; there was no time to write and all the romantic words that used to swim in my mind dried up.

Fast forward nine years. I opened my laptop one day and the *Come Back* file caught my attention. As I read the manuscript I winced at the not-so-great writing and I cried. The story broke my heart. The characters stayed with me. I dreamt of them. I thought of them as I drove to work and on the way to pick my daughter up from school and on the way home. Soary, Gwen, Jason, and even Gabriel haunted the outskirts of my mind. Their voices grew stronger in my head and heart. I knew these people. I understood them; each of them. They were people I would be friends with and love.

There was a lot wrong with the first draft of *Come Back*. But I knew Gwen's story was one that needed to be told. I knew there were a lot of girls, young women, suffering the same anxiety Gwen suffered. I knew there were women who needed to believe in a future. I started rewriting it. The final version was not what I intended. And I had more than one publisher suggest I change it. I did a bit. But in the end Gwen's story is her story and I am just the catalyst for how it is told. Although it wasn't the happily ever after some may have been waiting for it is an ending full of grace. So, I thank you, all of you who are reading this and all who were a part of the early stages.

To Jen L. Grey, you are an awesome writer, friend, and mentor. I pulled so much confidence from your encouragement, advice, and guidance. You always have a fan in me.

To my first Beta Readers, those to be named and those who are not, your feedback and guidance were valued and appreciated: Lanie, this book would not be the book it is today without the candid advice you shared as an academic, a reader, and a friend. I thank you so much!

To my mom, thank you for reading my poetry and telling me I should write a book because I really know how to capture how people feel.

To Meghan, April, Lindsay, and Greg, I couldn't have finalized this book without your feedback and support. Thank you for spending your time reading it.

There are so many friends who cheered me on; some expected and some not. But there was one unexpected surprise: Little Star. Your enthusiasm motivated me on a daily basis. I pray you experience the same encouragement from someone as you delivered to me. You will never know how much your words meant to me along the way.

To all who voted on my cover (OMG that was a stressful decision) and to Danielle who was so patient with me; thank you, thank you, thank you!

To my editor, April, I could not have gotten here without you. Thank you for stepping outside your comfort zone to give me the guidance I needed to make this book the best it can be.

And to my amazing daughter, Eden, I give the biggest thanks. She was such an inspiration to me. She was curious about this story from the moment she knew I was writing. While the theme is too old for her; the concept was not. Her interest and encouragement throughout the process pushed me forward even when I thought the mountain too high; the task too severe; the work too much. She drew the first images for my cover. She believed in me and knew her mom would be a published author. Her faith in me made my faith in myself increase. Thank you, Eden, for being the most amazing human I know. I will love you more and the most times Googleplex to Infinity always. I win. 😊

And finally, to my Granny. All of my fond childhood memories circle around you. You were always there for me. I wished I had gotten more than sixteen years learning from you. You were my world as a child. I love you and I know you are watching over me.

To all my readers, I appreciate all your encouragement, reviews, and support. I can't wait for you to read my next story. Thank you.

Made in the USA
Monee, IL
12 May 2021

67358039R00164